Because of Logan

Because of Logan

RIGGINS U SERIES - BOOK ONE

ERICA ALEXANDER

To anyone who has ever felt like an ugly duckling:

You're not an ugly ducking.
You're not a swan.
You are a phoenix.
Reborn from the ashes of whom you were yesterday.
You get to choose who you want to be every day.
Choose to love yourself.
Choose to be kind.
Choose you.

CHAPTER ONE

Skye

"YOU'D BETTER NOT PUKE IN MY CAR!"

River waves a hand at me, dismissing my warning.

I've lived in her shadow my entire life.

River has the kind of beauty that stops people in their tracks, be it male, female, old, or young. Even little kids gawk at her. She doesn't flaunt it, doesn't even try. Never has to. Teachers go easier on her and people trip over their feet in her presence.

I sometimes resent her for hitting the jackpot in the DNA lottery, but she's my sister, and she's never held her beauty over my head.

I do it on my own. River can't help the way she looks any more than I can.

We are opposites. She's beautiful, where I'm plain. She's a brunette, where I'm blonde. She's an extrovert. I like to hide. She's confident and full of life, while everything about me is blah.

Just once, I'd like to be truly seen as me instead of a faded copy of the woman sprawled in my passenger seat.

1

I'm glad my fraternal twin has enough sense to call me to get her from the party when her ride hooked up with some guy and left her to fend for herself, but I'm so mad at River for being drunk.

We come to a stop sign and I look at her.

"What did you do, take a dive into a vat of beer? You stink."

The words sound harsh, but there's no bite in them and River knows it.

"Nope. But someone spilled a full cup on me."

She lifts her left arm to show me the damage. She's wearing a black sweater, so there's nothing to see, but I sure can smell it.

My eyes are back on the road as we make our way home. Not a lot of traffic at 2:30 a.m.

A few more minutes and I'll be back in my warm bed.

"I'll never understand it. What's the point of getting so drunk?"

I have the urge to shake some sense into her and hug her at the same time. Something is eating at my sister and I have no idea what.

"I'm not *that* drunk. And why are you so mad? It's not like I interrupted a hot date or anything."

Her response burns me a little, and my face flushes in anger and embarrassment. The curse of fair skin is that everything shows. My shoulders tense and my jaw clamps shut in the way I've grown used to. This happens whenever someone says or does something that hurts me. True, I haven't dated anyone in two years, but still, hearing those words upsets me. I suck in a deep breath and will my body to relax, my jaw to unlock, and I open my mouth so words can come out.

"I had a date with a book." Lame, I know.

"Please, that's all you do, Skye. Read, study, work, bake. You should try living a little. Like me."

Her speech is slower, a little slurred, but River's quick wit is not dulled by the alcohol she consumed.

Easy for her to say. You'd think with being twins, even if fraternal twins, the gene distribution would be somewhat even. It isn't. But as much as I sometimes wish to be more like River and have her confidence, her cleverness, and yes, her looks, a bigger part of me is glad I'm nothing like her. I wouldn't be able to handle all the attention she gets. I love my sister and I know she loves me. She always has my back, and she stands up for me and tries to include me in whatever she's involved with.

I'm the one who can't rise to the occasion.

I'm the one who would rather be alone than in a crowd.

I can't fault River for her blunt honesty. It's the truth. And I'd always rather have the truth, even if it stings a little. Or a lot.

"You're living enough for the both of us. Someone has to be the responsible one. We're not even two full weeks into the school year."

I shake my head in disbelief and mutter under my breath.

"So? I have the whole weekend to recover, and what better way to start our senior year in college?"

I have no answer to that. I can feel her watching me, waiting, head resting on a hand, elbow propped on a raised knee. A yawn followed by a loud hiccup interrupts the brief moment of silence, making me jump. I expect the smell of sour beer to fill the small space between us in the car, but *no*. Her breath smells minty, like she's just brushed her teeth. It's not fair. If I hadn't shared a womb with her, I'd think she was a fairy, a vampire, or some other beautiful and mystical creature. That annoys me even more.

"Seriously! Did you have to drink that much? We're not even twenty-one yet."

"Pfft. Another week."

I give her a quick side-eye glance and put my full attention on the road ahead of us.

The light turns from green to yellow as soon as I reach the intersection. I curse under my breath. My right foot leaves the gas, but it's too late. I can't brake now. My hands grasp the wheel tighter as I step on the gas again and speed up in an attempt to get through the wide intersection before the traffic light turns red.

"I went through a yellow light." I speak more to myself than River. She hears me anyway.

"It's just a yellow light. You need to relax. You need a drink," River slurs.

Ugh. No, thank you. I can't imagine what kind of drunk I'd be, but I'm sure it wouldn't be the beautiful, sexy, and fun kind like Miss-Drop-Dead-Gorgeous-Every-Guy-I-Ever-Met-Fell-In-Love-With-Me. AKA, my sister.

No.

I'm not bitter at all.

Red and blue lights in my rearview mirror catch my attention a second before I hear the police siren.

"Shit!"

There's no denying that River is drunk, or at least very tipsy if the claim of her beer bath is to be believed. The smell of alcohol fills the car and hangs heavily in the heat I have blasting through the vents. With one last glance at the rearview mirror, I turn the blinkers on and drive into an empty strip mall, park below one of the light poles, turn off the ignition, and look down at myself.

"Shit! Shit! Shit!"

When River called, I rolled out of bed, slipped on my pink bunny slippers, grabbed my keys, and left. It's just a four-mile drive to the party, and I wasn't planning on leaving the car. I didn't even grab a jacket. I'm wearing a pink tank top and red boy-shorts PJs. And did I mention pink bunny slippers? It's an early birthday gift Mom shipped to us. Mom's idea of a joke, because Riggings University has a D1 hockey team. Mom said this is our last chance to be puck bunnies since we're graduating in May.

River leans into me, squints, and giggles when she sees what's on my feet.

"You're wearing Fuzzy One and Fuzzy Two!"

She named our slippers when we got them—hers are called Dick and Cock. Don't ask—but right about now, both Fuzzy One and Fuzzy Two have the urge to kick my sister's ass.

I'm angry at her for putting us in this situation, for all the drinking in the last few months. For not letting me in and talking to me. I don't know what's going on with River. She's always been a free spirit, full of life, but she's never been irresponsible before.

Not like this.

She's leaning over my knees, the seatbelt stretched to the max, and is trying to pet my slippers. I grab her by the shoulders and push her off me and back into her own seat. My death glare never fazed her before, so I try sweet instead.

"Don't say a word, okay? Please stay quiet and let me handle it."

A knock on my window makes me jump, and I push the button to roll it all the way down. I find myself staring at someone's narrow waist and hips.

Just how tall is this guy?

A light shines on my face and then over to the passenger and back seats before returning to my face. I instinctively raise my hand to block the light in my eyes.

"Do you know why I pulled you over?"

"I went through a yellow light. It changed as soon as I reached the intersection. I'm sorry, Officer."

My voice is steady, even. It doesn't betray how nervous I am. I can't quite see his face, the flashlight still somewhat shining in my eyes.

"Going through a yellow light when it just turns from green wouldn't get you pulled over, but you also have a brake light out."

"I do?"

And idiot that I am, I look over my shoulder as if I'd be able to see the broken light.

"Yes, you do. The left one is out. Make sure to get that fixed. Can I have your license, registration, and insurance, please?"

I've never been pulled over before. This feels a little like being in a movie or TV show. Hopefully, not an episode of *Cops*.

Reaching across the car, I open the glove compartment—thank God, River is quiet for once—and take the registration and insurance cards and hand them to him.

He looks at them for a minute.

"Who's David Devereux?"

"Our dad."

The car may be ours, but it's still under Dad's name.

He looks at the IDs again. I still can't see his face. "You're a little far from home."

"We go to Riggins."

He nods. This is a college town, so I'm sure I'm not the first RU student he's stopped. Nor the last.

"And the driver's license?"

"Oh, yeah. Sorry about that."

I turn around to grab the license from my purse and it's not there.

No, no, no. A moment of panic hits me like a punch to the chest. Did I lose it? Did River lose it? I search for it in a rush, behind our seats, the car floor, and back where it's supposed to be—on the console between the two front seats—as if it would magically appear there.

Then I remember. I know exactly where my purse is. Back home, on the chair where I left it minutes ago. I squeeze my eyes shut, trying to gather a calmness I don't feel before turning to the window.

"Officer, I'm sorry, but it seems I forgot my wallet at home, and my license is in it."

He shifts outside the door, as if in slow motion. I watch as broad shoulders fill the entire space of the open window. He's illuminated by a parking lot light, and when his face comes into view and he looks at me at eye level, my chest contracts as air leaves my lungs in a rush.

He's beautiful, like someone took the genes of Chris Hemsworth and Ian Somerhalder, put them in a bottle, shook it all around, and poured this perfect representation of the Y chromosome. His clear blue eyes are in sharp contrast with his tanned skin and dark hair. A strong, square jaw, his bottom lip a little fuller than the top.

He narrows his eyes at me, his lips a thin line. He looks angry. *What did I do?*

"Step out of the car, please."

"What? But . . . why?"

For a moment, he doesn't look like he'll answer me. His eyes shift over my face, my shoulders, my chest. My heart is beating so furiously, I imagine he can see it hammering against my breasts. *What's happening to me?* I don't understand my body's reaction. My stomach clenches, my breath catches, and I feel the need to squeeze my thighs. A small gasp leaves my lips when I realize . . . I'm aroused. I'm nervous, embarrassed, worried about my sister being drunk, scared even, but the primary emotion running through me at this very moment is . . . lust. *What the heck?* This is so not me.

My brain and my body are at war. The even-tempered and rational me is being challenged by a hormonal reaction the likes of which I've never encountered. I suck in a breath, shake the lustful thoughts off, and try to get back to the task at hand. My missing driver's license. When our eyes meet, I'm certain he can see all of it in my face. My cheeks burn.

His eyes open slightly, and his lips move but stay silent. He blinks a few times and his pupils darken. He hesitates. His gaze falls to my chest again, then he looks away.

"Step out of the car, please."

His voice is a little huskier now.

"I smell alcohol on you."

"What? No, I'm not drinking—"

"Nope! That's me, Officer."

River leans into me again, not heeding my plea to stay quiet. Half of her body is on top of mine. Thank God for the seatbelt or she might have face-planted into my lap.

And then the giggles start.

Oh, please, no. Not the giggles. River giggles a lot when she's drunk. The fact I know this is evidence of how often I've seen her in this state in the last few months. I try to push her back, but she weighs about a ton right now. What is it about alcohol? Add a few ounces to a one-hundred-twenty-pound girl and suddenly, it feels like she has the body mass of a football player.

I manage to guide her back, and River flops to her seat and squirms, trying to tuck her long legs under her.

He moves impatiently outside my window, his attention now on River. Maybe he'll go easy on us, if what they say about cops and pretty girls is true.

"Is she okay?" he asks me, but he's looking at her.

"Yes, she'll sleep it off and be fine in the morning."

He studies my sister for a long moment, and whatever he's looking for must satisfy him because he looks back at me.

His eyes do a quick once-over of my face again, lingering on my lips for a second and back to my eyes. *Is that . . . interest?* No. There's no way this gorgeous guy is checking me out. I'm out of my mind for even thinking it. Plus, hello? This is not the place nor time to even think such a thing. Damn hormones!

He clears his throat. "That's twice I've asked you to step out of the car. Don't make me ask you again." His tone is half command and half plea.

He taps the door and opens it for me.

I remove my seatbelt, step out, and stand to the side.

In pajamas.

And bunny slippers.

He leans into the car through the open door and looks at River, studying her again.

For a fraction of a second, I think maybe, just maybe, I've found a guy who's immune to River's appeal. Maybe he's my unicorn.

Stupid.

Stupid.

Stupid me.

Of all the things I should be worrying about right now—my getting a ticket, River being drunk and underage, although he doesn't know it, what I'm wearing, River saying or doing something River-like, and my having to call our parents to bail us out—my out of place unrequited insta-lust is not one of them.

Like I said. Stupid.

CHAPTER TWO

Logan

I OPEN THE DOOR FOR THE DRIVER AND OUT STEPS A WISP of a girl. Her eyes meet mine and slowly drift away as if she, too, is having a hard time not staring back at me. I have to make a conscious effort to drag my eyes away from hers. There's something about this girl that has me acting like an idiot. And it's not just the crazy outfit she's wearing and all the skin she's showing. There's a softness about her I'm drawn to.

I check inside the car once more, evaluating the passenger. I'm looking for any red flags, any signs she's in distress or needs medical help. She's drunk but coherent, and her demeanor is calm and compliant. My gut and training tell me neither of them is a threat to me or themselves, and the intoxicated girl is safe with the driver. Even under the influence, she's absolutely stunning. She smirks at me like she knows something I don't. But she's not driving nor disrupting the peace, and smirking is not illegal in the state of Vermont. She's just another college kid having fun.

I close the door and turn my attention to the little blond pixie in front of me. I need to shake off this attraction. This has never happened before, not like this. I'm at a loss. I like to take my time to think things through, but time is a luxury I don't have right now. Training kicks in.

"I want you to walk a straight line. Use the markings on the ground."

I point at the white line that marks the division between parking spots.

"One foot in front of the other. When you get to the end, turn around and walk back to me."

She's shivering in the next to nothing outfit she has on. It takes tremendous effort to keep my eyes from wandering all over her petite body. The bare legs, the little boy shorts PJs that barely cover her small but round and firm ass, the tight tank top that does absolutely nothing to hide the fact she's braless, and it's freezing cold tonight. Her nipples are so hard they might rip a hole through that top any moment now. I have to hold off a laugh when I notice her pink bunny slippers. This is a nice change of pace on an otherwise boring night in this small college town. Other than the occasional streaker running down Main Street, noise complaint calls, and a few drunk frat kids here and there, the town of Riggins, home of Riggins University, my alma mater, is quiet and safe.

Just four years ago, I was one of those college students.

Her blue eyes meet mine, and something stirs inside me, and it's not only my dick. He's been paying attention for a while now. I'm not a creep. I don't ogle girls, and I'm very much in control of myself and how I act. My reaction to this girl surprises me. It brings up a part of me I thought dead long ago. I don't like it, and yet I'm fascinated by the sudden impulse to let my guard down, to bend the rules a little, to be more lenient than I otherwise would be.

This is a college town, after all. Young, beautiful girls who think they can get away with breaking a traffic law because of the way they look are everywhere. I've never given any of them a break because they flashed a smile or cleavage at me. And I had my share of invitations for more. Turned them all down. Politely, of course. They still got a ticket. Maybe I'm an asshole for following the rules so strictly. But a pretty face and a pair of tits are not the thing I'm going to sell out my integrity for. And yet, I find myself treading that very line right now. Something about this girl calls to me, and it's not just her body. There's kindness and honesty in her eyes. She's not trying to manipulate me. It's easy to see how very uncomfortable she is. She wears her distress like a second skin and it tugs at me.

I tamper down my inconvenient lust with my next exhalation.

"What's your name?"

"Skye."

"Do you have a jacket, Skye?"

I like the sound of her name on my lips.

She shakes her head.

"Hold on."

I go back to my car and return with my jacket. She looks at me with big, pale blue eyes, confusion and anticipation on her delicate face.

I place the jacket over her shoulders, and before I can help myself, I pull her hair from under it. It's silky soft. My fingertips brush her neck and she shivers on contact. I freeze. Her pouty, full lips call to me. *What the fuck am I doing?*

I take a big step back and away from her and look down, trying to get a hold of myself. I don't know what it is about this girl that affects me so.

She's nothing like the women I usually go for. It's been a while. I just need to get laid. *Yeah, lie to yourself. That's always helpful.* I'm starting to get pissed off at myself for my less than professional behavior.

She grabs the sides of my uniform jacket and closes it around herself, turns around to walk the line, stops, and looks at me.

"Thank you."

It's just two simple words I've heard and said a thousand times, but for whatever reason, that something inside me no longer stirs.

It churns.

I watch her walk the line in her pink bunny slippers and back again until she's standing a couple feet away. I take a step closer to her. The car door opens, saving me from whatever stupid thing I was about to do. I'm acting like a teen boy and not the twenty-five-year-old man I am.

The other girl steps out. She half walks, half stumbles to the front of the car and leans on it until her gaze steadies on me.

Normally, this is where I'd tell her to get back in the car and stay there. But I don't. Everything about this stop is off the books, and it bristles at my sense of order and love of rules, and yet I can't make myself do what I know I'm supposed to.

It's like I'm under some kind of spell. Except, I don't believe in magic. Never did.

"Officer, she's not drunk. My sister never drinks. I am, though."

She giggles as she lifts a hand, pointing at the sky. Even drunk, she looks perfect, with long legs in skinny jeans, a tight sweater that shows off her large tits, and high-heel boots adding a few inches to her already tall frame. She's slim and curvy in all the right spots. She's exactly the kind of woman I go for. Gorgeous, confident, unapologetic. But when I look at her, I feel nothing. My brain recognizes what my eyes see, a beautiful woman, and yet I have no interest, no attraction.

Maybe a few hours in the can will sober her up. But as soon as I think it, I dismiss the idea, imagining what kind of distress it would cause her sister.

The blond pixie steps into my line of vision, between me and her sister.

"I'm so sorry, Officer. My sister was at a party and she needed a ride. I was already in bed—I didn't expect to have to leave my car. I just ran out to get her," the petite blonde explains.

Skye. I remind myself of her name.

The brunette points a finger at me and then at her sister.

"My sister doesn't like parties. She likes books."

I'm still looking at the brunette when Skye responds to her.

"Yes, I do, and I was reading a very good one when you called me to rescue your ass, yet again!"

"She likes to read smut."

More giggles.

"I do not!"

"Yes, you do. All those books have half-naked men on the cover."

Normally, this is where I'd halt the conversation, gain control of the situation, and put a stop to it. Well, if I'm honest, it would've never gotten this far. Instead, I repress a smirk, still trying to do my job, but relaxing and enjoying myself for a change. This is the most fun I've had in a long time. Too long to count, and it almost makes me feel like I'm back in college again. The poor girl stammers.

"I—I'm not responsible for what an author puts on the cover of their book."

"You need the real thing. You should just get laid. I bet

officer Hot Cop can help you. You know, protect and serve. He can *service* you."

Now, there's an idea I can get behind. I shake my head as if doing so would get rid of all the random thoughts in it. I cross my arms over my chest and try to pull my head out of my ass and do what I always do when something doesn't go as planned. I take a step back and analyze the known facts.

One: I'm attracted to this girl.

Two: She's scared, embarrassed, and out of her element.

Three: I'm in a position of authority, in uniform, at work, and behaving in a way that's not professional or up to my own personal standards.

Four: There's no way I can act on this attraction. *Maybe not right now . . .*

Five: I have to get this mess under contr—

"River!" Despite the cold, her face burns with embarrassment.

"Or not. I know! You should use your vibrator," the brunette quips, like it's the greatest idea of the century.

"I.

Do.

Not.

Have.

A.

Vibrator."

Skye enunciates each word.

"I'm buying you one for your birthday. It's a great twenty-first birthday gift!"

The brunette slurs between giggles and looks at me.

"We're twins, you know. Fra-ter-nal twins."

And now she's confessed to underage drinking, which for a college town is common, but damn it! I walk up to the front of the car to get a closer look at her. It doesn't matter if she's just buzzed or drunk. It's still underage drinking. She's able to hold eye contact, her breathing is normal, not labored, and her words are clear enough, a little slow and a slur here and there, but still coherent. She's tipsy for sure, but not plastered.

"Can I see your driver's license, please?"

She fishes in her back pocket and hands it over. I tilt it to the light to get a better look. Her birthday is September twenty-second. She'll be legal in a week.

I scratch the back of my neck. I have a decision to make. Take her in for underage drinking, in which case they'd probably just keep her until morning so she sobers up, or make sure they get home safely.

"I'm buying my sister a rabbit," she tells me.

"River, they don't allow pets in our building."

Skye says this with more patience for her sister than humanly possible. As if humoring a little kid in the middle of a tantrum.

The brunette—River—is laughing now.

"You don't even know what a rabbit is?"

"A rabbit is a furry animal that comes around on Easter," Skye says, hands going to her hips.

She's swimming in my jacket, it's so big on her.

River is bent over the hood of the car, holding her belly and laughing.

"O-M-G, Skye! A rabbit is a vibrator! It has these little rabbit ears that go right on your—" She holds a hand up, showing two wiggling fingers up like a rabbit's ears.

"River, there's no such thing!" blondie interrupts before her sister can go on.

I feel like a spectator in a verbal tennis match. Okay, enough of this. I have to get control of this situation.

"Miss?"

I give the brunette her license back.

"You have to get back in the car. It's for your own safety."

She looks at me, more sober than before, and she takes her license, and again, I wonder how drunk she really is. *If at all.*

"Help me out here. Please tell her there is such a thing."

River throws the words over her shoulder as she makes her way back to the car.

Skye turns my way, eyes wide. I have a primal urge to hold her and protect her from her sister's taunt. *What the hell is wrong with me?*

"Miss, in the car. Now."

She eyes me warily. I wait until she gets in and closes the door before turning my attention back to the driver.

"Officer, I'm not drunk. I was home. My sister called for a ride, and I went to this party to pick her up. Please just let me blow on your stick and you'll see that—"

The brunette is in the car but leaning out the driver's window.

"You want to blow his stick? Well, that's a way to get out of a ticket."

The little pixie—Skye—looks down and covers her face with her hands for a long moment before looking up at me again.

Her eyes shine with unshed tears.

"Officer, I live fewer than two blocks away. Could you please just follow us home, and I can show you my driver's license there? I swear I didn't drink a drop of alcohol."

I should just let her go. End this foolishness right now. Chalk it up to a late night and a long self-imposed dry spell. Forget about tonight. But I don't. I can't.

There's something at play here, something I have no clue

about, but the cop in me needs to know why. What about this wisp of a girl has me so out of sorts?

I need to know what. And then make it stop. I'll follow them to make sure they get home safely and are off the street. That's all. I just want to make sure they're safe.

I take her in, her small body hidden by my jacket, eyes wide and expectant, full rosy lips, cheeks flushed with embarrassment. Again, it's like I've fallen under some sort of spell. I draw in a breath and attempt to shake off whatever hold this girl has on me.

"Okay."

I FOLLOW them home to a street I'm all too familiar with. There's a moment of awkward silence as Skye and I stand by her door, staring at each other while her sister makes her way inside the building. We both speak at the same time.

"I'll go get my license—"

"No need to get the license—"

The low sound of a laugh escapes her mouth. I can't help the smile that tugs at my lips when her face pinkens.

Her eyes go to the name tag on my chest.

"Thank you again, Officer . . . ?"

"Logan Cole," I say.

I need her to know my full name. Not just the last name on the tag.

"Skye Devereux."

Her right arm rises, but her hand is lost inside the sleeve of my jacket.

"Oh, your jacket! I'm so sorry. Forgot I'm wearing it."

Another awkward moment follows as she unzips and shrugs

my jacket off. Her skin pebbles with the loss of the heat it provided.

I take the jacket back and give her my hand to shake. It's an innocent enough gesture, but I can't fool myself into thinking there's nothing to it. *I need to touch her. Just once.*

Her hand is so small, it disappears into mine. Delicate bones and soft skin meet my roughened hand. Her left arm drapes over her chest. I know she's trying to hide her near-nakedness from me. Too late. I memorized it all. But I don't ogle or make it even more embarrassing for her. Too soon, I let her hand go and gesture to the door behind her back.

"Good night, Skye. Be safe."

Walking away, I put the jacket on, still warm from her body. A faint scent of orange blossoms lingers on the heavy fabric and it makes me smile. I look back when I get to the cruiser, just in time to see the door close. She'd been watching me.

CHAPTER THREE

Skye

"GREAT! THIS IS JUST GREAT," I BLURT, HOLDING THE empty bag of coffee beans.

It had been River's turn to go grocery shopping yesterday, but she slept until noon, showered, took the shopping list, and left right after. She hates food shopping and always tries to bribe me to do it. I'm sure she only went out to avoid me. She did a pretty good job of that. Between her being out and my having to finish a paper yesterday afternoon, she'd managed to avoid me all of Saturday. I'm not sure what I'm more annoyed with— her avoiding me, avoiding talking about her drinking the last few months, or her forgetting to buy coffee even though it's on the list.

I can't go without coffee. I need my morning fix, so getting dressed and facing the Sunday morning chill it is. The weather app on my phone says the current temperature is a crispy forty-three degrees. It's a little on the cold side for early September but not unheard of. I pull on my favorite pair of yoga pants, extra soft from many washes, a thermal, and the red hoodie with the Riggins University logo. Then, I step into my shearling boots and grab my jacket.

I'm one of those people who's always cold. Being born and raised in Vermont should have made me less susceptible to the cold, but I'm not. Which again, for the umpteenth time, makes me wonder what I was thinking when I went out late Friday night—or Saturday early morning, rather—dressed in pajamas.

I leave a note on the fridge for my still-sleeping sister, letting her know where I am, and walk to Pat's Cafe, half a block away.

A couple of minutes later, I wave to Pat behind the counter as I step through the front door of the café. The scent of coffee and sugary goodness makes me instantly happy.

The décor is what one could call bohemian chic. The hardwood floors are dark with age and use, but the space is bright with sunlight and color. The café is decorated with a mismatch of tables and chairs of all different colors, textures, and sizes. A couple of couches flank one of the walls along with a few oversized beanbags. Those are always taken first.

I'll miss this place when we graduate and I have to move closer to wherever I can find a job. I first met Pat when we moved into our apartment three years ago to attend Riggins University, and she promptly declared herself our college mom.

I sigh, eyeing the big clock on the wall, and wait in line for my chance to order. The place is busy for 8:00 a.m. on a Sunday, but it's mostly locals hanging around. I see a few RU students, but they usually arrive later in the day after having slept the morning in. Pat's Cafe is always busy with college kids despite the food plan the university offers. The chance to eat a meal that tastes like homemade with a side of free Wi-Fi and Pat's ever-loving mothering of anyone who comes into her café is not something many can pass up. Pat knows everyone by name and has no qualms about giving them a verbal smackdown if she thinks they're misbehaving. Or an actual smack to the back of the head if she thinks they deserve it.

As I wait, memories of the last *River rescue mission* take residence in my mind, and I smile to myself thinking of the police officer who pulled me over. *Logan Cole.* I let his name roll off my tongue silently, and I like the way it feels. My chest expands and contracts as I release a resigned sigh. It's just like me to have met the most beautiful man I've ever seen during the most humiliating moment of my life. Just thinking about it, my face flames again. I can't deny the heat that pools low in my belly, either. Just thinking about him turns me on. Embarrassment and lust take turns, fighting for dominance over me. Maybe I'm going through some delayed hormonal puberty.

As if being pulled over and thought to be driving drunk wasn't bad enough, I just had to be wearing PJs that barely covered my ass and pink bunny slippers because, you know? That's not awkward or anything. Who goes out in public like that? Apparently, me. I do. And all because of River.

I take another step forward. It's finally my turn.

"Good morning, Skye. What can I get you today?"

Pat asks me with her big momma smile. Her brown hair is always in a ponytail. She has one of those faces that's impossible to tell the age, but if I had to guess, I'd say she's in her mid-fifties. The crinkles around her eyes are proof of someone who smiles and laughs often. Pat wears her happiness in the wrinkles of her face with pride.

I eye the goodies behind the glass and decide to be bad. I need a pick-me-up after the last couple of days.

"A red velvet muffin and a chocolate cappuccino, please."

It's not so much a muffin as a giant cupcake covered in cream cheese icing, and it's just what I need right now. I pay for it and step to the side, waiting for the barista to make my cup of heaven as Pat takes the person behind me. Then I hear a voice I never thought I'd hear again and shiver.

This time, it has nothing to do with the cold.

CHAPTER FOUR

Logan

I'M CROSSING THE STREET WHEN I SEE SKYE WALK INTO Pat's Cafe. If I'd planned to meet her there, it couldn't have been more perfect. She doesn't see me walk in right behind her. She's completely distracted, and I take advantage of it to study her, letting my gaze drift over her small figure. I take in the long blond hair falling down her back and the way the ends curl in different directions, my eyes lingering on the curve of her ass in those tight pants she's wearing. She moves forward and I step closer. Her scent fills me with longing. She smells like orange blossom flowers—the scent of my childhood and teen years.

Grandpa loved Vermont and the cold. Grandma loved summer and the heat. They compromised, traveling back and forth between Vermont and Florida, always making sure to be around whenever my brother Liam and I didn't have school. We spent every school break and vacation with them. Every summer, Liam and I would fly down to Florida where we spent weeks on end with our grandparents. Grandma loved to garden, and she had several orange trees in the large back yard. The fragrance of orange blossoms hung in the humid, warm night air like a thick blanket. It's been a couple of years since I made my way down south. I didn't realize how much I missed it until I caught my favorite smell on Skye.

Pat's voice brings me back from memory lane.

"Hey, hon, good to see you here today. You got the morning off?"

I answer Pat, but my eyes are fixed on Skye. She turns as soon as I speak. A look of surprise comes over her face as her cheeks pinken in that way I'm getting used to.

"Yeah, I worked a late shift last night."

"What can I get you, Logan?"

I glance at Pat then, and she's watching me with eyes that miss nothing. She's already doing the math in her head as her eyes move between Skye and me. Pat has clearly missed her calling. She should have been a detective. Just one glance from Pat, and I feel the need to confess all my sins and beg for forgiveness. I think of her poor kids growing up under that stare and shudder.

It takes me a second to get my bearings again, and I make it appear as if I'm thinking, but I can tell by the twinkle in Pat's eyes that she knows better.

"What do you suggest, Pat? Do you have my favorite?" I ask, trying to buy time.

Pat snorts at that—yeah, I'm so busted—and goes to the glass case to get the pastries I'm addicted to. I very well know she always has them. I stop by almost every day to get a to-go coffee and something to eat.

I pay for it, place the small plate with the sweets on top of my coffee mug, and take a step closer to Skye, who's still frozen in place.

The barista is trying to get her attention, but her eyes are locked on mine, and as I get closer, her head tilts up, still looking at me. I'm about a foot taller than her. I reach around her, brushing her shoulder with my chest, my face inches away, her eyes never leaving mine. She takes a quick breath in and holds it. With my free hand, I grab the drink she ordered, take a small step back, and nod back at the counter.

"Is that yours?"

She blinks and looks over to her side, breaking the connection as she grabs a plate with the muffin.

"Yes, thank you."

I search for an empty table and find a small one in the corner near the window. Taking her mug hostage with me, I nod toward the table and hope she'll follow me. She does.

Skye sits with her back to the large window. The still weak sun filtering through the morning haze shines over her head, making her hair even more golden. I'm mesmerized by the way the sunlight plays on her hair, trickles around her small frame, and glows around her. An unfamiliar ache in my chest has me questioning my sanity. What is it about this girl that has me so attracted to her? She's cute, but not in an overt way. Certainly not as beautiful as the women I've been with before. Skye has a certain vulnerability about her that speaks to my hardened soul. I'm intrigued, and I can't remember the last time anything had me this eager to figure out. I need to understand what it is about her that fascinates me so I can control it. She challenges me without even knowing it.

It's just lust, I tell myself. It's been a while. I push all the questions away, and an unbidden fantasy of what I'd like to do to her if I had a chance takes me by surprise.

I want to wrap those golden locks around my wrist as I tug her head back and nibble on her neck, working my way up to those full lips that are begging me to bite, lick, and suck on, and then reverse my path and work my way south.

Jesus!

I shift in the chair, trying to release the pressure building inside my jeans and shake off the dangerous track my thoughts are trying to lead me on. I'm sitting across from Skye—a small table between us—and the space underneath is not enough to contain my long legs. Her knees brush against mine and it sends a shiver up my spine. I get harder. Fuck! My dick is acting like I'm fifteen again.

Her eyes rove over me, taking in my gray hoodie, and I can almost hear all the questions swirling in her head.

She takes her jacket off and drapes it over the back of the chair.

"What are you doing here?" she asks in a low, unsure voice.

I push her mug closer to her on the table.

"The same as you. Having breakfast."

"But why here?" she says, but what I hear is, *Are you following me?*

She looks nervous.

I try to ease her worries with a smile.

"I live right there."

I point at my house, almost directly across the street from the café.

She turns to look over her shoulder.

"The blue house?"

"That's the one."

"Wow! What are the odds?"

Pretty good, I hope.

She bites her lip, thinking hard.

"I want to thank you again for Friday night."

The words are followed by a lovely blush.

My smile grows. Hers wanes. She's uncomfortable. And that's the last thing I want. I want her to like me if I'm to have a chance of getting into her bed. *Because that's all this is, right?* A normal hormonal-driven attraction to a pretty girl.

Except that for the last few years, I didn't give a fuck if anyone liked me or not. The women I've been with knew the score. And like me, they were in it for the sex and nothing more. I vowed to never be trapped into a relationship again. But for some reason, I want this one to like me. *Me.* Not my family name or what it represents. And not the fulfillment of some *'I want to fuck a cop'* fantasy. I get a lot of those too.

"Don't worry about it. I know you were telling me the truth. It's all good."

And to take the attention away from her and me, I ask about her sister.

"How's your sister? Was she okay after I left?"

I'm used to reading people, seeing their thoughts in the expressions on their faces, hearing the words that are not said. Something crosses her mind when I ask about her sister. Not anger. Annoyance, maybe, and a touch of resignation? It happens so fast, I almost miss it, but I could swear she wanted to roll her eyes.

"Yes, River is fine. She's such a lightweight. I don't even think she drank that much. She said someone spilled beer on her shirt. One or two drinks will do her in. I wish she didn't do things like that."

She sighs with a note of concern in her voice.

"She does that a lot?"

"No, not really."

Skye's quick to defend her sister. *Loyalty.* That's another thing I haven't experienced much of either.

I can feel her opening up a little more, now that she's not the center of the conversation. Skye is not used to being the center of attention or does not like the spotlight on her.

"Well, since we were kids, she's always been the fun one, but drinking, no. This is something that started a few months ago . . ." Skye trails off.

Okay, new subject, I think.

"Are you going to eat all that?"

I point at the giant muffin.

She laughs as her gaze drops. She's shy. "It might take me a couple of tries, but I think I can tame this monster."

I break off a chunk of the large slice of lemon pound cake and save the three chocolate chip cookies for last.

"You have a sweet tooth too, I see."

Her eyes land on mine and move away again as if she's unsure of where to look, but her shoulders drop, and her gaze lingers a little longer each time.

"If you make a donut joke, I'll give you that ticket after all," I say but follow it with a laugh so she knows I'm teasing. "Yes, I have a weak spot for sweets, and this"—I pick up one of the chocolate chip cookies—"is my greatest weakness."

"Oh, Pat's cookies are good, but mine are better," she whispers with a guilty look toward the counter where Pat is.

I don't look back as to not give away that we're talking about her.

"I love to bake. You should eat my cookies. You'd love them."

I can't help the smirk that comes over my face.

"I want to eat your cookies, and I know I'll love them."

I know she did not mean the double entendre as I did, but I can't help myself.

Her eyes go wide as she gets my meaning.

"Sorry," I'm quick to apologize. "I'm teasing. I didn't mean to embarrass you."

Skye sighs, and her shoulders drop a little more. The tension leaves her, and she settles into her seat, either finally relaxed in my presence or defeated, accepting there's no forgetting the embarrassing moments we shared a day ago. I sense it's the latter, and it bothers me.

I watch as she picks up her mug with both hands, brings it to her lips, and blows on it. Steam and the scent of chocolate hang in the space between us. She licks her lips before taking a tentative sip, and finding the temperature acceptable, she takes a long drink. Her eyes close in bliss as the flavors of her chocolate cappuccino touch her tongue. The entire moment lasts no more than a few seconds, but it's so sensual, so captivating—I'm utterly lost in it. My pants get tighter. I shift, trying to give my inconvenient growing erection a little space. She opens her eyes and a smile of pure joy graces her face. There's no subterfuge. Her innocent enjoyment of the drink in her hands turns me on even more. I'm surprised by the appeal it has to me.

She puts the cup down on the table, small hands still wrapped around it.

"This weekend was a disaster. I don't think I've ever been so embarrassed in my entire life. And believe me, I have stories to tell."

"I wouldn't say that. It was the perfect ending for a boring night. I don't remember ever having so much fun on a traffic stop."

She narrows her eyes at me.

"Glad someone enjoyed it."

Her words drip with sarcasm.

There's a little fire to her after all. I find that I'm enjoying myself and her company. There's something about this cute and awkward girl that makes me feel lighter. I can't remember the last time I've been this carefree.

"So you have a birthday coming soon, right?"

I know her birthdate because I read it on her twin's driver's license.

She looks confused and I clarify.

"Friday night, or Saturday morning, rather, your sister said you had a birthday coming."

She averts her eyes, remembering the exact circumstances in which her birthday had been mentioned and what her sister had said she'd get her.

"This Saturday. I'll be twenty-one."

Skye looks at me and away again as she smiles her shy smile.

"What are you doing to celebrate it? A party?"

"I don't know. River always comes up with something crazy, but I doubt it will be a party."

"Books before parties, I remember."

"Yeah, I'm boring like that."

"Liking to read doesn't make you boring. It makes you smart. Do you always celebrate together?"

She smiles at the compliment and takes another sip of her drink before answering me. I force myself to break eye contact and take a drink of my coffee, making a mental note not to come on too strong. I like this girl. I have no idea why, but I do.

"For the most part, yes. I'm sure River will have some big plan, being a milestone birthday and all, but I don't know if I want to do anything she has in mind."

"Why not?"

"Well, River can get a little crazy with our birthdays. She's an all-or-nothing kind of girl and I'm more of a stay-out-of-trouble type."

"What do you mean, a little crazy?"

"For our eighteenth birthday, we went skydiving. She

dragged me to this small airport and made me jump off a perfectly good airplane."

My eyebrows curve up and my mouth drops open. This surprises me.

"For our nineteenth birthday, we went on a hot air balloon trip. There's nothing like seeing the fall colors from a hot air balloon in Vermont. That was cool. Still scary, but cool."

"And last year?"

"Last year, we went bungee jumping. Off a bridge. It was terrifying. A thousand times worse than the hot air balloon and the skydiving."

I wonder if she ever says no to anything her sister comes up with.

"I see a trend. Everything has to do with heights. Your sister must love the thrill of being up in the sky."

"Nope. She's afraid of heights and that's why she does it. Confront your fears and all that."

"She's an interesting character. If this trend continues, rock climbing might be a possibility in your near future."

"We did that when we turned sixteen. And whitewater rafting at seventeen. I didn't see the connection until we got to the ten-foot drop in the middle of the river."

"I think I'm scared of what twenty-one will bring."

"Tell me about it. I just want to stay home and do nothing."

"But you should do something. Twenty-one is a big milestone. You don't want to look back on it when you're ninety and regret not doing something special."

"What did you do when you turned twenty-one?" she asks.

"Yeah—I don't think you want to do that," I reply, thinking of my last year in college when my friends took me to a strip club and bought me lap dances and enough alcohol to float a boat.

I'd never been so drunk and vowed to never be that drunk again. Stupid stuff happens when people get drunk, and I can't afford for anything slightly unsavory to tarnish the family name. Even after years of being away from home and shunning my father altogether, his influence still reaches me. It pisses me off. Something must show on my face because she frowns at me.

"Was it something bad?"

"No, not at all, just not the wisest of decisions."

She bites her lip.

"Now I need to know. You got me all curious."

She reminds me of a cat—reserved, curious, graceful—and I want to make her purr.

Blurred images of asses and tits come to my mind, but I spare her the details.

"My friends got me drunk. I advise against that."

"Yeah, after last night's fiasco, I have no inclination to be drunk, not that I've ever been."

"Never?" I ask.

It surprises me.

"I've tasted champagne and wine, but I didn't like them. Alcohol is bitter. I don't understand why anyone would drink to the point of losing control."

"Sometimes, losing control can be a good thing."

Her eyes widen, and it tells me that behind the innocent face hides a dirty mind. I didn't intend my words to sound dirty, but somehow, she went there. I like that. I like that a lot.

"And I'm not twenty-one yet," she counters.

"Not being of legal drinking age wouldn't stop most people."

Our eyes linger on each other for several seconds and it's not awkward.

I hesitate for a moment and then think, what the hell, just go for it.

"Would you like to celebrate your birthday with me?"

"With you?" she repeats.

"Yes, with me. I have next Saturday off, and I don't get many since I work on a rotation, and being one of the youngest and single, I usually let the guys with kids have the weekends so they can have family time. But it just so happens that I'm free this Saturday, and I'd love to take you somewhere for your twenty-first birthday."

"You would?" Her eyes widen.

"Yes."

"*Me?* You want to take *me* out?"

There's something unsaid between 'me' and the words that follow. Like she can't believe I want to spend time with her.

"Yes, I do."

"To celebrate my birthday?"

"Yes. Is that so hard to believe?"

A shadow crosses her eyes, but she doesn't deny it.

"Why?"

Her simple question comes out in a whisper. I find it troubling that so many unsaid words can be conveyed in just three letters. Doubt, insecurity, and even some fear flash in her eyes. It tugs at my heart, and that's an unfamiliar feeling. I'm truthful. Well, partially truthful. I can't exactly say everything that's running through my mind right now.

"There's something about you I'm drawn to. I like you."

She's silent for a long moment, and I wait. I give her time to get used to the idea of my being attracted to her. She seems to have a hard time wrapping her head around the concept. When she answers me, there's still doubt in her voice.

"I don't know. I don't want to get drunk."

"You won't get drunk," I assure her.

"I promise, you'll be safe. And we can do anything you want. Have dinner. Go to a movie, or a show, or dancing. Or you can let me surprise you. What do you like?"

"You mean, besides reading smut books?"

She makes a joke at her own expense and I love that about her. I've never cared for people who take themselves too seriously, and I've had a whole lot of that growing up among the richest families in New Canaan.

I laugh.

"Yes, besides that. Would you like to go out on a date with me and celebrate your birthday? I can arrange for a police escort," I joke.

"On a date?"

Her voice is breathy, and it's doing things to me that are decidedly not PG.

There's so much doubt in her tone, and it bothers me. I see disbelief and vulnerability. And then it hits me. *The vulnerability.* I'm drawn to it. I'm drawn to the doubt in her eyes and the timid way with which she carries herself. A small part of me, the part that sees some of my father in me, is repelled by it. But a much bigger part is fascinated by the openness I see in her.

There's a tremendous amount of power in being vulnerable, in being open, in taking risks. Often, courage is measured against how brave one is, but now I wonder about a different kind of courage. The courage to expose oneself and the willingness to get hurt in the process. If I'm to measure myself by this yardstick, I'm a coward.

Before I can answer her, the chair next to Skye gets dragged back and River sits on it. The four-person table now sits three.

"Officer Hot Cop! I didn't expect to see you this morning."

And then she attacks Skye's untouched muffin.

"Who's going on a date?" River asks after a bite.

I relax into my chair, my forearm on the table holding the cookie I have yet to bite. I look at River and point at Skye and then back at myself with the cookie.

"We are."

River narrows her eyes at me.

"Did my sister work out a deal so she wouldn't get a ticket?"

"No! There are no deals," Skye grumbles.

"I didn't say I agree to going out with you yet. It's both our birthdays, and I haven't talked to River about what she wants to do."

She said *yet*. That's not a *no*.

She looks at her sister. *Is it a plea for help in her gaze?*

"Well, I was thinking of going hang-gliding. Looked up a couple of places, but Becca organized this surprise party for me and a few friends pitched in, which is no longer a surprise since she had to tell me about it when I told her of my plans for our birthday."

River takes another bite of the muffin.

"I would've told you before, but you got distracted by Hot Cop—"

"I got distracted? You were drunk! And then I didn't see you all day."

River ignores her.

"Anyway," she continues, "they're taking me to a male strip club. You're invited too. Becca paid for our tickets."

"You're going to a strip club?" Skye asks.

"Yes, but it's for girls. With guys dancing, like *Magic Mike*."

Skye is already shaking her head in a silent no.

"That was my initial reaction too. I don't much care for some guy shaking his junk in my face. Watching it in a movie is one thing, but in real life and 3D? But you know Becca," River says with a sigh. "I agreed to go, as long as they aren't buying me any lap dances."

River breaks another piece of the muffin and into her mouth it goes. Skye is mute.

"I can't picture you in a stripper club. I hate to be apart on our birthday, but maybe you should go on a date with Hot Cop."

River says it like I'm not here and can't hear everything that comes out of her mouth.

"He has a name. It's Logan. Not Hot Cop."

River lifts an eyebrow at that, a little smirk forming on her face.

Skye is about to say something else when her phone starts vibrating. She pulls it out of the jacket pocket behind her.

"It's Bruno," she says distractedly.

"He's at our door and wants to know where I am."

She replies to the text message and puts the phone between us on the table, noticing for the first time that River is eating her muffin and pulling it back to her side. Half of it is gone.

"I told him we're here."

"So about this date," River says, glancing at me. "You're not going out with Bruno?"

"No, Bruno is going away for the weekend with Sidney."

River huffs at that.

"Who's Bruno?"

My voice is casual, but I'm feeling oddly irritated by this guy I don't even know.

"Bruno is her fuck buddy," River says with a shrug and a side glance at Skye. She does it on purpose, I can tell. Sisterly tease, or something else?

"He is not!" Skye is quick to deny.

"Friend with benefits, or whatever you want to call it. It's all the same."

River says it with such a casualness, as if she's talking about her favorite color and not her sister's sex life.

Skye looks upset.

"Bruno is my friend, my best friend, and there are no benefits at all. At least none of what you're talking about."

River just rolls her eyes and tries to get another piece of Skye's muffin. Skye pulls it farther away, so River takes one of my cookies.

I raise an eyebrow at her but don't say anything.

"I'm hungry. She's not sharing hers with me, and you're not eating yours."

The playful, fake innocent smile on her face tells me she's used to getting away with this type of thing. She's not exactly rude, but somewhat forceful. I pity the fool who falls for her. He'll need balls of steel to put up with River.

I may know her for all of five minutes, but I can already tell she's a force to be reckoned with. She manages to be pushy and cute about it.

There's no denying she's used to getting her way. And yet she doesn't seem to be full of herself.

Another chair drags back, and a tall, lean, and good-looking guy sits down opposite to River, but not before giving Skye a quick hug and kissing her on the top of her head.

They have similar coloring, but his hair is a darker blond, his eyes are also blue, and it's obvious he works out often when he takes his parka off and drapes it over the chair. His arms are ripped with lean muscle. And that annoys me. Not that I look any worse than him. Playing hockey for the last twenty years has made me strong and muscular as well, even if I no longer play for hours every day. I still get together with friends to play, and I work out almost every day. But this guy has an in with Skye and he looks like competition. I do not share well.

Just the thought of another guy near her pisses me off. The unwelcome possessiveness startles me. I'm not the jealous or possessive type.

The alpha-male domineering bullshit I witnessed growing up with a father like mine always made feel uneasy. I'd never been jealous of Amanda in all the years we were together. Or anyone else, for that matter.

I don't like the way it makes me feel. Not at all. I don't know what to do with these feelings. They don't sit well with me—feels like trying to put on clothes that are a few sizes too small. It doesn't fit and makes me feel constricted.

So much for hoping this Bruno would be a bookish nerd. He's anything but.

Bruno nods at River and then gives me his hand to shake, introducing himself.

"Hey, I'm Bruno. Nice to meet you, man."

"Logan," I say as I shake his hand. He has a firm handshake.

I'm looking for something to hate about the guy, for something to be wrong with him, but he's friendly and seems nice. He puts an arm around Skye's chair and nudges her toward him with a big grin.

"What's up, Sugar? One more week and then I can get you drunk."

A surge of irritation comes over me. I want to grab him by his preppy pink polo shirt and throw him out. *Jesus Christ! What's wrong with me?*

"Oh-oh, better not say that in front of Officer Hot Cop. He hates drinking."

"Who?" Bruno asks.

"Him."

River points at me with my own cookie. Or half of it, rather.

"He's a cop, and we got pulled over last night, and I don't even want to know what Skye had to do to get out of the ticket. And now he's taking her on a date so he can do more things to her I don't want to know about."

Bruno looks my way, assessing me with new eyes, and his hand curves protectively over Skye's shoulder.

"Oh my God, River! Would you stop that? Nothing happened, okay?"

She glares at her sister.

"We got pulled over because I went through a yellow light and had a broken tail light. Logan thought I was drunk, but it was not me. It was River, and then he let us go. I ran into him a few minutes ago. That is all, end of the story."

"Well, not the end of the story. Don't forget your birthday date with me," I say, gauging Bruno's reaction.

Bruno surprises me when he says, "That's cool. I won't be here, and God knows what River would get you into. At least with a cop, I know you'll be safe."

He looks pointedly at me.

"Won't she? Be safe, I mean."

"She will."

He earns respect from me with that question and the veiled threat behind the friendly words. *Cop or no cop, I'm going after you if you hurt Skye.*

"We didn't decide—we're just talking about it," Skye says, looking uncertain still.

I don't want to force her to go out with me. Hell, I'd never force a girl to do anything. I'm about to say something and give her an out. As much as I want to get to know her better, maybe I should run the opposite way. I'm much too interested, and I barely know more than her name. If I allow myself to go down this path . . . I don't want to think about it.

Bruno leans closer to her and whispers something in her ear, then pulls back and asks her, "Okay?"

She glances at me, her face pink, and then back at Bruno and nods at him. When her eyes find me again, the blush intensifies. She bites her lower lip and speaks, her voice tentative, as if she's not used to the words she's saying.

"Okay, I'll go on a date with you."

Then she adds, "For my birthday."

As if that's the only reason anyone would want to take her on a date. It bothers me, but I don't let it show and smile instead. I'm excited about it. It feels like the first real date I've had since high school. The newness and expectation of it send a thrill through me.

At that, Bruno grabs her phone, enters the lock screen code, and taps the screen a few times and then points it at me and takes my picture before I even know what he's doing.

"What's your number?"

I give him my number and he enters it into the phone.

"So, should I put this under Logan or Officer Hot Cop?" he asks Skye with a smirk.

"Logan Cole," I say at the same time River says, "Officer Hot Cop."

He taps the screen a few more times and my phone vibrates.

"There, now you have her number too, and I sent you a picture so you can add it to the contacts."

"You sent him a picture? Which one?"

"Don't worry," Bruno says. "It's a cute one."

She tries to grab her phone from him, but he holds his arm high, keeping it away from her.

Curious, I grab my phone and key my code in and look at

the picture. I can't help the smile that spreads over my face. It's a beautiful picture. It had to be taken in the summer because Skye is wearing a sundress, and the sun is low on the horizon behind her, giving her face an ethereal glow, her hair floating in the wind. She's not looking at the camera but is lost in thought, and I wonder what she was thinking about then.

Oh, man, *fuck*! I have to stop this giddy high school crap I have going on right now.

It's just a pretty girl.

Nothing else.

Soon enough, she'll show her true colors. *They always do.*

Don't get stupid over it. A plan. I need a plan so I know where I stand before this goes any further.

Pat stops by, gives River and Bruno their own cups of coffee, and puts a plate in the middle of the table filled with pastries. She ruffles Bruno's hair like a mother would. "Hey, big boy. How's the family?"

He shrugs.

"Same as always, Pat."

He reaches in his pocket for his wallet, but Pat waves him off.

"Pay me next time."

"You always say that. But next time never comes."

Pat puts a hand on his shoulder and squeezes. He covers her hand with his.

"Thank you."

She waves him off again and walks back to the counter.

All eyes are on Bruno, but he makes no eye contact with me or River. He looks quickly at Skye, who in turn squeezes his hand on the table and then turns to the plate of food.

"Dibs on the chocolate croissant."

River is studying Bruno with intent eyes, but surprisingly enough, she says nothing.

Bruno pushes the plate over to Skye. She grabs the croissant and pushes the plate to River, who takes a cupcake before offering me the plate.

I shake my head.

"Still got my cookies, thanks."

"So, this date you two are going on," River says to me.

"Where are you going and what are you doing?"

CHAPTER FIVE

Skye

I HAVEN'T SEEN LOGAN SINCE THE MORNING WE MET AT
Pat's. If it wasn't for the texts he's been sending me every day,
throughout the day, I'd think he's changed his mind.

My phone rings, and the sound of *Girls Just Wanna Have
Fun* by Cyndi Lauper tells me Mom is calling me.

"Hi, Mom."

"Hi, sweetie. I heard you got yourself a hot cop."

Freaking River. She already blabbed about my date
with Logan.

"Oh, River told you?"

"Yes. Are you excited about it?"

"Mom."

"Honey, it's a date, not marriage. Just go and have fun. If
you don't like him by the end of the date, say thank you and
goodbye. You're not obligated to do it again."

"Have you met me? I'm so bad at this."

"You worry too much. Live a little. Enjoy yourself and your
body while you're still young."

"I'm not good at that either."

"There's nothing wrong with some casual dating and hooking up. As long as you both know it's just that, casual, so no one gets hurt."

I have the most open-minded mother in the universe. Dad is not far behind her.

"You know what I always say, Skye."

"What's good for the goose is good for the gander," we say at the same time.

It's her personal motto and a not so subtle stab at misogyny. Gender equality and all that, starting at the very core of what makes men and women different—sex.

"I know it's cliché, but what people have between their legs should not dictate how they live their lives."

"I know. You're right."

"Honey, don't allow what happened before tarnish who you are today and how to live your life."

"Mistakes have a way of following you around."

"There are no mistakes in life. Only lessons. You learned from it. Now you have to bless it and let it go, or you'll be chained to it for the rest of your life."

"You make it sound so easy." Ugh, I sound like Eeyore.

"I know it's not easy. The mind has a way to loop back to the very things we want to forget. Not wanting to think about something is the same as thinking about it. The trick is to replace those thoughts with new ones. Until you create a new loop."

Create a new loop? Could Logan be it? Could he be the man to give me something new to think about?

"Okay, Mom. I promise to give this date a real try."

"You have to step out of your comfort zone. Take a risk. Listen to your heart."

"I will. Love you, Mom."

"I love you too, sweetie. Talk to you soon."

I TRIED THIS BEFORE. After my high school boyfriend disaster, I thought maybe it was just what I needed to do. Be less picky and hang out with a guy and not think beyond the moment. But I can't do casual. It doesn't work for me. I can't make myself be with a guy just because he's cute or I have nothing better to do on a Saturday night.

There has to be something more. Maybe something is wrong with me. Unlike most of the girls in high school, I was never boy-crazy. I very rarely felt attracted to a guy. My one and only high school boyfriend was pretty much the only guy I'd been interested in, and we were together for six months. Until he got what he wanted, that is. He was one patient jerk, I'll give him that. I don't think many guys would have stuck around, pretending to love me for so long, just so they could take my virginity and then brag about it.

Three years later, and I still can't believe I fell for his smooth talk.

I went on a few dates in freshman year at Riggins and dated Jon for all of three weeks in sophomore year. And what a mistake that was. But he'd been so charming and so insistent, and I thought why not? Ugh. He turned out to be a douche of the first order.

River hated his guts on sight. I didn't miss how Jon's greedy eyes fell all over her when they first met after we'd been on a few dates. We broke up not long after that.

It has always been every guy's reaction when they first meet my sister. They forget I exist the moment River walks into a room. It can't be helped. It's nothing that she does. It's just her. They're all drawn to her.

It's like she has her own gravitational pull. I'm just the moon hanging around, and she is the sun, and as soon as any guy enters her stratosphere, they're hooked.

Except for Logan. I expected it. I looked for it but found . . . nothing. He doesn't seem to be attracted to her at all.

THE WEEK'S FLYING BY. It's already Wednesday, and this class, Structure of English Language, is putting me to sleep.

My phone vibrates in my backpack. I grab it and hide it under the desk. I'm seated toward the back. I don't think the professor can see me, but we're not supposed to use cell phones in class and I try to be discreet.

Logan's texting me.

I keep waiting for him to change his mind. Why is this gorgeous guy interested in me? I key in the unlock code and open my text message app. I can't help the smile that comes over my face.

Logan has been texting me all week, asking all kinds of questions, and he will not tell me what he's planned for Saturday. We haven't been able to see each other even though we live on the same block.

This double major in English and Communications is kicking my ass. Between classes, my daycare job, and his odd hours at work this week, all we manage are text messages.

Three more days until I see him again. The thought fills my belly with butterflies. I'm nervous and excited at the same time. I don't remember being this eager to see someone since high school when Blake asked me out for the first time at a Halloween party our senior year, and we all know how that ended.

I had to change his contact name back to Logan again this morning. River keeps changing it to variations of Hot Cop. This morning it was *I hope Hot Cop Has a Big Cock.*

She has the sense of humor of a fourteen-year-old boy. I should change the passcode, but I know she'll guess it within a few tries. I need a number I can relate to or I'll forget it completely, and River knows them all.

Logan: What's your favorite food?
Skye: I love Italian food.
Logan: Like?
Skye: Lasagna. Nothing better than homemade lasagna. And garlic bread too. You?
Logan: I make a mean lasagna. I'm going to cook for you one day soon.
Skye: You'll be my chef?
Logan: I'll be anything you want.

I have no idea how to respond to that. He'll be anything I want? A picture of a naked Logan served on a platter pops in my mind. My face burns with the image.

I type and delete my answer three times. I know he can see the dots on his side and I have no idea how to respond to him.

Logan: Are you blushing right now?
Skye: No?
Logan: Liar
Skye: Maybe
Logan: I knew it! Back to work. Talk to you soon.

What do I want? I ask myself again, this time not thinking

of Logan but myself. I'm not sure. I want to be happy, and I am happy.

I count the blessings in my life every day. I have a loving family, parents who dote on me and support me in anything and everything. A sister who, as crazy as she is, always has my back even if at first glance it doesn't show. But I want more. I'm just not sure what that more is. *No.* I'm lying to myself. I do know what I want, but I'm afraid to want it. I'm afraid to say it aloud because then I might jinx it somehow.

I can rationalize it all I want and make plans to venture out of my carefully constructed shell, but I know not everyone can be a leader. Some people are happy to follow and are content in the way they live their lives, but I'm not one of them. I could lie to myself and stick to the shadows, but of late, I'm craving the light. This self-imposed shell feels constrictive. I'm outgrowing it, and I have no idea what to do with myself.

Sometimes, I wish I could be first in something. Leave the first tracks on the road. Guide instead of follow. But the thought terrifies me as much as it draws me in.

CHAPTER SIX

Logan

I thought that by now, three days after seeing Skye that morning at Pat's Cafe, my lust for her would have settled. It hasn't. I find myself thinking about her more often than I like to admit. And it scares me. I've never been one to text girls all the time. But I can't help it. I think of something and want to ask her about it.

A part of me wants to retreat and call the whole thing off. But the bigger part is excited about this girl. I like her, and I'm not so blind to my own flaws that I can't see how being into her shakes the walls I've built around my heart.

I wish Liam were here and I could talk to him about it. I can't imagine opening up to anyone else. I can't talk to him, so I do the only thing I can. I text him. I do this every so often. I don't expect him to answer. Last time we spoke, Liam said he was going to turn his phone off. Something to do with phone signals being tracked by insurgents and safety. By the time he finally gets his phone back on, he'll have a book's worth of texts from me.

Logan: I met a girl.

I don't expand on that text message. For now, that's all I'll allow myself to say. I just need someone to know, even if that someone is stuck somewhere in the Middle East and has no way of replying to me right now. Again, I wish my brother were here with me instead of wherever he is. As proud of Liam as I am, I can't help the fear in my heart for him.

I can lie to myself and say the images in my head are an exaggeration of the truth, and her lips are not as pink as I remember, her eyes not as blue, her body not as sexy, and her hair not as golden, but the problem with lying to yourself is that in the end, you still know the truth.

It's funny how I think about her in colors when my entire life has been black and white.

WE'VE BEEN TEXTING BACK and forth. She has responded to all my texts but has initiated none. I wonder if it's just shyness or if she's not as interested in me as I am in her. It will be easier to walk away if she's not into me. The thought of walking away —of her not liking me—triggers a dull ache in my chest. I'm not looking for a serious relationship. Not now, maybe never.

Then, why do I keep thinking about her as if she has a place in my life, in my future?

Only one way to find out.

I have a night shift again, and the clock on the cruiser dash says it's 1:11 a.m. She must be asleep by now, but I send her a message anyway, not expecting her to see it or respond until morning.

Logan: Sweet dreams.

Skye: Thank you. I would wish you the same, but I guess you're working.

Logan: What are you doing up this late? You should be sleeping.

Skye: Some guy keeps texting me.

Logan: That must be very annoying.

Skye: Nah…I kind of like it.

I stare at her response for a full minute before replying, smiling the whole time.

Logan: I kind of like it too.

Skye: Be safe, Logan.

Logan: I will. Have a good night.

CHAPTER SEVEN

Skye

Our date is tomorrow, and I have yet to know what we're doing or where we're going, except that Logan said to keep the entire day open and that he'd tell me more about it later. I haven't heard from him today yet, and it's already the afternoon. I got used to hearing from him every morning and throughout the day.

My fingers hover over his name on my text app. For once, River hasn't changed the contact name. I think she ran out of words that rhyme with cop and cock.

I have yet to initiate a text to him. I wonder if he thinks I'm playing hard to get or snubbing him. That's not it at all. I just don't know what to say.

Skye: Hi.

His response comes right away.

Logan: Hey, there. Was just about to text you.
Skye: About tomorrow...

Logan: I hope you're not texting me to cancel.

Skye: No. Not at all.

Logan: Curious?

Skye: If I were a cat, I'd be dead.

Logan: LOL, clever.

Skye: So……

Logan: I'll pick you up at 10 a.m. Dress comfortable and warm.

Skye: Where are we going again?

Logan: Nice try.

Skye: >: (

Logan: Is that supposed to be a mad face emoji?

Logan: Cute!

Skye: What kind of comfortable are we talking about? PJs comfy or business casual comfy?

Logan: I've seen your PJs. They may be comfortable, but definitely not warm.

Skye: …

Logan: Don't think too hard. A favorite pair of jeans and a sweater will be fine. And no fancy shoes needed.

Logan: Got to go. See you tomorrow morning.

RIVER FINDS me staring at my open closet.

I look over my shoulder when I hear her behind me. I don't know what to wear.

"What are you guys doing?"

"I have no idea."

"How do you know what to wear?"

I continue to stare at my closet as if an outfit will jump out of it and say, *pick me, pick me.*

"He told me to wear something I love and something comfortable."

"So, what will it be, pajamas or yoga pants?"

I smile. "Hmm, he's seen me in both, so I thought I'd try something new."

River walks around me into the small closet and comes out holding a blue peasant dress in one hand and skinny jeans and the blue sweater that's an exact match to my eyes in the other.

"Go with the dress. Easier access. He can just slide his hands up your legs and get to home base—"

I take the dress from her and hang it back in the closet.

"He said to dress warm and suggested I wear a favorite pair of jeans and a sweater."

She thrusts the jeans and sweater at me.

"Well?"

I grab them and put them in front of me, looking in the mirror.

"I know. I was trying to find something sexier, you know. I still can't believe he's asking me out. If this will be my one and only date with him, I want to at least look good for it."

"Why would it be a one and only date?"

"Have you seen him? I know the first time, you were drunk, but the second time, you were in full possession of your faculties—"

"Awe, shucks. Thank you." River grins at me.

"Correction, the second time, you were sober," I say.

She play-punches me in the shoulder.

"Skye, any guy would be lucky to have you. You are kind, smart, beauti—"

I stop the compliment train before it derails into utopia territory.

"Guys like him? They don't go after girls like me. Not

when there are so many women available who are far more beautiful and sexier than me. This is a college town. They're everywhere."

And I still can't believe he asked me, and not you.

"Why would he ask me out? He only had eyes for you. Plus, Law and Order is so not my thing," River replies.

Ugh. I guess I said that out loud. I'm always very careful not to let River know about the many guys who passed me over for her. She'd be upset about it, and it's not like she tries to get their attention. They can't help it.

I exhale and ignore her question.

"Okay, jeans and a sweater it is. He also said no fancy shoes."

"Hold on," River says and walks to her room.

When she comes back, she's holding her favorite pair of dark brown suede boots. They're soft and warm and so comfortable, they feel like being barefoot. I can't believe she's letting me borrow them.

"Okay, you can borrow these, but I expect you to name your firstborn after me."

I reach for them before she changes her mind, but she pulls them back just as my fingers graze the soft as butter suede.

"Better yet, you have to name all of your children after me. River the Second, River the Third, River the Fourth, and River the Fifth. It's a very versatile name. It will fit both boys and girls."

"I'm having four kids?"

"Yes. I want lots of nieces and nephews since I plan on having none myself. I can be the fun auntie who spoils your kids rotten and then returns them to you sugared up and cranky. They're gonna love me."

It's not the first time I've heard River say she doesn't want to have kids, but every time she sees a baby, she goes all mushy over them. I'm not buying it.

"Okay, got the outfit and the boots. What else?"

"Make sure to put on some sexy underwear. Even if he never sees it, it will make you feel sexier and confident."

I riffle through the dresser drawer.

"I need to go shopping."

"Nope. I have it covered."

She reaches under my bed and pulls out a shopping bag.

How long was that there?

"Here."

River hands me two wrapped boxes.

"I thought we weren't exchanging any gifts. You said—"

"I know, we're saving to buy a second car, but you're only twenty-one once."

I don't point the flaw in her logic that we're only any age once.

"Well, in that case, here."

I grab a box from my nightstand and give River a gift of my own.

"We're terrible non-gifters."

"I don't think non-gifter is a word."

"It is now. I'll even submit it to *Webster's* if it makes you feel better, Miss Proper English. Come on, open the bigger box first," River instructs me.

I rip the paper off to find a familiar looking pink box. "Victoria's Secret?"

River laughs.

"I had a hunch you'd need it. Go ahead. Open it."

"Well, my underwear problem just got solved." I pull the lingerie set from the box. A panties and bra set in a soft lavender. It's delicate and feminine, without trying too hard to be sexy.

"Open mine."

River rips through the paper and opens the box.

"You didn't."

I smile at her.

"I know how much you loved it."

"Yes, but we'd agreed it was way too much money for a scarf and I was going to wait for a sale," River says as she wraps the purple silk scarf around her neck.

It's made and hand-painted by a local artist, and each is a unique piece of wearable art. This one has various shades of purple, violet, and deep blue. The colors blend in such a way that it's like looking at one of those pictures of a nebula in space. Some people frame them. They're that beautiful. Purple is River's favorite color, and she almost cried when she saw the price tag on the scarf a few days ago when we first saw it. We both knew it would never go on sale and would most likely be sold within hours. River got a phone call and stepped out of the store to talk, and I bought it without her knowing.

"The color goes perfectly with your eyes and hair. And don't worry about the cost. I found a great coupon," I lie.

She knows I'm lying, but she doesn't call me on it. That's what grateful sisters do.

"Thank you, Skye."

She hugs me.

"Now open the other box."

I start to rip the paper off the rectangular box when I catch the look on her face.

"River?"

She's full-on smiling now. A very devious smile.

No, she wouldn't. Would she?

I pull the wrapping paper away from the box and—she did. Yes, she did. I am now the owner of a Rabbit—a pink one. "River!"

She falls back on my bed laughing.

"I told you I'd get you one. If Logan doesn't cut it, you've got a friend to help you out."

"River, I can't even—"

"Or better yet, just bring it on your date tomorrow. Double the fun!"

"What? No—just no. There's no way I'd bring this on a date or even suggest it."

I open the drawer on my nightstand and put it inside.

"And don't even think about saying anything to Logan about it."

"Ah, c'mon, Sis! It's just between you and me. I won't tell a soul. Unless I forget and it slips out."

"I'm not feeling a whole lot of confidence in you right now."

"Come on. I'm hungry. Let's get something to eat and talk date strategy."

CHAPTER EIGHT

Logan

I'm at her door at ten. I don't think I've ever had a date that started in the morning, but what I've planned requires daylight.

The sound of the lock being turned sends a shiver of excitement down my spine and right to my groin. I haven't even seen her and my dick is already trying to stand at attention.

She smiles a shy smile, and I feel like I'm fifteen again, going on my very first date.

"Hi, is this okay?" she asks, pointing at herself.

"I wasn't sure what to wear since you're keeping wherever we're going a secret."

"It's perfect. You look beautiful."

"Okay."

Her smile grows bigger.

"Let me get my coat."

She waves me in, and I follow her down the hall and into her apartment.

"Happy birthday, Skye."

"Oh, thank you."

She grabs a jacket and zips it up.

River comes into the living room.

"Hey, Hot Cop! How are you?"

"I'm well. Happy birthday, River."

"Thanks."

She smiles.

"Now I can drink and you can't arrest me."

I laugh.

"I could still arrest you."

"Not if you want to get into my sister's pants. I'm sure arresting me would not put her in the right mood."

"River!"

I look at Skye, and yes, she's already blushing. I love the way her cheeks pinken. I glance at River, but my eyes return to Skye before I reply.

"I'll keep that in mind."

I OPEN the passenger door of my truck for her. The red pickup truck is tall and doesn't have a running board for her to step on. Skye holds to the top of the door and pulls herself onto the seat. My hands go around her hips and give her a little boost. The brief contact speeds up my heart. Sitting inside the truck brings her to eye level with me, maybe even a little taller.

A mild breeze ruffles my hair, and her hand reaches out to run through it. I freeze at her touch. My eyes drop to her mouth and Skye pulls her hand back. Her lips part, but all that leaves her mouth is a shallow puff of air.

"Buckle up, please," I say before closing the door and walking around the front of the truck.

"Ready?"

"I hope so. I have no idea what you're planning on doing to me."

I can't help the smirk on my face. Skye says the most innocent things, but somehow, it always sounds like an invitation to do something dirty. Or maybe it's just my overactive imagination.

She touches both cheeks with her hands.

"I curse the genes that made me so light-skinned and prone to blushing," she says.

"I love the way your skin flushes. It makes me want to come up with naughty things to say just to see how pink you'll get."

As if by command, she flushes even more. My fingertips trace the color on her cheek in the gentlest of caresses before tucking a lock of hair behind her ear.

I linger for a moment, and she holds her breath, but the leaping pulse on her neck betrays her.

I've never been this affected by anyone else before.

I give both of us a break and buckle my seatbelt and start the truck. I let air into my lungs, taking in slow breaths.

I pull into traffic and navigate the local streets until we get to the highway. I'm grateful for the few minutes of silence. It gives me a chance to get ahold of myself. You'd think this is the first time I ever went on a date.

Skye runs a hand over the weathered bucket seat. It's an old truck. The red paint is faded and the leather seats have lost their sheen, but the interior is spotless.

I wonder what she's thinking. I could have driven the Escalade, but this old truck is also part of my plan. A plan that's starting to look dumber by the minute.

"I love this truck," she says.

What? That's the last thing I expect her to say.

"You do?"

"Yes, I learned to drive in a truck just like this one. But it was blue and nowhere near as well-kept."

The coincidences keep piling on.

"This truck was Grandpa's. He taught me and my brother, Liam, to drive in it. I have so many fond memories associated with it."

"Yeah? Tell me some."

"God . . . Liam and I as kids, riding in the back on country lanes at what we thought were great speeds, but now, I know we were hardly moving. Us sitting between our grandparents during long drives all over the state."

I run my hand over the same spot Skye did, as if I could touch those memories somehow.

"Camping and sleeping on the truck bed on piles of blankets. My first kiss at fifteen, one early summer when Grandpa let me borrow it even though I was too young to even have a driver's permit."

The bright red color has long ago faded, and the truck is now a dull terra-cotta. The fifteen-plus years show, but I love this truck and could not part with it when Grandpa died and Grandma told me to sell it and take the money.

The old fella shows its years, but the engine is in mint condition. Grandpa had a knack for mechanics and taught my brother and me everything he knew.

I glance at her and she's smiling at me. Sharing these memories makes them alive again. I can almost smell Grandpa's aftershave. He was an Old Spice man.

"Where are you originally from?" I ask.

"Born and raised in Vermont. A couple of hours' drive from here, actually."

"Yeah? Where about?"

"A tiny little town, barely on the map. You've probably never heard of it. Apple Hill."

The corner of my mouth tilts up in a smile.

"I'm familiar with Apple Hill. You're not going to believe this, but when we were kids, our grandparents took us to Apple Hill every fall. We'd hit a few small farms and fill ourselves with ice cream, apple cider, chocolate, donuts, and bring home all kinds of food. We never made it more than five minutes awake on the trip back."

I'm lost in happy memories again, but her laugh brings me back to the present. The sound warms me from the inside out.

"No way! Apple Hill is so small. We probably crossed paths a dozen times."

"I have to make it back there. It's been too long," I murmur to myself.

I glance at her and her eyes are on me. I wonder if she heard me.

"I guess fate is trying to bring us together. I visited your home town dozens of times growing up, and now you live across the street from me. Do you go home often?"

"As often as school and work allow us. We try to go any time we have a long weekend or more than three or four free days. And all the holidays, of course."

"Will your parents be upset you're not going back for your birthday?"

"No, not really. This is the first time our birthday falls on a weekend since we began college, so they're used to our not coming home for it. We usually do something after, the next time we can make it home or meet for lunch halfway between Riggins and home."

"You're close to them. And your sister too."

"I am. We're very close. We hit the parent lottery. I couldn't have asked for more loving and supportive parents."

I can't say I know what having loving parents means. There's an empty spot in my soul where that should have been.

"That's good. I'm glad you have a loving family."

I'm not sure what else I can say.

"How about you? Are you from Vermont?"

"No, I'm from Connecticut. But I grew up in Vermont as much as back home. My grandparents on my mother's side lived here. The house where I live now belonged to them."

"It's cool that you can live in the same house your grandparents lived in."

"I spent the best moments of my life with my grandparents. We came up as often as we could. Every school break, and the entire summer vacation too. But we spent most of the summer in Florida with them."

"When you say we . . ."

"I mean my baby brother, Liam, and me. Our parents were always busy with work and social functions."

There's a long silence between us, what I'm not saying heavy in the confines of the truck.

"I take it you're not very close to your parents then."

Her voice is soft, as if she's unsure whether she should ask me about it.

"No, we didn't hit the parent lottery, that's for sure."

Before she can say anything, I smile and announce in a much happier voice, "We're here."

I WATCH HER CLOSELY, expecting to see displeasure on her face or anything that will tell me she's less than impressed to be spending her birthday and first date with me in an amusement park.

The place is not huge and caters more to teenagers than adults, and this early in the morning, it's not busy, as the mostly empty parking lot can attest. But it has a particular ride I want her to try.

Her face is pure joy. She's smiling like a kid at the—well, the amusement park. She gets out of the truck so fast I don't have a chance to open the door for her.

Amanda, my ex, would've still sat in it and waited for me to open the door even if it was on fire. Well, if I'm to be honest, Amanda wouldn't step foot inside a truck, especially not this old, beat-up one. I do a mental shakedown and tell Amanda to go fuck herself. There's no room for her in this date.

"You brought me to an amusement park?"

Her eyes dart among the rides she can see as she walks my way.

"Yeah, I hope this is okay."

She looks at me then and her smile is so big, something inside of me cracks. I smile back, and she steps up to me, her feet on tiptoes as her arms go around my neck. She barely hits my shoulder, and I tuck her into my side. A muffled *thank you* leaves her mouth and goes straight to my heart. She pulls my head down and kisses my cheek, a shy smile playing at her lips. I can't remember the last time someone looked at me with such joy and gratitude. The crack widens a bit more.

I take her hand and it feels right, like her hand belongs in mine. I buy us both wristbands, and she tries to pay for hers, but I don't let her.

"No, this is all part of your birthday celebration. Your money is no good today."

I can tell she wants to insist, but I stop her before she can say anything.

"How about this? On my birthday, you can take me out and pay for it, deal?"

She looks at me suspiciously.

"When is your birthday?"

"July fifth."

"That's nearly a year away."

"It should give you plenty of time to plan then. I expect it to be epic."

I can see the wheels turning in her head, and the thought of having Skye with me for the next ten months makes me smile.

"Come on, there's something I want to try first, before it gets crowded."

I tug her behind me to the back of the park. When we get closer and she sees where I'm taking her, she starts to laugh. She's in on the joke. That huge smile is back on her face.

"Oh, you're going down, Logan."

I want to go down, all right—between her sweet thighs—but I don't think that's what she meant.

We show our wristbands to the attendant at the Go Kart gate. We're the first ones here. He hands us the mandatory plastic disposable shower caps for hygiene purposes and helmets. When Skye is not looking, I slip him a twenty and ask him to give us some extra time and exclusive use of the ride. He's glad to oblige.

Skye is trying to put her long hair inside the plastic cap, but it keeps falling off.

"Hold on," I say. "I have something that might help."

Then I reach into my jeans pocket and pull out the hair tie I bought yesterday, along with a large box of condoms. But I don't let her in on my extra purchase.

"It's brand-new. I just bought it. I figured you'd need it today, and I didn't want to say anything to you before and give the surprise away."

Her mouth drops open as if she could not believe I thought of such a thing. I can't believe it either. I never imagined I'd be buying hair ties one day. First time for everything.

I step behind her and run my hands through her hair and gather it in a low ponytail. Another first, putting a hair tie on someone. Then I put the cap and the helmet on her and do the chin strap before doing my own. She searches my face for something.

I smile.

"What?"

She shakes her head. The attendant, whose name I now know is Mike since he put a name tag on, points to two of the carts and tells me they're the best two. We take them.

The ride has tires and bales of hay around the entire track. I haven't done this in years, but I remember having a lot of fun with my brother and grandpa here. This track is one of the longest in the country at almost one mile long, and the carts can go up to fifty miles per hour.

No one under sixteen is allowed to drive them.

I help her into her kart and get into mine. Mike signals us to make sure we're ready and turns the starting lights on. Red gives way to yellow, and I glance at Skye.

Her eyes are on the track ahead of her. As soon as the green light turns on, Skye takes off, burning rubber in a cloud of smoke. I'm so surprised, it takes a few extra seconds to hit the gas pedal. She's already a good fifty feet ahead of me. I can't help the smile that covers my face.

It seems Skye is a speed demon. I spend the whole race trying to pass her, but she closes me in every turn and doesn't let me by. Having the whole track for just the two of us gives her a chance to go as fast as she can without holding back.

We ride until I notice Mike waving at me and circling his hand above his head in the universal signal to wrap it up. His voice comes over the loud speaker and announces it's the last lap, and Skye wins. I never even had a chance to pass her.

When we coast the cars back to the starting line, there are quite a few annoyed faces looking at us. But we're both too excited about our little race to care.

The look of joy on her face is well worth the angry glares. When we hand our helmets back to Mike, he laughs at me.

"Dude, you got smoked. She handed your ass to you. You might have to turn your driver's license in."

I laugh and look at Skye. She tosses the plastic cap in the trash can and is running her fingers through her now loose hair. The hair tie is on her wrist. She has an *I told you so* smirk on her face.

I slap Mike on the shoulder.

"If you're going to get your ass smoked by a woman, make sure she's a beautiful one."

We turn to walk away, and Mike yells after us, "Come back. I'll be here all day."

I look at Skye and her smug face. Sounds good to me.

CHAPTER NINE

Skye

"I would've never guessed this was what you had planned. What made you think of it?"

He looks pensive for a moment, as if looking for the right words.

"I didn't want to have the pressure of a first date hanging over our heads. I wanted to do something that would allow us to talk and just be."

He smiles, still lost in thought.

"To be honest, I didn't think of this place until yesterday morning. I was cleaning the truck and I remembered Grandpa telling me about his first date with Grandma. He took her to the fair and they spent the day at the rides. As soon as the thought popped in my mind, I knew it was what I was looking for. I came here a few times with my grandparents and with friends when I was at Riggins. It seemed like the perfect place for a date."

There are butterflies in my stomach. I love that Logan is recreating his grandparents' first date for us.

"Maybe your grandpa whispered the idea in your ear," I say.

This is something Mom would have thought. She's rubbing off on me.

"Maybe he did."

Logan takes my hand.

"I've always loved amusement parks. When we were old enough to go alone, Dad used to drop us off, and River and I would spend the entire day at the rides. Go Karts were always my favorites and the one thing I beat River at every time."

"You like speed."

He's not asking.

"I've always loved the feeling that comes with it. Love the wind on my face, the sliding into a tight turn, and the way my whole body vibrates with the kart as if an extension of it. I even love the smell of burned tires."

I laugh.

"Gosh, it's been at least a couple of years since I went Go Karting. River was more of a roller coaster thrill seeker. I didn't like roller coasters as much, so we compromised."

Logan is smiling at me and shaking his head. He tugs me to a concession stand and buys two water bottles. He cracks the seal open on mine before handing it back to me. I've never had a guy do this before. I don't think anyone has done this for me since I was a little kid and not strong enough to open the bottle myself.

"Good thing I didn't have a bet going against you, or I'd be paying up right now."

"I told you, you were going down."

I can't help the laugh that escapes my lips.

"You did. How did you come to be a little speed demon?"

"I've been riding Go Karts for as long as I can remember. Dad used to take us all the time. At first, I'd sit in his lap because my little legs couldn't reach the pedals, but Dad always let me steer. Eventually, I was tall enough to drive them by myself, and the older I got, the faster I went. I didn't know this place was here."

"Is this something you still do often?"

"Gosh, no. Not for a couple of years. The last time was when we went back home for Thanksgiving in my sophomore year. There's a fair every fall. Dad and River raced me. They lost too. The three of you have something in common."

"I'm glad I picked this place then. I wanted to do something low-key without the pressure of trying to dress up or impress each other. But I guess it kind of failed."

"It failed?"

"I'm totally impressed with you. And now you raised the bar so far up, how will I ever be able to impress you?"

"No worries there, Logan. You already did. This is officially the best date I've ever had."

"We just started."

He reaches around me, runs his fingers through my hair—the tips graze the back of my neck and send a trail of shivers down my spine. My skin rises in goosebumps and I'm glad the long sleeves hide it.

My confidence falls. I can only imagine what my post-helmet, wind, and bad ponytail hair looks like. I reach over to comb my hair with my fingers, but Logan beats me to it.

His hand is gentle as he combs his fingers through my hair and places the locks around my shoulders, his eyes watching me the entire time. My eyes want to drift closed. I think a little moan escapes my lips. His smile confirms it.

"I don't look like Medusa anymore?"

"You couldn't look like Medusa if you tried."

"You haven't seen my bedhead first thing in the morning."

"I'd like to."

And right on cue, my face turns red. The burn in my cheeks raises the temperature a few degrees.

His smile widens.

"I love to make you blush."

A finger traces the edge of my sweater where it meets my clavicle.

"I wonder how far down the pink goes."

It feels like his words have a direct connection to whatever part of my body is responsible for flushing because the heat on my face spreads down into my chest. I press the cold water bottle to one cheek and then the other. Maybe it's hot flashes.

Can a twenty-one-year-old have hot flashes?

"I walked right into that, didn't I?"

He laughs and takes my hand again.

"Come on. Let's see what else you can beat me at."

CHAPTER TEN

Logan

HAVING SKYE'S BODY AGAINST MINE IS THE SWEETEST OF tortures. She can't stop giggling, and her ass is shaking and rubbing me in all the right places.

I want to drag her into the trees that line the park and have my way with her. Vermont doesn't have any laws against public nudity, after all, so we can't get a 311 for indecent exposure, but we could get a 2601 for lewd and lascivious conduct. It would definitely be worth the three-hundred-dollar fine, but not the up to five years' stay in jail. And I don't think Skye would be up to it just yet. I'm so hard, it hurts.

Down, boy. He does not go down. My dick is a terrible listener.

She puts the air gun down and turns in my arms. My hands fall to her hips.

Skye is all smiles.

"I guess it's safe to say I won't be applying for a sniper job anytime soon."

Our faces are inches apart, and the urge to kiss her is almost painful. I lean into her when some kids bump into me, trying to squeeze into the spot Skye just vacated, and the moment is broken. It's probably for the best. It would have been the least-PG kiss in the history of kisses, and we are in a very PG place.

Her stomach growls so loudly, the kids who just bumped into me give me a dirty look as if I did it. One of her hands goes to her stomach and the other covers her mouth. Her eyes widen in surprise. We stare at each other for all of three seconds before busting out in loud laughter.

I take her hand and grab the giant Minion I won for her in the target shooting game. I didn't feel the need to tell the guy manning the game that I'm a cop and an expert marksman.

"Let's go, woman. I'll feed you. I'm getting hungry too."

"I'm so sorry."

She begins to apologize, but I stop her.

"Don't. I'm obviously failing the feeding part of this date. It's entirely my fault."

"I didn't even think I was hungry until my stomach decided to let me know it was not happy."

She looks at me with the sweetest of smiles.

"Thank you, Logan. I can't remember the last time I had this much fun."

It hits me then. Her words unveil something in me. Something that has been missing. A need, a want I didn't know I had. I've never been this carefree. I've never laughed this much or had so much fun with anyone. Not even as a kid.

My entire life had been so carefully orchestrated that there was never any room for spontaneity. And even after I was out of my father's reach, his influence continued to mold me. To dictate my behavior, to make up my mind for me.

The realization nearly knocks me on my ass and I do an internal shake-off. I'll revisit this later, when I'm alone.

"So, how do you feel about tacos?"

Her stomach grumbles again. I place my hand over it and she tightens the muscles there.

"Okay, one rumble for yes, two rumbles for no?"

The sound of happiness spills out of her lips and fills my heart. For everyone else, it may have just sounded like a laugh.

"Yes. I love tacos."

"Great! Let's put your yellow friend in the truck and go for a little ride. I know a great place not far from here."

"His name is Stuart."

"You named it already?"

"No, that's his actual name."

"You know the Minions' names?"

"Don't you?" She smiles.

"I work with kids. Minions are very popular."

I unlock the doors with the remote and open hers first. My hands go to her hips to help her into the truck. I miss the touch the second I let go. I walk around the hood and open the back door to toss the minion inside.

"Can you please put a seatbelt on him?"

"You want me to put a seatbelt on the doll?" I ask in half a laugh.

"He's not a doll. He's a minion, and his name is Stuart. And yes, please. You, of all people, should know. Safety first."

She's teasing me, I know. And this is another first in a day that seems to be made up of them. I've never put a seatbelt on a plush toy before.

THE FIVE-MINUTE DRIVE is done in comfortable silence. I don't even miss having the radio on. I glance at Skye, trying to read her reaction when we pull into the makeshift parking lot for the food truck.

She nearly squeals when she sees the taco truck.

"Oh. My. God. You brought me to a taco truck?"

"Yeah, I hope that's okay. It's not fancy, but they have the best tacos in Vermont."

I worry if this low-key day and lunch will turn her off.

"It's perfect."

The way she looks at me makes my chest constrict and my heart skip a beat. There's pure and undiluted joy on her face. She radiates happiness. I don't know what to do with it, and for a moment, I'm struck mute.

"I love food trucks. Every year, my family goes to this huge food truck festival in Burlington. I eat so much, I get sick every single time, but they have the best food. I can't help myself."

I find my voice again.

"Well, let's make sure you don't eat so much that you get sick today. I want to race you again and try to beat you."

She laughs.

"You think you can beat me?"

"I hope so. If you stick around long enough, I might be able to."

"You got me Go Karts and tacos. You may never get rid of me now," she jokes.

The idea of keeping her makes my heart speed up. Something is seriously wrong with me.

We find a shady picnic table to sit and eat at, and the look of bliss on her face with every bite makes my jeans tighter in the groin area.

Where have you been my whole life, Skye?

CHAPTER ELEVEN

Skye

I CAN'T BELIEVE HOW MUCH I'M ENJOYING MY BIRTHDAY date and how at ease I am around Logan. This has been the perfect date. I would never expect him to take me to an amusement park and then to a taco truck for lunch. It's almost 2:00 p.m. and I'm already regretting the fact this day will end.

We've been talking in between rides and games, but nothing deep. The way Logan is looking at me tells me this is about to change. I can tell there's a lot on his mind by the way he watches me when he thinks I'm distracted, as if he's trying to figure something out. What, exactly, I don't know.

"Tell me more about you. I met your sister, and you told me a little about your parents. Which friends do I have to impress?"

His voice is light, and he's smiling, but there's an edge to it anyway, as if he's trying to figure out a puzzle.

"You know Bruno. We met during orientation and bonded over our mutual love of *The Princess Bride*. We've been good friends since. Some people think we're more than that, my sister included. River is jaded, and she can't believe a guy and a girl can be friends without one of them developing feelings for the other. In her defense, pretty much every guy she ever met wanted to date her."

"I don't," he says.

"I really like her sister, though."

I forget what I was about to say and take another bite of my taco. Two down, one to go.

"So, you and Bruno are just friends, no benefits involved?"

"Exactly. Nothing remotely romantic has ever happened between us, and it never will. We have a few of our classes together since we share the same major, and we hang out often as well. He's my best friend."

Logan takes a moment to think it over while taking a sip of his water bottle.

"Is Bruno interested in your sister then?"

The thought of Bruno and River together makes me burst out laughing.

"Oh, God, no. Bruno is in a long-term relationship with someone who lives out of town. That's where he is today. He spends most weekends away."

I can see how from the outside, someone might think Bruno and I are more. But friends with benefits, we are not. I know all of Bruno's secrets, and he knows mine. We're each other's rock.

Bruno is the kind of guy everyone loves and wants to be friends with. Having people think we have some sort of fuck-buddy relationship is sometimes mutually beneficial. It keeps guys from badgering me and keeps most girls off his back too. Not everyone cares that he's in a relationship. It's easy to ignore it when no one but me has met his person.

"So, what do you want to be when you grow up?"

"Work in a magazine or newspaper as an editor. I'm doing a double-major. Communications and English."

My real dream is to be a writer, but I don't tell him that. I take a sip of my water before shifting the conversation back to him.

"What about you? Who are your friends?"

What I want to ask is what a guy who looks like him is doing with me. He could have anyone.

"I stay in touch with a lot of the guys from college. We have an alumni hockey team and play all year long, just for fun. RU gives us some ice time a few times a month. Less so during the season. I'm the youngest at work, so the older guys like to call me rookie and pull pranks on me. I don't have anyone like Bruno. I guess I have to agree with River. Most of my female friends wanted more. I dated some over the years, but nothing serious."

"No one serious? Ever?"

He hesitates before he answers. His blue eyes go stormy at my question, but he covers it up so fast, I wonder if I imagined the whole thing.

"There was someone I dated for a long time, but it didn't work out. We wanted different things. I've been single for the last four years."

I've been single for almost four years too, with the exception of those three weeks I was with Jon—I don't know what I was thinking back then. I'm glad his relationship ended a while ago. It must mean he's over her, right?

"And what about your family? You mentioned a brother before. Is he your only sibling?"

"No other siblings. Just Liam. He's two years younger than me, and he's a marine deployed somewhere in the Middle East."

"A police officer and a marine. Your parents must be so proud."

"Not exactly. Our parents don't approve of our career choices."

There's a thunderstorm is his eyes. Then I remember what he said earlier about not being close to his parents. I want to smack myself in the head and kick his parents in the ass.

"Why the hell not?"

I'm so mad at myself and put off on his behalf, the words are out of my mouth before I have a chance to think them over.

Logan laughs and the storm clouds leave his eyes. They're sky blue again.

"They had different ideas for what our lives should be. We don't get along that well."

"I'm sorry to hear that. I sometimes forget not everyone is as lucky as I am. Holiday dinners must be difficult."

"They would be if I attended any. I haven't been back home in four years."

That surprises me and touches something inside my chest. I feel for him. I'm not so naïve as to think everyone has a loving and supportive family, and even then, there are always differences. But to have no one? That's heartbreaking.

"What do you do for Thanksgiving? Christmas?"

"I work. I've worked every holiday for the last four years. It's not like I was going to my parents' house. I figure I may as well volunteer to take the jobs and give someone with kids a chance to spend the holidays with them."

Logan's response tugs at my soul. I can't imagine not having anyone I'd want to spend time with. I wonder about his friends, but I don't ask.

"Nope. Not this year. You're officially invited to spend the holidays with my family. They're crazy, but I think you'll like them."

His smile is almost sad, but his words hold a touch of gratitude.

"I'll have to put a request in, but I'd like that. I'd like that very much."

CHAPTER TWELVE

Logan

I SURPRISE MYSELF WHEN I ACCEPT SKYE'S INVITATION TO spend Thanksgiving with her. Hearing about her family and seeing the love she holds for them in her eyes touches something inside me. It makes me realize how very lonely I am, how very lonely I have been—not only for the last four years, but most of my life.

She's all smiles when we stop by my truck, and I unlock the passenger door for her. But I don't open the door just yet. I brace myself on the truck, my arms on either side of her head, and lean in.

Her eyes widen at my proximity, and she bites her lower lip, but she doesn't look away, and I'm lost in the clear blue of her eyes. I have to hold in a groan. I want to bite that lip. I want to kiss her and find out if she tastes as sweet as I think she does.

I want to dive in head-first and run like hell. I know I don't make any sense. I spent far too long keeping everyone at an arm's length, and I do a damn good job at it. I have to learn to trust again. I have to learn how to let someone in.

No. Not someone. *Her.*

Skye awakens something in me. Something I can't name quite yet.

I lean in a little closer still but hold off from touching her. I'm glad she's keeping her eyes on mine, because if she looks down, she'll get an eyeful. If my dick had hands, it would be opening the zipper from the inside.

"I want to kiss you, Skye."

"Okay."

"Is that a yes?"

When it comes to sex, I don't want vague responses. Everything about Skye's body is saying yes, but I need to hear the words. I want her to trust herself and take charge of her needs and wants. I'll hold off until she's ready if I have to.

She bites her lip again and her eyes start to drop. No, that's not good. The situation south of my belt hasn't changed.

"Skye?"

She looks back at me again.

"I won't push you into doing anything you don't want to or aren't ready for. Don't feel obligated because we're on a date and I said I want to kiss you. You don't owe me anything. I can wait until—"

She surprises the hell out of me.

With her feet on tiptoes and her small hands on my chest, she kisses me. It's shy and tentative, but so fucking sexy, I groan. It takes everything in me not to press her against the truck and dry hump her in the parking lot.

I'm so fucking over my head in this. She tastes even better than I imagined and I haven't touched her tongue yet. I can feel her pulling away, and my hands go to her face, keeping her in place. I gently guide her and my tongue slips past her lips. My mouth tastes hers. She moans. I'm completely immersed in her, in her taste, in her orange flower scent, in the softness of her skin under my hands.

Her arms go around my neck and she pulls me closer. There's zero space between us now. Her small frame curves into mine, the heat of her body setting my own on fire. One of my hands finds its way around her back and the other behind her head, and I pull her into me even closer.

Jesus! This is supposed to be just a taste. Just a chaste kiss. And now, I'm practically fucking her mouth with mine. I feel like an asshole, but she's taking all I give her and giving it right back.

This kiss went from PG to XXX so fast, I half expect to hear a sonic boom.

There's no sonic boom, but there are some honks and whistles.

Reality crashes over us then. We break the kiss but don't pull apart. She hides her face in my chest, and we stand there for a couple of minutes, catching our breaths, willing our hearts to slow down. I can't help running my fingers through her soft hair. The color's more golden under the light of the afternoon sun.

She makes a move to pull away from me. Her eyes are still downcast. Her lips are red and swollen, and some kind of caveman primal pride fills my chest with the knowledge that I did that. I left my mark on her somehow.

Great.

Next, I'll be pissing a circle around her and thumping my chest.

She raises her eyes. Her cheeks are pink. I tuck a lock of hair behind her ear. I should say something, apologize for attacking her mouth the way I did.

"Sorry, I got carried away."

"I was there too. You didn't do it alone. I was a willing participant. No need to apologize. Unless you want me to say sorry too."

"Hell no!"

She bursts out laughing and it's beautiful.

"I'm not really sorry. Not at all. As far as first-date kisses go, this one was a perfect first-date kiss."

She smiles.

"Just a perfect *first-date* kiss? And here I thought it was the perfect kiss, period."

That caveman in my chest? He's flexing his muscles now.

"I might have to try it again just to be sure."

Her eyes fall to my lips, and I'm about to kiss her again, but there are too many people around us now, so I kiss her forehead instead, my lips lingering on her skin for a few moments.

My eyes closed so I can feel her better.

CHAPTER THIRTEEN

Skye

We went back to the park, and I beat him twice more in the Go Karts. We talked and held hands and stole kisses on the Ferris wheel.

We're driving back now. He glances at me every so often, and neither of us feels the need to fill the silence with words. The bright day is giving way to evening as the sky changes colors from blue to pink, purple, yellow, and orange, blending in with the fall colors on the horizon until it looks like an impossible painting on a day made up of impossibles. It still feels surreal. I kissed him. I can't believe I just up and kissed him.

I don't know what got into me. He'd been so perfect the entire day, so sweet and funny and attentive. I've never had a guy be so into me before. I've never wanted to kiss someone so badly. I can't believe I kissed him first, and the way he kissed me back! If I were a cartoon character, my feet would be floating off the ground and there would be hearts jumping out of my eyes. I bite my lip to keep from smiling like the Cheshire Cat.

Then that old voice I know all too well starts chipping away at my joy.

Of course he had to kiss you back. What choice did he have?

Shut up.

This isn't going to last. A guy like him? He can have anyone. Why would he want you?

Shut up, shut up.

As soon as he gets into your pants, he'll drop you, and now he knows you're easy too.

I don't respond to the last accusation in my head. Experience tells me it's right.

"Hey?"

He grabs my hand, lacing our fingers together and kissing the back.

"Everything okay?"

I smile, but I know it doesn't reach my eyes.

"Yes, I'm fine."

His eyes stay on me for a moment longer, look at the road, and then glance back at me.

"Stay with me, okay? I had a blast today. Whatever doubts you're coming up with in your head right now? Get rid of them."

How did he know? Am I that transparent?

I don't respond, just nod and let the sound of the road under the truck tires lull me into acceptance. I can hear Mom's voice in my head.

Whatever happens, happens. But nothing will ever flourish and grow if you don't give it a chance. The seed may turn into a beautiful flower or it may just be a weed. And only you can decide which it is. Just remember, one person's weed may be someone else's flower. And the world needs both.

CHAPTER FOURTEEN

Logan

WE DRIVE BACK HOME. MY HOME, THAT IS, SO WE CAN GET
to the second part of our date. I've never spent this many hours
on a date before. When we pull into my driveway, Skye looks
back at me, a question in her eyes.

"Ready for part two of our date?"

"Part two?"

I smile. "You'll see."

This time, she stays in the truck while I walk around the
bumper, her eyes tracking my every move. Until I open her
door, that is. Her gaze drops, her cheeks blush, and her shyness
returns. I help her out of the truck and take her hand until we
get inside the house.

"May I have your coat?"

"Sure."

I watch as her small hands lower the zipper, and my imagination is a dozen steps ahead and already picturing her naked.
I've gotta get ahold of myself.

She gives me her coat and looks around, taking everything
in, and I try to see my home through her eyes. The walls are

painted a soft sand color with white wainscoting around the entire room. The furniture, dark chocolate brown sofas and tables, are decidedly masculine. The seventy-inch TV above the brick fireplace is the central focus of the room, but her eyes are immediately drawn to the dozens of framed pictures on the wall. A good portion of them are black and white pictures of my grandparents and other relatives long gone. I love old pictures and the history they hold. A moment frozen in time on a piece of paper. I love how something so fragile can capture life and hold so much history in it.

I kick off my sneakers and put them in the closet by the front door. I hate wearing shoes in the house. I hang both of our coats.

"Get comfortable. Be right back."

When I return, she's standing by the wall looking at the pictures, and her boots are off. Her socks make me laugh.

"Purple unicorn socks?"

She looks at her feet as if seeing them for the first time.

"Yeah, they're River's lucky socks. She made me wear them. She's obsessed with unicorns and the color purple. You didn't hear it from me, though. She'll deny her love of all things unicorn if you ask her. It doesn't exactly go with her tough girl image."

I think about making a joke about getting lucky and her socks, but I pass.

"Her secret is safe with me."

I stand at her shoulder and see the picture she's looking at.

"Tell me about this one," she asks.

It's one of the bigger frames. I had the image restored and blown up.

It's a picture of my brother and me on the back of the truck, parked in the very same spot it is now. Grandpa is holding a hose and is spraying us. The water is making rainbows in the air. Our skinny bodies are taller than our ages. Grandma is right next to him. We all have huge smiles on our faces. It's a candid image. No one is posing. I have no idea who took this picture.

"This was summer. I was ten and Liam was eight. It had to be a Sunday. We washed that truck every Sunday, even in the rain. As long as the temperature was above sixty-five. Grandma's rules."

Skye looks around the room, pausing in front of a few other pictures, but she doesn't ask any other questions about them.

"We have about an hour until the food is ready. Come on, let's get dinner going."

I take her hand and we walk to the kitchen. Unlike her apartment, I kept the original structure of Grandma's house when I renovated it two years ago. The kitchen is spacious, with honey-colored granite countertops, stainless steel appliances, and a large island that doubles as a kitchen table. It opens into the dining room.

Music is playing softly in the background.

"What do you like to listen to?"

"I love classic rock. Aerosmith, Pink Floyd, Queen."

"I do too. I always have music playing when I cook."

"You like to cook?"

"Yes. And I can bake too."

"You can cook and bake?" she asks, incredulous.

"Yes. And I made dinner for you."

She makes me laugh.

"How did you learn?"

"We had a cook growing up. My brother and I spent most of our afternoons after school doing homework at the kitchen table and watching Mary cook and bake. She'd make us a fresh batch of cookies every day. I guess I watched her enough over the years and picked up a thing or two."

What I don't tell her is that Mary is the closest thing we had to a mother. And we stayed in that kitchen long after homework was done.

"That explains your cookie addiction."

"I have no idea what you're talking about."

"Sure, you don't," she says with a laugh.

"We have about an hour. Can I get you something to drink?"

"Just water is fine."

I get us both a glass of water.

"Tell me more about your family. What are they like?"

"Mom and Dad are so unlike any other parents I've ever met, especially Mom. If you think River has no filter, wait until you meet my mother."

She takes a sip of her water.

"Our parents never judged or questioned us. My parents guided but never pushed. For starters, they never enforced any kind of punishments on us or forced us to do anything. Not even homework. If we decided that we didn't want to do homework, then it was up to us to tell the teacher at school, and we quickly learned that not doing it at home meant losing recess and doing it at school, anyway."

"They taught you responsibility by allowing you to be responsible for your choices."

"Yes. And consequences. Our parents explained that for every action or lack thereof, for every choice we made, there would be consequences. They didn't leave us to fend for ourselves or allow us to do anything that would put us in danger. But they gave us the freedom to make our own choices to the measure we could handle them and let us deal with the consequences of those choices."

"So, you didn't so much learn from their telling you, but from your own experiences."

"Exactly. Nothing teaches a kid that eating half of a chocolate cake in one sitting is a bad idea like actually doing it and dealing with the stomachache that's sure to follow. Let's just say River and I never did that again."

Her words radiate love, and it makes me want to kiss her and capture it with my lips.

"They were preparing us to be independent, to think for ourselves, and to blaze our own path. That's Mom's favorite thing to tell us, *'There is only one person who can live your life: You. So you may as well do what makes you happy. Create your own path. Leave your mark in the world. Make it something you're proud of.'*"

"I like that."

"I do too. The thing is, as much as I want to, there's a part of me that's terrified of taking that leap of faith."

She stops abruptly, as if in confessing her fears, she has said too much.

"I can understand that."

"You can?"

"Yes. Faith requires trust. And trust is not something that comes easily to everyone."

"No, it doesn't. Especially if that trust has been broken before."

The word *trust* floats between us long after it was said, as if suspended in wait. Invisible, intangible, and yet heavy with fear and need.

The need to trust.

The fear of trusting.

Two sides of the same coin.

We don't say anything for a while, and the first cords of a familiar melody start to play, "I Don't Want to Miss a Thing" by Aerosmith.

I wonder if Grandpa is whispering in my ear again. The first time I heard this song, he played it to me and told me to make sure to never hold back because I don't want to miss anything.

CHAPTER FIFTEEN

Skye

I'M LEANING ON THE COUNTER AND WATCHING AS HE makes us coffee. It's not late, but it's been a long day. I stifle a yawn.

"I'm sorry."

He smiles as he turns to me and kisses me on the cheek. It's such a sweet gesture, so filled with tenderness. My heart skips a beat.

"Nothing to be sorry for. It's been a long day. But I enjoyed every minute of it."

His hand is on my hair again. He twirls a lock on his fingers and then lets it drop. He's done it a few times tonight.

"Take a seat."

He guides me back to the now cleared kitchen island where we had dinner less than an hour ago.

He gestures for me to wait and gets us both coffee. Then goes back to the fridge and brings out a cake. He places it in front of me. A homemade cake, twenty-one colorful candles on top of it. A rainbow of colors against the dark chocolate ganache.

He lights the candles, but it's my heart that goes up in flames.

"Happy birthday, Skye."

Words I'm not capable of saying try to spill out of my eyes. I blink to stop the rogue tears. Of all the things he could have said or done, this simple gesture, a birthday cake he's clearly baked himself is what touches me the deepest. I throw myself into his arms. He hugs me back. A muffled *Thank you* leaves my lips as he squeezes me harder and kisses the top of my head.

This moment, with his arms tight around me—it feels right. Maybe we can give trust a chance because I just realized I don't want to miss a thing either.

I pull back just enough to look at him, and like before, I go on my tiptoes and kiss him. It starts as a gentle kiss, a pass of lips, a chaste taste. My lips part for him, and he dips in once, twice, and then pulls back.

He looks over my shoulder.

"As much as I hate stopping myself right now, you'd better make that wish before the cake burns the house down."

We burst out laughing.

I look at him and back at my twenty-one candles. I make a wish and blow them out. Twenty-one little spirals of smoke rise up and dissipate, each one of them a message to the universe, a reminder to make my wish come true.

Logan plucks the candles off the cake and grabs a single plate and two forks. He cuts a huge slice.

"Vanilla cake with chocolate ganache is my favorite. How did you know?"

He shrugs.

"I didn't. It's my favorite too."

I moan at the first bite. He stills, eyes on my lips. I freeze too. Logan leans in and licks the corner of my mouth. Then he smiles.

"You had a little bit of chocolate right there."

I have the urge to cover my entire body in ganache.

His smile widens and turns into a knowing smirk. And I don't know if I said that out loud or if he just read my mind. I'm pretty sure my entire body is flushed red right now. He laughs and stands up.

"Be right back."

When he returns, he's holding a gift bag and pushes it toward me.

"Got you something."

The surprise must be evident on my face.

"Don't look so surprised. You didn't think I'd forget it's your birthday, right?"

"No, it's just that I wasn't expecting anything else. You didn't have to do this—all of this."

I gesture at the space around us.

"I know, but I wanted to."

A small smile plays on his lips. He watches my every move.

"Go on, open it."

Curiosity takes over me, and I reach for the plain brown paper bag and look inside. Two packages wrapped in tissue paper. I reach for the smaller one and unfold the paper, revealing a narrow powder-blue box. I find a beautiful silver bracelet inside with three charms dangling from it—a book, the number twenty-one, and . . . is that a cop car?

"This is beautiful, Logan. I don't know what to say. Thank you. I love it."

"I figured the book for your love of reading and the number for your birthday, and the cruiser for the day we met."

He looks at me and there's anticipation in his eyes.

"This is so thoughtful. I really do love it."

He takes the bracelet from me, opens it, and looks at me, waiting. I give him my left wrist. His fingers brush my skin, sending shivers up and down my spine. My nipples get hard and send a little thank you to whoever invented padded bras, glad that Logan can't see how his simple touch affects me.

I turn my arm so I can see the pendants, and the silver shines under the kitchen lights.

"There's one more," he reminds me.

I can't imagine anything that would top the bracelet. When I reach inside the bag one more time and remove the next wrapped gift, I can tell it's a book and get that old feeling of anticipation every time a new book comes my way. When I remove the tissue paper, words escape me.

He smiles at my reaction. I look at him and then back at the book and back at him again. And repeat this another half-dozen times. Still fighting to find my speech, all I can say is, "How?"

He shrugs.

"I don't understand. This book is not out until next week. How did you get it?"

I look at the book again and open the cover. A fangirl squeal leaves my mouth and Logan laughs out loud. My face heats with embarrassment.

"Does it mean you like it?"

"I love it, but I don't understand. How do you even know about this book, and how did you get it?"

"I ran into River at Pat's on Monday and asked her for ideas for a birthday gift. She said I could never go wrong with a book. I asked her what kind of book and she gave me names of your favorite authors but said you most likely had read all of their books already. Except for this one, because it wasn't out yet."

"River never said anything about it."

"I asked her not to."

"But, how did you actually get it?"

"When I got home, I looked up the author and found her webpage."

I look at the paperback in my hands, the last book in my favorite series. I've been waiting for this book to be released for months, and not only do I have a hard copy in my hands, but it's also signed *to* me.

"I can't believe you did this. You got this book for me?"

The words come out like a question even though I intended them as a statement.

"Yes, for you. I sent her an email and explained that I met this amazing girl and our first date was on her birthday and I wanted to do something special for her. And that you loved her books."

"And she sent it to you?"

"Yes, she said she had a few paperbacks on hand and that she'd be glad to mail me a signed copy."

"Wow, I can't believe it. This is . . . I have no words. Thank you, Logan."

I step around the counter and wrap my arms around his neck and pull him into a hug. His hands go around me and he tugs me between his legs.

I can feel him breathing into my hair, sending a dance of shivers on my skin. I kiss him on the cheek and pull away. His eyes linger on my lips for a few seconds before he dips his head and his mouth finds mine.

He savors me. There's no other word to describe the way Logan's lips move over mine.

Unhurried.

Knowing.

Skilled.

Each pass of his lips, each nibble, each lick of his tongue on mine is a contained invitation for more. We kiss for a long time, his hands never straying into second-base territory.

HE WALKS ME HOME. His legs are much longer than mine, but he adjusts his pace and I don't have to lengthen my stride to keep up. Something in me trusts him. I feel safe. And it has nothing to do with his being a cop. It's him. The way he looks at me, the way he smiles, the way his eyes light up when I blush. The thought makes be blush again. I'm glad it's dark out, and save for the few lamp posts here and there, there isn't enough light for him to see my blushing face.

The sides of our bodies touch, his arm around me spreading heat over my back and other places he's not touching. His body is like a warm blanket at my side. I want to wrap myself in him.

I look up, taking in his beautiful profile, the strong, chiseled jaw darkened by the shadow of whiskers, the mouth I've wanted on mine since the first time I saw him.

We walk up the three steps to the building's front door, and I punch in the code for the keyless entry. He opens the door and guides me in first.

I take a few steps into the hall and hesitate in front of my apartment door before unlocking and leaving it open for him to follow me inside. I drop my new book and my purse on the side table near the couch and unzip my jacket, glad for the warmth inside. I expect to see him behind me, but he's standing just outside my door.

For the space of a breath or two, we look at each other in silence, the moment filled with expectation. He takes a step, then another and another until there's only inches between us. His fingers push a lock of hair behind my ear and trace my cheek and chin just before rubbing my lower lip with his thumb. On instinct, my tongue licks the spot he touched as if trying to capture his taste. He groans a little and comes closer to me, his hands around my waist, fingers spread, his touch spanning from my hip to the band of my bra.

"I had an amazing day, Skye. I hope you did too."

"I did. Thank you. It was the best birthday ever."

We stand there for a few seconds, no words between us, and yet so much is said. We both want more. Neither of us wants this day to end. But it's too soon for anything else. As much as I want to give into the need growing inside me, I know I'd regret it come morning. Not that there's anything wrong with it. It's just that I'm not that comfortable in my own skin. Taking what I want has never been something I could easily do.

Logan seems to understand this. I can see the need in his eyes, in the way his breath comes out in short pants, and in the possessive touch of his hands on my body.

"I should go. It's been a long day. But I want to see you again."

"I'd like that."

He leans into me then. His mouth is soft on mine, teasing. He licks and nibbles at my lips before going in deeper and opening my mouth with his tongue.

Jesus, the man can kiss. His body presses into mine and he pulls me closer, lifting me off the floor a few inches to adjust for our height differences. One arm wrapped around my back anchors me to him and the other holds my head where he wants it. I can feel all of him, the thundering of his heart against mine, the muscled arms and the way they flex, the hard flat of his stomach, and his erection pressing into me. My hands move over his shoulders and biceps and tangle in his hair. I don't think I've been this turned on since . . . well, never.

When we finally break the kiss several minutes later, his forehead touches mine, our mingled breaths rapid and shallow. We stay there in each other's arms, in each other's space, until both our hearts return to a steady beat and our breaths are no longer hurried. He lifts his head, his eyes lock on mine, and he lets me slide down his body. The friction nearly undoes me. I almost ask him to stay. Almost. My lips move, but the words stay stuck inside. His thumb brushes my bottom lip again.

He steps away from me slowly.

"I'm going now. I'll talk to you tomorrow. Have a good night."

He pulls the door closed behind him, and I'm still frozen in place when I hear the soft click of the lock.

CHAPTER SIXTEEN

Logan

I LIE IN BED, AND MY SKIN STILL DAMP FROM THE SHOWER, is chilled, but I'm burning on the inside. I grab my phone and find Liam's contact.

Logan: That girl I met? I spent the entire day with her.
Logan: God...she's a tiny little thing, and so full of life. When I look at her, I feel like a blind man seeing colors for the first time.
Logan: I'm so fucked.
Logan: Where are you, Liam? Talk to me.
Logan: I wish you could respond to this. I'm trying so hard to do what you said. To let go, but it feels like taking my clothes off in the middle of a parade. Like being completely exposed.
Logan: Come home, baby brother.

I think of the last time I talked to Liam and his parting words.

"If you change who you are because of him, because of what Dad did to you, he wins. The biggest 'fuck you' that you can give

that bastard is just being you. The real you. Not some made-up version. What they did to you was beyond wrong and fucked up. But they did you a favor. Imagine if you'd never found out. You'd be trapped right now."

God, when did my little brother get so smart?

Always. He was always the smartest one. The kindest. The most generous. I wonder where Liam is and how he's doing now. It's been months since I last heard from him. He's too gentle a soul to be in the middle of a war.

"Okay, Liam, I'll try." I hope you're right and I hope you're okay.

"Come home, baby brother."

I say it like a prayer.

CHAPTER SEVENTEEN

Skye

THE FAINT RUMBLE OF THUNDER OUTSIDE AWAKENS ME. I blink, chasing away sleep, glad it's Sunday and we don't have classes. I can see the rain beating against the window through the partially open curtains. God, did it all really happen? I can't help the smile on my face. I'm still in dreamland when River walks into my room with two coffee mugs. I push myself up and fluff up the half-dozen pillows on my bed. She gives me one of the mugs and settles under the covers with me. This is something we used to do a lot, but River hasn't come to my bed in the morning for several months now.

"Thank you, Sis."

"You're welcome. Now tell me everything."

"Hmm, the first sip is always the best."

I look at my sister. Her beautiful hair is messy and loose around her shoulders, and like always, she's wearing a purple sleep shirt and panties. River hates pants. She drinks her coffee and waits for me.

"It was such a perfect day."

"Yeah? You look happy."

"I am, I really am. He's sweet and funny and he surprised me."

"What do you mean?"

"I don't know. I guess I expected him to be like Blake or Jon. My previous experiences with guys don't really give me the warm fuzzies, you know?"

"Yep, I was there. I know. Where did you go?"

"First, we went to an amusement park, and get this, they have Go Karts!"

"Oh, no. Please tell me you didn't beat him and then gloat about it."

"I sure did."

"And what did he do?"

"Nothing, he just laughed."

"He didn't get mad or annoyed?"

"No, not at all. One can tell a lot about a person by the way they handle competition and losing a game or a bet. You know how I get with Go Karts, and I decided that if I beat him and he got mad about it, then that would be it, right? I'd endure the day, be polite, and be done at the end. But he didn't get mad or annoyed. He got a big kick out it, actually."

"Yeah, I remember how pissed Blake would get if you beat him on the Xbox. He'd stop talking to you for days."

"I know. I made so many excuses for his behavior. But I'm not seventeen anymore. I've learned my lesson. No second chances for assholes. That's my new motto."

"I'll toast to that."

She touches my mug with hers.

"What else?"

"Then we had lunch at a taco truck and went back to the park, where I beat him two more times, just to be sure, and all he did was laugh."

"He seems like a nice guy. I have a good feeling about him. He's nothing like Asshole Jon."

"No, he's not."

"Did he kiss you?"

"Yes. Well . . . technically, I kissed him."

A giggle escapes my lips.

"Shut up!"

"I did. I don't know what came over me, River. But one moment, I'm just standing there looking at those blue eyes, and the next, I have my mouth on his."

River high-fives me.

"One to ten?"

"It was a twenty."

When we were kids—teens, really—River came up with a kissing scale from one to ten on how good a kisser a boy was. Silly teenage stuff, and we hadn't used the scale in years.

"That good, huh?"

"God, yes. And then we drove back to his house, and he cooked and baked. Can you believe it? He made lasagna and baked me a birthday cake. He even had garlic bread. And it was delicious. We talked a lot, and he gave me this bracelet."

I show her my wrist.

River fingers the charms with a smile on her face.

"And this."

I reach to my nightstand, put the coffee down, and show her the book.

"Son of a bitch. He got it. I thought this book wasn't out until next week."

"It isn't. He emailed the author and asked her about the book, and she mailed it to him. I still can't believe this is happening. I expect to wake up at any minute now and be disappointed that was just a dream. Thank you, by the way, for the part you played in it."

"I didn't do anything other than answer his questions. Can't take credit for it."

River watches me, and I know what she'll ask next.

"Did you sleep with him?"

"No. I wanted to. But, you know me."

That's a first too. I've never felt so attracted to a guy that I wanted to sleep with him.

River nods at me.

"I think it's better this way. Let him marinate a little."

"What about you? How was the strip club?"

"Ugh."

"Not good?"

"It was okay until Becca got really drunk and puked on one of the guys and we got escorted out."

"No!"

"Yep. It was my birthday, and she's the one who got drunk. I had one margarita, and she was already five tequila shots into the night. Her last boy toy found someone else, and you know how she is with that. She doesn't take rejection very well."

"I don't understand. She doesn't even like those guys. She uses them for a few weeks and then moves to the next one. Why would she care if they move on?"

"She doesn't care if they move on. She cares if she's not the one to dump them. Becca has major control and abandonment issues."

"Her way to deal with it is to break up with them first?"

"I've tried talking to her, but she shuts down and tells me I don't have a psychology degree yet, so save it for someone who needs real help. And then she tells me I have a hang-up because I'm not hooking up with a different guy every other week. Been there, done that. This is not high school or freshman year anymore. I'm kind of tired of the same old jocks and guys who can't have an interesting conversation. Last night, this one dude walked up to me and asked me if I wanted to fuck. No hello, no can I buy you a drink, no nothing. Stick it in dry, will you?"

"What an ass. I wonder if that line ever works in real life. I mean, how often does a guy walk up to a strange girl and asks if she wants to fuck and she says yes, please, I was sitting here waiting for someone to come up and ask me that."

"I know. I guess there's nothing wrong with it, if that's what you want. But I'd like, just once, for a guy to look me in the eyes for more than five seconds instead of at my tits."

"At least you have tits."

She rolls her eyes at me.

"Is it asking for too much to meet a guy who wants to get to know me a little? Sometimes, I feel like a thing people want to use and show off rather than a real person with feelings and flaws."

"Flaws?"

This is the most open River has been in ages. I don't want to say the wrong thing and have her shut down again.

"Yes. They don't even see it. I did a few experiments. I was rude, mean, shallow, completely obtuse, boring, and dull, and guys still looked at me, hanging onto my every word like I'm a rock star or something."

"Some guys will do anything to get in your pants, River."

And there goes the conversation. She visibly puts her walls back up and shifts the attention back to me.

"So, what's on the agenda for today?"

"Nothing. No plans. It's raining, so it's a perfect day for TV and books."

My phone buzzes, and I grab it from the side table. A smile

is already on my face when I see Logan's name.

Logan: Good morning, Skye. I had a great time yesterday.
Skye: I did too. It was so much fun. Are you off today?
**Logan: No, I'm already at work. What are your plans for
tonight?**
Skye: Nothing. Just hanging out with River.
**Logan: Got enough leftovers for another dinner. Want to come
over tonight?**
Logan: You can bring your sister if you want.

I show the phone to River. The old doubt tugs at my chest. What if Logan comes to his senses and falls for River? Men are visual beings. He can't deny that she's beautiful. I have the urge to say no, so he won't be around her, but I ignore it. I'm being stupid. It's not like I can keep them away from each other. If I end up dating Logan—if this is not just a fluke—they will be around each other a lot.

"Leftover lasagna and cake? Heck, yes. It's always best the next day. I'm in."

Skye: Yes, we'll be there.
**Logan: You forgot your little yellow friend in my truck
last night.**
Skye: Stuart!
Logan: I got a good ribbing about it at work.
Skye: LOL. Sorry?
Logan: No worries. See you at 8. Back to work now.
Skye: Be safe, Logan.

I look at my phone for another minute, but he doesn't text

me back. My mind goes back to doubting myself. What if this whole thing is just to get closer to River?

"What's that look for? What are you thinking?"

Her too-perceptive eyes study me.

"Nothing. Hungry. Let's go make breakfast.

"You're weird."

"You're weirder."

"You're weirdest."

And just like that, we're back to normal.

CHAPTER EIGHTEEN

Logan

FOR THE FIRST TIME EVER, MY JOB IS ANNOYING ME. AND not because of the array of bad or sad things I come across every so often, but because it's getting in the way of my seeing Skye.

Logan: Hey, Liam. I haven't texted you all week, so we have some catching up to do.

Logan: That girl I told you about? Her name is Skye. I saw her three times last week.

Logan: Had dinner with her and her sister the day after our first date. Wish you were there. I made Mary's lasagna and the cake she used to make for our birthdays.

Logan: On our second official date (I'm not counting the dinner with her sister as a date), we went to the movies and dinner at Domenic's. We stayed there talking until they invited us to leave so they could close the place. I don't even know what we talked about. I just know that spending time with her makes me happy.

Logan: I texted Skye earlier today, asking her what she was doing for lunch. She said she was just grabbing a bite to eat

at Riggins since she only had an hour between classes. And now, I'm here. Stalking her.

Logan: She's coming. 10-73, baby brother.

The police radio codes came in handy when we were kids. I memorized them early on and taught Liam. It was a great way to communicate and not get caught by our father. Saying 10-73 instead of goodbye doesn't make it any easier, though.

I see her small frame and blond hair shining in the sun before she sees me. She's wearing skinny jeans and an open blue ski jacket over the navy Riggins hoodie. Pink sneakers on her feet.

Bruno is on her left and another girl on her right. The girl is tall, and her two friends dwarf Skye. They're laughing as they walk the path to the cafeteria among the dozens of students going in the same direction.

Bruno nudges her in a playful way, and she pushes him back, her hands on his chest in a way that feels too familiar for comfort, but I remind myself they've been friends for years and she told me they're just friends and that he has a girlfriend out of town.

Her eyes land on me then and her step falters. Bruno holds her arm and steadies her. A second later, a warm smile spreads over her face as she veers off and away from her friends and stands in front of me near the curb by the cafeteria entrance where I'd been stalking her. Her smile turns shy, and she casts her eyes down for a moment before looking back at me.

"What are you doing here?"

Her eyes shine with anticipation and excitement. She's happy to see me.

"I wanted to see you."

I step closer, my hands on her hips, and I inch her toward

me, lean in, and kiss her forehead. What I really want to do is push her against the wall, a tree, my car—any flat surface will do—and kiss her until she forgets her name. But it might be too much for the lunch crowd around us, and I'm in uniform, so I refrain. She can see the intention in my eyes because her face blushes prettily. My fingers press a little tighter into her hips.

Her friends stop a few feet away from us. Bruno is the first to speak.

"Joining us for lunch, Logan?"

"Yeah, if you don't mind my crashing in."

My words are friendly, but I'm sure the way I'm looking at him says clearly that I don't like the way he's so comfortable around Skye, who luckily missed the exchange since it's all happening right above her head.

The bastard laughs and shakes his head a little.

"Sure, we don't mind your company, if you don't mind the cafeteria food."

I make sure to place my hand on Skye's back and put myself between her and Bruno. It does not go unnoticed by her friend, and she gives me an odd look. Skye introduces us.

"Sabrina, this is Logan. Logan, this is Sabrina Giorgi, and you already know Bruno."

I shake her hand and nod at Bruno. *Yes, I'm the jealous-for-no-reason asshole. Nice to meet you.*

I feel like an ass. I'm not a possessive or jealous guy. I just can't shake what River said about them being fuck buddies and how familiar they are with each other. I'm not so stupid that I would say anything about it, but I can tell Bruno is on to me. I hope he says nothing. I don't want to look like an idiot.

I DIDN'T EXPECT her to be onboard when I asked if she would like to go fishing with me this weekend. Skye keeps surprising me. Saturday looked to be the warmer day, so that's what we picked. The day is perfect, sixty-five degrees and warm for Early October, even with the breeze. It's hard to believe that just three weeks ago, when I first met Skye, it was over twenty degrees colder.

The ride to Lake Dillon takes a little over an hour. Twenty minutes of that hour-long drive is through an unmarked dirt road in the woods. And another five-minute hike through the trees.

I don't expect to see anyone on this side of the lake today. In all the years I've been coming here, we'd only run into other people three times.

Most people who fish at Lake Dillon come from the other side, where it has a paved road access and a boat ramp. But that's about a mile downstream. Lake Dillon is not really a lake, but a river. This spot is actually a cove and just the right size. It's also very private. It can only be accessed through the road we drove on or via a boat.

"This place is beautiful. Do you come here often?"

I look around. It's the same as I remember. Trees, grasses, and bushes compete for attention in a riot of colors, greens, yellows, and oranges with a touch of red here and there. There's a small concave beach, about thirty yards wide, that slopes into the lake. Grass gives way to sand and pebbles the closer it gets to the water.

I set the picnic basket and fishing gear down before I answer her.

"I haven't come down here in a few years."

I take the large blanket she's holding against her chest and shake it open on the grass. Skye helps me straighten it. I put the basket on one corner and Sky drops her backpack next to it.

"How did you find this place?"

I laugh. I knew this question was coming.

"I've been coming here for as long as I can remember. I learned to swim in this very lake."

"Let me guess. Your grandparents brought you," she says with a smile.

"Yes. Liam and I spent many days and nights here. We used to camp overnight with our grandparents before we went to Florida for a few weeks every summer, then do it again just before school started."

"Is it me, or is your grandpa playing wingman again?"

"That would be so like him. If he were here now, he'd be telling you all about me, the most embarrassing but endearing things he could come up with."

"I don't know their names."

She sounds almost sad.

"Bill and Maggie Valentine."

"Your grandparents' last name is Valentine?"

There's a laugh in her voice.

"Yes, it means strong. What's so funny?"

"Isn't it a little funny that your wingman's name is also the name of a holiday dedicated to lovers?"

My eyebrows pop up. And I laugh too.

"I never made the connection between Valentine's Day and my grandparents' last name."

I can almost hear Grandpa laughing at me.

I set up two beach chairs and sand spikes near the water's edge and prop the fishing poles in them.

"Have you ever gone fishing before?"

"A few times when we were younger. But River and I would

make such a racket about killing the poor fish that Dad had to throw them back. After a few trips like that, he decided if he wanted to actually bring the fish home, he'd better not take us with him. Wait! Are you cooking the fish?"

She looks so alarmed, I have to laugh.

"No, I never bring it back with me. Strictly catch and release. Grandma is a vegetarian. She never allowed Grandpa to bring the fish home either," I say as I finish setting up the rods.

I HEAR A CLICK, and when I look, Skye has her phone out and she's taking pictures. She points the phone at me.

"Is this okay?"

I smile and she takes a picture.

"That's okay," I say as I get closer to her and take the phone, switching the camera view, "but this is better."

I hold the phone and take a dozen pictures of us smiling, me kissing her, her kissing me, and her laughing when I pull her body in front of mine, holding her with one hand and taking the pictures with the other.

Then I step back, grab my phone, and take a few more pictures of her alone, the kaleidoscope of fall colors at her back. Her looking shy, eyes downcast, and of her looking straight at me, lips parted and inviting.

I give her phone back to her.

"I want all of those. Send them all to me."

We sit at the water's edge for the next two hours, talking in hushed tones as if in church and listening to nature's songs, birds chirping, the rustle of trees, and the ripple of water over rocks and sand. We don't catch a single fish.

"Hungry?" I ask.

"Yes. I'm always hungry when I'm outdoors."

We walk to the blanket, take our shoes off, and sit on it. I'm in charge of lunch and Skye is in charge of dessert. I start unpacking.

"I got us some sandwiches, fruit, veggies . . ."

I stop talking when I see the container she pulls out of her bag and opens it. Three different kinds of cookies, chocolate chip, peanut butter, and sugar cookies.

"Marry me."

She laughs, and I swear I hear Grandpa's voice saying, *"attaboy."*

"Tell me about your home."

Skye packs away the food we didn't eat before answering me.

"I grew up on a farm. An organic farm, to be exact. It's not huge, but it's not small either. We grow different fruits, depending on the season. But we have a line of organic maple syrups we produce year-round. Traditional and flavored ones. We even have an adult-only version. It has bourbon, and you have to be over twenty-one to buy it."

"You can harvest maple all year?"

"Not harvest. Produce. Harvesting time is late winter into early spring. But we have different flavors being produced at different times of the year."

She leans back, propped on her elbows, back arched, face up to the sun, and eyes closed. The sides of her gray zip hoodie fall back, revealing a white T-shirt and a sliver of skin where the shirt meets the top of her black yoga pants. The outline of a pink bra is visible under the thin and nearly see-through fabric in the bright daylight. I watch, fascinated as the breeze swirls locks of golden hair around her face and shoulders. Eyes still closed, she inhales the cool, clean air deeply, her chest expanding, her flat stomach contracting.

It takes everything I have not to pounce on her. This level of trust she's giving me is something I'm having a hard time wrapping my head around. If I were her and a guy I'd just met drove me to the middle of nowhere, I'm not sure I'd be so relaxed.

Skye drops from her elbows to her back, arms crossed behind her head and legs crossed at the ankles. She's a picture of peacefulness. I envy her ability to just be.

Unguarded.

Open.

Artless.

"This place is beautiful."

When she speaks, the words startle me, so quiet and intense the moment is.

I lean over her, my knee touching her thigh, my hand at her waist.

"No, you are."

She looks at me with confusion in her eyes.

"I'm what?"

"Beautiful."

She reaches up and folds a hand behind my neck, fingers playing with my hair.

"Come here," she whispers.

I comply, half of my body hovering over hers as she lies back down. She traces the outlines of my face. My eyebrows, the curve of an ear, the bridge of my nose, my chin, and finally, my bottom lip. The touch is light as air.

"Kiss me," she says.

"As you wish." I quote *The Princess Bride*.

She smiles as my lips touch hers.

The kiss starts slow, teasing. But her hands tangle in my hair and pull at my back, urging me on, asking for more. She tugs me closer, and I let my body touch hers, a thigh between hers, my hard-on pressed into her hip. I brace myself as to not drop my full weight on her. She's half my size.

Skye presses up into me, and the last thread of restraint is gone. My tongue invades her mouth, and she whimpers and presses into me harder. I push my thigh into her center, and she pushes back, seeking relief. Her small hands grab at me, move down my back, and flex on my hip. I move on top of her, between her legs, never breaking the kiss.

She moans when I press my hardness into her, and Skye wraps her legs around mine. I move, grinding my erection into her clit. Our lips part then, and I kiss her neck instead. Her hard nipples are pressed to my chest, and I can feel her need, her desperation in the way her hands open and flex on my hips. She's close to orgasm. If I keep this up, I'm going to come too. I can't remember the last time I had an orgasm from just grinding into a girl. High school, maybe.

And then it happens. Her body arches under mine, and her mouth is open, but no sounds escape her. Her skin is flushed red. I slow my movements as she comes down from her orgasm. I didn't come. I'm hard as steel. That's okay. I'll take care of it later, picturing this moment in my mind over and over.

Her body relaxes and she goes limp under me. Then her eyes fly open as if surprised by what just happened. The expression on her face tells me exactly that. She tries to move her hands to cover her face, but my position on top of her makes it awkward.

"Hi," I say.

She closes her eyes.

"I'm sorry."

"Sorry for what?"

"I lost control, and I feel like I kind of molested you."

I would laugh, but I know she's really concerned.

"Skye, you didn't molest me. You turn me the heck on."

"I feel like I lead you on and . . . and . . ."

I know what she's trying to say. I didn't get off. She didn't plan on it going past a kiss. But it did, and I'm glad.

"Shh. I'm a big boy. I can handle myself. I know you're not trying to lead me on. And I'm glad you lost control. It was hot as fuck."

"Well, not quite hot as fuck, since technically, it was more like hot as dry humping," she says.

I burst out laughing. I love her ability to infuse humor into the most awkward of situations.

"Oh, Skye. What am I gonna do with you?"

"Hmm, some more of that?"

"As you wish."

CHAPTER NINETEEN

Skye

"So, did you do the deed yet?"

I roll my eyes at River and don't bother to answer her.

"You guys are dating for what? Almost a month now, and nothing?"

"Trying to read, River."

"Pfft, you're always trying to read. When don't you have your nose stuck in a book?"

"You should try picking up a book every so often. It would open the world for you."

"I am in the world. Living it in real life and 3D. And I do read. I'm just not as obsessed as you are. Now stop trying to change the subject and tell me why you haven't slept with him yet."

I try to ignore her and read the same line for the third time now.

"I know you're not using the rabbit either. I checked the box, and the seal is untouched. Much like your vajayjay. What gives? I thought Hot Cop would have you under arrest by now."

River snort-laughs at her own joke.

There's no getting away from this conversation. When River gets like this, it's easier for all involved to just go along with her. She's tenacious. I close the cover on my new iPad Mini, a birthday gift from our parents. I know River won't let go until I give her some kind of answer.

I pull myself up on the couch so I can face her, sitting on the other end from me.

"We're just taking it slow. I don't want to rush into things. And between his odd work hours and how busy we are with school and my job at the daycare, it's not like we're seeing each other every single day. Even if he lives right across the street."

"But you're making out and stuff, right?"

"Yes, River, we make out and stuff. He's very . . ."

What's the word I'm looking for?

"He's very what?"

"I don't know how to explain it. He's nothing like Blake or Jon. He's the complete opposite of them."

"That's good, because they're assholes, the both of them."

I have to agree with River. So far, my pick of guys hasn't been great.

"Logan is careful with me. I can tell he wants more, but he's holding back. Like he's waiting for me to make the move, you know?"

"He's waiting for you to take initiative? In sex? The poor guy will wait forever."

"Hey!"

I throw a pillow at her.

"I resent that. Just because I'm not dropping my panties at every guy who looks at me, doesn't mean I couldn't take initiative. I kissed him first."

Her reaction is not what I expected. There's a look of hurt

in River's eyes and she doesn't bother to cover it like she usually does when something hurts her feelings.

"What?"

"Just because I have a big mouth and joke about sex a lot, it doesn't mean I'm dropping my panties at every guy who looks at me, Skye."

"What? No, no. I didn't mean you. I didn't mean it like that at all. I'm talking in generics. This is not a jab at you or anything like that. I wasn't trying to slut-shame you. I'm sorry. I guess it came out that way."

She still looks upset, but it's more anger than hurt right now.

"And even if I were fucking every guy on campus, it still doesn't give you or anyone the right to judge me."

Gosh, how did this get so out of hand? She's right, of course.

"I was just making a joke, River. An exaggeration. You're right. I have no right to judge anyone. Their choices are their choices, and there shouldn't be different rules for women and men."

There's less heat in her eyes now. Again, I wonder what's going on with my sister. Jokes like this never upset her before. I get to see the River I know, for the most part, but then, in moments like this, there's something that's not right and I have no idea what it is or what to do about it. I want to help my twin with whatever is hurting her, but she won't let me in. I go back to her question.

"We haven't had sex yet. I know he wants to, and I want to. I think it will happen soon. Maybe I should buy condoms and keep them in my room. What do you think?"

"You're going to the pharmacy to grab a box of Trojans?"

She laughs at me. She knows I'd be mortified. Thank goodness I can Amazon Prime all the embarrassing stuff.

"Ugh, with my luck, one of my professors would be standing right behind me in line when I go pay for it. Maybe you can buy them for me."

Yeah, right. She can't even remember to buy coffee. Coffee! Who forgets to buy coffee?

"Sure. I'll get you some of those glow-in-the-dark, and the flavored ones too. Ribbed, for her pleasure. XXL."

"No, River. Just no. Forget I asked."

Knowing my sister, she would do it too.

And give it to me during dinner.

With our parents.

CHAPTER TWENTY

Logan

MY EYES ARE ON SKYE AS MUCH AS ON THE PUCK. I should be playing like shit with my attention split between her and the black rubber disk flying across the ice. But somehow, I'm playing one of my best games ever.

Twenty-seven seconds left on the clock and the score is three to one. I scored two of those goals. I think we can squeeze one more in. I glance one more time at Skye and get my attention back in the game.

I'm right outside the face-off, sticks battling for the puck, and I catch the rebound, turn, and skate across the ice, zigzagging between the other players. I can see number sixty-seven on the opposing team coming at me at full speed. He'll try to smash me into the boards. I slow down, and just before he hits me, I spin out of his way and shoot. The next thing I hear is the sweet sound of the goal horn confirming my score.

The clock zeros just as the sound ends. Game over. All I want to do is skate to Skye, but I have over a thousand pounds' worth of teammates hugging me and smacking my helmet. We do the customary glove pounding. The players skate to the tunnel and the few dozen family and friends who came in today are making their way out of the rink as well. Through it all, I keep my eyes on her.

Skye walks along the boards until she gets to one of the gates. I make my way to her, and when I get close enough, she throws herself at me. I catch her.

"Hat trick!" she yells at me, referring to the three goals I scored tonight.

You'd think I'd just won the Stanley Cup, she's so excited about it. I drop her to her feet. The skates add another three or four inches to my height, and she has to crane her neck to look at me. I bend to kiss her.

"I'm all sweaty. I'm sure you don't want to smell like a locker room," I say, a little self-conscious.

Her small hands grab my jersey.

"Nope. You smell like victory."

I kiss her again. I just have to.

"I have to go clean up and change. I'll be right back. Then we can grab dinner."

I kiss her one more time before I skate across the rink and into the tunnel.

I CAN'T BELIEVE we've been dating for a month already. And it's perfect. I miss Skye when we're not together, and we spend just about every free moment we can match up between us together. This is the first game I've played since we started dating.

We're seated in a booth, our legs tangled under the table. We're both wearing jeans, so there's no skin contact, yet this feels as intimate as if we were naked. I feel close to Skye, more than anyone else I've ever known.

"It was so exciting! When is the next game? Can I come again?"

I can't stop smiling.

"Yes, I want you there. You're my lucky charm. I never scored a Hat Trick before."

She pinkens with the compliment.

"That's the training rink, right? It was my first time there. I've been to the arena many times, but never that rink. I like it. I can get a lot closer to the ice."

"Yeah. Usually, just the family and friends of the players come to watch. The bleachers are not exactly comfortable."

"I'll say. I think my butt is still frozen. Did your family come to your games often?"

I hesitate. We're getting closer, but I've done a great job at skirting around family questions. She knows I don't get along with my parents, but we haven't talked much about my family.

"My grandparents did, and Liam. My parents never came to any of my games."

Some of the light leaves her eyes. I grab her hand and lace our fingers.

"It's okay. I got over it a long time ago."

But have I? Can anyone ever get over not feeling loved by their parents?

"Wanna talk about it?"

I never talked about it with anyone. Not even Liam.

"Growing up, my father never attended any of my games. He never attended a game when I was in college either. It just wasn't on his radar. If it wasn't something that was making him money, it had no place in his life. Liam and I were no more than pawns in his power and money games."

"What about your mom?"

"My mom did whatever my father told her to."

Skye tilts her head, questions in her eyes.

"I resent her. Not because she's like my father, but because she never went against any decisions he made. Even when I could see she disagreed with him. When she wanted to say or do something else, she never did. In a way, she was as much of a captive of his influence as we were as little kids. But we grew up and got away. Mom never did. I'll never understand why she stayed by his side all these years. She had a wealth of her own. She didn't need him. She couldn't possibly love him. Not after all the years of neglect and cheating on his part."

"You'd be surprised at the lies people tell themselves in the name of love. Even if that love is misplaced or unwanted."

Skye is right, I know. But a part of me, a part that's angry at my mother, still refuses to feel bad for her. I tried. I tried so many times. But you can't help someone who refuses to be helped.

"She turned a blind eye to everything he did and went along with it. I'll never understand the power he holds over her."

"Was he . . . was he abusive toward her?"

"No. I know my father was never physically abusive toward her. He would have thought it beneath him. Looking back, the emotional scars are clear now. I didn't see them back then when I was under his control. I thought she was just as cold as him. After I cut ties with him, I tried reaching out to my mother. I asked why she stayed with him and she had no answer for me. I flat-out asked her to leave him. To just go. I asked her to move in with me until she figured what she wanted to do. But she said she couldn't, and that's when years of repressed anger came out in a spectacular manner. I told Mom that my father was dead to me, and if she chose him over her own children again, so was she. That was the last time I saw my mother. Haven't spoken with her since. It's been nearly four years now."

She moves from her side of the booth to mine and pulls me into a hug. I feel like an alien in my own skin. Opening up like this is foreign to me.

"She never made an attempt to reach out to me. I feel like an asshole. In making that ultimatum, I'm no different from my father, and I hate myself for it."

Skye pulls away from the hug.

"No. You are nothing like your father. You may have allowed anger to speak for you, and I understand that. But you'd never treat your children the way he treated you. Never."

I never thought about having kids, but I know she speaks the truth. I'd never treat my children the way my parents treated me. I would love them unconditionally.

Still, I can't go back to that place. My mother knows where I live. She has my phone number. She knows how to find me, and she's never tried. Mom made a choice, and it wasn't Liam or me.

My entire life up to the day I left for good had been a web of lies, manipulation, and control. And I refuse to be a willing participant. But even now, four years later and with no contact with them, I can still feel the reach of my father in the way I live, in the decisions I make. It's been four years of trying to shed the conditioning he imposed on me.

Skye is a step in the right direction. A step away from him. I would've never gotten involved with her in my old life. She wouldn't have been good enough for my father.

Logan: Guess what, baby bro?

Logan: She likes hockey.

Logan: And fishing.

Logan: We've been together four weeks now.

Logan: I like this girl, Liam. I really, really do.

Logan: Mary is worried about you too. Please call us.

CHAPTER TWENTY-ONE

Skye

STANDING IN FRONT OF MY CLOSET, I CONSIDER MY options. My eyes find the flirty blue dress. It's kind of cold for it, but a long coat will solve the problem.

Next, my underwear drawer, which now houses several new panties and matching bras.

Today is the day, I tell myself. I can't help the smile on my face. I feel good. It feels right.

For the first time in years, I don't feel like less. For the first time in years, I'm not comparing myself to River and finding I'm in the loser column. Not that it was ever a competition, but being the lesser twin has always weighed heavily on me.

I will never be as beautiful as she is. Not even with all the plastic surgery in the world. When I look at myself, I see a small, timid girl who's plain and boring looking. My skin is pale. My hair is pale. The only pop of color on me are my blue eyes, but even they are a watered-down blue. I'm not curvy or tall like River. I can't think fast and toss comebacks at people when they say something rude. I don't know how to stand up for myself or be assertive.

As far back as I can remember, I was ignored. People would comment without any regard for the little blond girl hiding behind her mother's legs while River sucked up all the attention. Every single time, whenever we were out in public, the comments would be about how beautiful River was. How funny and assertive.

And me? It would be . . .

Oh, who's that?

Is that your friend?

You can't be sisters!

Twins? No way. They look nothing alike.

Way to go, people. Say I look nothing like my sister right after gushing about how beautiful she is.

It didn't take long for me to catch on. Even at a very young age, I was aware of our differences, and the shy little girl I was retreated into herself even more. When I was too old to hide behind my mother's legs, I started hiding behind books.

Sometimes, I'd hear, 'Oh, she likes to read. She must be very smart.' But as I grew older, smart turned into nerd, bookworm, and weirdo. And then there were the braces. The braces made the nerd-ugly-duckling-without-hope-of-ever-becoming-a-swan package complete.

My parents tried to compensate the unkind words of strangers by telling me how beautiful I was. But they were two people, and there were so many strangers, relatives, and friends repeating the same words again and again. The words of strangers carried more weight than my parents' words did. As they tend to.

Your mom and dad are supposed to say you are beautiful, right? How could I believe them when everyone else and the mirror said differently?

You'd think all that attention would have made River

shallow and conceited. But it didn't. Our parents made sure of it. They instilled in us values that have nothing to do with physical appearance or possessions. For River, having heard she's beautiful her whole life is just empty words. She has always been my defender, the force that stood between me and the world. She fought my battles, put mean people in their places, squelched rumors before they started, and made sure I was invited to every party and event, even if I didn't much want to attend. If people wanted to be liked by her, they had to be nice to me first.

I was as intensely grateful to my sister as I was resentful for needing all that protection from her as young teens. Not that I've ever let it be known—except to Mom, with her sixth sense, the woman knows everything. I love my sister. I can't fault her for my own insecurities, even if she has indirectly played a part in making me feel this way.

A petty and shallow part of me wishes I could trade places with her, just once. I've always wanted to know what it was like to be looked at with such admiration and adoration. To have strangers come up to me to say I'm beautiful. To have guys tripping over themselves. And I never thought it would happen.

Not until now.

Not until Logan.

He makes me feel beautiful and wanted. He makes me feel like I'm enough.

And I want to let him know this. So, today is the day.

CHAPTER TWENTY-TWO

Logan

THE MOVIE IN THE DVD PLAYER IS LONG FORGOTTEN AS our bodies move in tandem with each other, seeking the same thing. We tease, push, and retreat, move back and forward, pressing in and pulling back. I'm so hard it's painful, but it feels so good to have Sky sitting astride me, rocking into me, her tongue in my mouth and my hands under her dress, grasping her ass and guiding her over me. I push up and she presses down.

The moment I saw her walk through the door in the flirty baby blue dress, I knew I'd have my hands under it. There was just no way she could come over and go home without it happening, but I'm getting so much more than I expected when Skye came over for a lazy afternoon of movies and snacks. She is my snack now, and I'm going to devour her.

If she'll let me.

Skye is so much smaller than me that even in my lap, I'm still taller than her, and as she tilts her head to deepen the kiss, I pull one hand away from her ass and caress my way up her waist and the side of her breast. She arches her back into me. I let my hand travel around her stomach and up until I cup her in my palm. She moans into my mouth and I squeeze her breast into my hand gently. Her nipple is as hard as my dick. Jesus! I don't think she's wearing a bra.

I pull my mouth from hers and let my lips travel down her neck with open-mouthed kisses. I lick the curve of her neck where it meets her shoulder and then blow on it. Skye shivers in my arms. I pull the hand still holding her ass down her thigh and up her side as I make my way to her other breast and then cup them both over her dress. The bodice of her dress is tight to her chest and my fingers slide under the cap sleeve seeking skin. I move slow, giving her a chance to stop me, letting her know of my intentions. Her mouth finds mine again and sucks my bottom lip into hers. My shy little Skye is not so shy anymore, and she's driving me crazy with need. I want to bury myself into her.

No. I *need* to bury myself into her.

I slide the top of her dress down, and I stop when the fabric is just above her nipples, the swell of her small breasts begging to be tasted.

"Skye," I whisper into her lips.

"Logan," she whispers back into mine.

I tug her dress down.

"Is this okay?" I ask, looking into her eyes and waiting for her response.

Her skin is flushed pink and her lips swollen. Her eyes are dark with lust, and I know they're a mirror of my own. She responds by pulling her arms away from my neck and tugging her dress down herself.

My eyes fall to her breasts, small but round and perky, and notice there are no tan lines on Skye's skin. She is so fair. My hands come around to cup her bare breasts. I love the contrast between my tanned hands and her creamy white skin. Skye moans and pushes into my hands, and I oblige by bending my head to her and taking one nipple into my mouth as my thumb caresses the other. Skye stretches up, her knees on either side of my legs, and grabs the back of my head as she brings herself up, eliminating the height difference. Her breasts are now level with my face, and I feast on them. I was never really a breast man, but I'm one now. I lick and nibble and tease her nipples with my fingers, tongue, and teeth. All I want to do is rip this dress off her and get her skin on mine. She slides her hands over my shoulders, down my back, and under my T-shirt, dragging it up. I break away from her just long enough to pull my T-shirt off and toss it to the floor. Then I pull her into me so I can feel her skin on mine and tug her in for a kiss. As soon as my lips touch hers, she opens for me, and my tongue dips into her mouth, tasting her, devouring her. Her breasts brush against my chest, and I can feel her hard nipples pressed into my skin. I'm on fire.

"Skye."

I pull away and close my eyes, touching my forehead to hers. My breath comes out in short pants and my heart is thundering.

"Skye, I can't—I can't—God, I don't even know what I'm trying to say."

Her hands palm my face and she tilts me up to meet her eyes.

"I don't want you to stop, Logan."

I search her face because I want her to be sure.

"Are you sure? We don't have to. I don't want you to feel like you have to. That I'm expecting you to."

She smiles at me. Her thumb caresses my lips and I kiss it.

I'm falling so hard for this girl, and it scares me as much as it excites me.

"I want to. And that right there, what you just said, makes me want it even more. You never pressured me into doing anything I'm not comfortable with. You always let me set the pace and make me feel in control. I want to, Logan."

There's such an intensity in the way she looks at me. This timid pixie of a girl is anything but right now.

"I need you, Logan."

Jesus! If I try to take her now, it will be over before it starts. We've been here making out for half of the movie, which I realize is over because the credits are scrolling through the screen on the TV behind her.

She bites her lip in that way I've become so accustomed to, and her face pinkens.

"Please?"

She shifts over me and presses herself into my dick and then hides her face in my neck, shy once more. I laugh because really, what other reaction could I have?

"Skye? Let me look at you."

I lace my hands into the pale blond locks and gently tug her head back. She moans—interesting—and then I tug a little harder. Another moan. She looks at me, and the heat in her eyes tells me what I want to know, but I have to be certain.

"Are you sure?"

"Logan, please, take me to your bed and make love to me."

She doesn't have to ask me again. I pick her up, and she wraps her legs around my waist. I take her upstairs and into my bedroom.

CHAPTER TWENTY-THREE

Skye

I'm so turned on right now, I'm going to burst if I don't get Logan inside me right this second. But Logan is in no hurry. He sets me on my feet by the bed. I'm painfully aware of my near-nakedness. My dress pools at my waist, and I can't help the awkward feeling that washes over me. My arms cross over my chest automatically. I'm so out of my league. I'm not a virgin, but I may as well be with the amount of experience I have. Logan walks backward to the windows, his eyes never leaving me, and closes the curtains. The intensity in his gaze sends shivers up and down my spine.

"No free show for the neighbors," he says with a smile.

I'm glad he's thinking of these things because I'm not. He pulls the covers back and tugs my hands free, exposing me to him again. His eyes travel up and down my torso, lingering on my breasts before finding my eyes.

"If you change your mind at any time, tell me."

"I won't."

"Tell me, Skye. As much as I want to fuck you, I also want it to be one hundred percent your choice. If you tell me to stop,

I will. No questions asked, and I won't be mad about it either. Okay?"

"Okay."

My voice is timid and the complete opposite of how I want to be right now. I need him to take charge. I need him to be in control because I don't know how to ask for what I want. I don't have the confidence to speak up.

His hands go to my waist, and he works the dress over my hips and down my legs. It falls to the floor. Blue fabric pools around our bare feet. His hands move to his own jeans next. The sound of the zipper is muted by my thundering heart. He sheds the pants but keeps the boxer briefs on. We stand there for a minute in nothing but underwear. Logan steps back and takes me with him. Skin to skin, breath to breath, lips to lips, mouths open, tongues tasting each other. Hands take charge and travel, discovering, feeling, enticing. It's both hurried and painfully slow, too much and not enough.

He picks me up and brings me to the bed. Cool sheets meet my heated skin. Logan's body covers mine. So many contrasts. I'm simultaneously cold and on fire. Everywhere his skin touches me, it burns. I crave the burn.

His mouth finds my neck, and he kisses a trail down to my chest. Lips and hands follow a path to my breasts. Logan nibbles and licks at my nipples. I hold on to his arms, muscles flexing under my fingers, and I love the feel of them. I touch him everywhere I can reach. I can't get enough of his skin under my fingertips. He presses into me, and his hardness soothes the sweet ache between my legs, but it's not enough. My hips move up, trying to find release. Logan obliges, grinding into me. The room is alive with the sounds of a song as old as time—moans, grunts, loud breaths, and low curses fill the empty spaces between our lips and bodies.

His body slides down mine, and a trail of kisses across my stomach follows. He stops right over my sex, his breath hot and wet on me. His eyes find mine, asking for permission yet again. The clear blue has turned into indigo.

"Yes, Logan, yes."

My voice is so husky, I barely recognize it as my own.

With a chuckle, he slides my panties down my legs and drops them to the floor. I'm completely naked now. Logan sits back on his heels and takes me in. I expected to feel shy and want to cover myself, but I don't. I thrive in the way he looks at me. He makes me feel beautiful and perfect. His gaze washes away all of my flaws and insecurities.

My body floats in lightness, and at least for now, free of the weight of uncertainty and years of thinking of myself as the ugly duckling. Right in this moment, I'm more than a swan. I'm a Phoenix, reborn from the ashes of my old self.

He lowers himself over me and pushes my legs open with his wide shoulders as his hands wrap around my thighs.

"You have no idea how many times I've fantasized about this."

His cheek scratches the inside of one thigh and then the other. When I think I can't take the anticipation of his mouth on me any longer, his lips find me. Wet and trembling.

"Oh, Logan."

His name is followed by a string of sounds and moans I'm certain have never come out of me before.

This is a first for me. I get it now. All the books I read before had me curious, but now I get it. This, his lips and tongue in the most intimate part of my body, the way he licks at me, the way he tastes me, the pleasure he gives and takes from it, and the trust it requires. I get it now. I do, and I'm greedy for more. My hips move of their own accord, seeking more of what Logan is giving me as an exquisite sweet ache builds inside. More, more, more, just a little bit more. I'm so close, so close.

Logan lets go of one of my legs, and a moment later, his fingers are in me. He pushes one finger inside and then two, and the pressure of them combined with his mouth on me sends me over the edge. The orgasm takes over my entire body. It spreads outward in waves of pleasure so intense, I'm robbed of breath. My entire body spasms in ecstasy. Too much, too much, too much.

Logan doesn't stop, and wave after wave takes over me. Like a broken dam, the orgasms can't be contained. I grab his hair and pull him away from me. My body folds on itself. I'm gasping for air. I have nothing left. He took everything I had.

Logan folds around me. I can feel the press of his erection nestled in my lower back.

He brushes hair away from my face.

"Skye, you okay?"

I try to speak, but I can't even open my eyes right now. I manage to lift one hand in a give me a minute gesture.

His body vibrates behind me with his chuckle.

After a minute, I turn to look at him. There's something more in his eyes. Something more than heat and desire. I dare not to hope. Too many orgasm endorphins in my bloodstream to think straight right now.

A slow smile spreads his beautiful lips. They're red and swollen, and I know I'm the reason. Right on cue, my face flushes pink. His smile gets bigger.

"I love it when you blush."

He turns me to him.

"It's beautiful, Skye. Watching you come is beautiful."

I cover my face with my hands, and he tugs them down

gently, kisses the palms, and places them on his chest.

"We can stop here if you want. We don't have to go any further."

I can feel how hard he is against my hip, and even after the orgasms he just gave me, I still want more. I want him inside me. I'm aching for it. So I tell him. With courage born from the way he looks at me, I tell him.

"Logan, I want you inside me. I want to feel you. I want to watch when you come inside me. Don't hold back, please?"

A growl escapes him just before he kisses me. It's not tender or sweet. It's hungry and dirty. My taste is on his tongue. He devours me. His body hovers over mine. I grab his ass and pull him into me. Logan leans over me and gives in but then pulls back.

"Fuck! Condom."

He pulls back just enough to grab a condom from the drawer in the night table.

"You're making me lose my mind. I never forgot to suit up before."

In seconds, the wrapper is ripped open, and he slides the condom down his length. I finally get a clear view of him. His dick stands long, thick, and proud between us. I have no idea when he took off his underwear. I guess it must have happened when I was having my out-of-body experience. His eyes roam over my body. He braces himself over me, elbows around my head, and lowers his body to mine.

"You said it's been a long time for you. This might feel uncomfortable at first. I'll try to go slow. Let me know if I hurt you."

"Okay."

I'm hit with apprehension. The two times I had sex with Blake were not pleasurable. It had been hurried and unskilled.

We were just kids, neither one of us knew what we were doing, and I hadn't been ready. Logan looks at me, still waiting for my consent. I push all thoughts of the past away and smile at him.

"Now, Logan."

He pushes into me, slow and easy. I can feel pressure, but no pain. He pauses, his eyes never leaving mine. He's reading me, waiting, letting me get used to the sweet invasion. When he deems it okay, he pushes all the way in. I gasp, not in pain, but from the fullness.

He stops immediately.

"You okay?"

"It feels so good."

A satisfied cat-who-ate-the-canary smile graces his face. Then he moves. Oh, God. I think my eyes are rolling back in my head.

"Logan?"

"Yeah?" His voice is strained, raspy.

"Don't stop."

His mouth crashes into mine then. The kiss is less refined the faster and harder he pushes into me. I wrap my legs behind his thighs, pulling him in deeper still. The chant of more, more, more is on repeat in my mind, on my skin, in the very center of me. Logan moves, friction and wetness bringing us a step closer to orgasm. I don't know how long he keeps at it. It feels like hours. It feels like seconds. Our mouths part in search of air and sweat slicks our skin. I'm burning hot and covered in shivers.

Contrasts, so many contrasts. I love all the differences between us. His tanned skin against my fair. His hardness and my softness. How his large body dominates my much smaller one. His confidence and my shyness. Our contrasts and differences complement each other.

"Logan!"

I gasp, feeling myself squeeze around him. The orgasm hits me again, not as intense as before, but no less beautiful and meaningful.

"Fuck!"

His movements are less rhythmic, more frantic, and he grunts and stiffens on top of me. Long seconds pass before his body relaxes and his weight drops on me. We melt into each other.

After a long moment, Logan tries to push away.

"I'm crushing you."

I hug him to me.

"No, I like it. I like the way your weight feels on top of me."

He nuzzles my neck and drops little, tender kisses on my shoulders, neck, face.

"You're good?"

He checks on me again.

"Yes, you?"

"Never been better. I'll be right back."

He pulls out of me gently, still hard, and goes into the attached bathroom. The sound of water tells me he's washing his hands after getting rid of the condom. I'm still lying on the bed, the exact same position he left, when he comes back. I can't move. I'm paralyzed by orgasms.

He fluffs the pillows and lies on them, pulling me to his chest and arranging the blanket over our bodies. I rest my head on his shoulder and my hand on his chest. His lips brush my forehead with tender kisses. Satisfied exhaustion claims me. My eyes flutter closed, lulled by the warmth of Logan's body and the quiet breaths moving his chest under me.

When sleep claims me, I dream of him.

CHAPTER TWENTY-FOUR

Logan

WAKING UP WITH SKYE NEXT TO ME IS SOMETHING I could get used to. Her small frame under the covers is barely visible in the low light filtering through shades covering the windows.

We made love once more in the middle of the night, and I could have gone for thirds, but she must be sore, so I held back. Not sure I can hold back again this morning.

Wait—made love? Did I actually think that? Sex, hooking up, fucking, all those are terms I've used before. Making love has never been a part of my vocabulary. And surprisingly, it doesn't make me want to run for the hills.

I can see the top of her shoulders and a lovely mess of golden hair on the pillow. She's sleeping on her stomach, facing away from me. I have the urge to pull her into my body and wrap myself around her. I went to sleep with her taste on my tongue and her scent on my skin, and I want more of that.

I need my next Skye fix, but instead, I get out of the bed soundlessly and grab my phone from the nightstand. I make my way to the bathroom and close the door behind me.

After a few minutes, I find myself texting Liam.

Logan: Baby Brother. This girl...
Logan: This girl has me wrapped around her little finger and she doesn't even know.
Logan: She's sweet and kind and funny. And so unlike anyone I ever met before.
Logan: I'm fascinated and terrified. And last night? Bro...last night was like no experience I've ever had before.
Logan: She's like sunshine in the middle of a storm. Colorful. Unexpected. Warm.

There's a soft knock, and I put my phone on the bathroom counter and open the door. She's wearing a hockey jersey I had folded on top of the dresser. I take her in with hungry eyes. She looks at me, looks away, and back at me again, and I remember I'm still naked, my erection pointing straight at her. She bites her lip and touches the hem of the shirt. It falls nearly to her knees.

"Is this okay?"

"Yes, I like you in my jersey."

I like her wearing my number and name across her back. Even though I can't see them because she's facing me, I know they're there.

She points at the bathroom, and I step aside to let her in.

"I left a new toothbrush out for you," I say and notice I never put the cap on the paste after I brushed my own teeth.

"Thank you."

I grab my phone.

"You're welcome."

Her eyes are fixed on my face, but I can tell she's making an effort not to let them stray.

I want to make lo—fuck her in that jersey. If she lets me, I'm going to do just that.

CHAPTER TWENTY-FIVE

Skye

When I go back into the room, he's sitting on the bed, waiting for me. A sheet around his hips covers his still-naked body. I know the gesture of modesty is for my benefit. I bridge the distance between us without hesitation. I'm letting my body take charge, getting out of my own head for a change. I think too much, I know.

I stand in front of him, and Logan gently pulls me closer. His hands low on my hips, he traces the horizontal lines across the middle of the jersey.

"How are you feeling?" he asks, his eyes flitting all over my face.

"I feel . . . happy."

Happy is not the right word, but as I search my mind for the correct one, none quite fits the flutter of emotions inside me. Elation, joy, giddiness, a soul-deep contentment, and satisfaction. I settle for happy.

"Yeah?"

His smile is coy.

"Yes. Last night was more than I ever dreamed of."

"You dream of fucking me often?"

The smile is unashamed now. He baited me.

"Logan!"

I try to push his chest in play. He doesn't budge. The man is solid.

"Are you sore?"

There's a hint of concern in his voice.

I do a mental check. Am I sore? I can for sure feel his touch on me still, but sore?

"No, not really."

"In that case, can I have you for breakfast?"

CHAPTER TWENTY-SIX

Logan

RIVER PERSUADED EVERYONE TO GO TO A HALLOWEEN party. A middle of the week party since Halloween falls on a Wednesday this year. The girls are dressing up, and I got roped into doing the same. I kind of cheated on my costume. I'm wearing jeans and a hockey jersey.

I'm picking up the girls. I'm glad I worked a day shift today and have tonight and tomorrow off. I haven't been to a Halloween party in years and it will be fun. Granted, I'd rather have Skye all to myself, but I can share her with the world for a few hours. Luckily, we got nice weather, and it's warm for this time of year. We don't see too many sixty-degree nights on Halloween.

Skye gave me the outside door code, and I let myself into the common hall and knock on her door and wait for one of them to open it. The door opens, but it's not the girl I want. River has her hair in a high ponytail and a knee-length coat on. Heels on her feet make her even taller. She's maybe a couple of inches shorter than me with those shoes. The door opens wide, and I step in. Sounds from the back of the hallway tell me Skye is coming into the living room. Can't wait to see her outfit.

Oh, fuck.

Holy fucking fuck.

No.

Nope.

Just no.

There's no way I'll make it through the next five minutes, much less through the night, with her dressed like that.

Jesus Christ!

She's a walking wet dream.

Thank God, my hockey jersey covers my groin because my dick is standing at attention and screaming *Sir, yes, sir!*

Fuck me now.

Skye halts as soon as she sees me in the room. I'm sure every thought in my head is visible on my face. She has pigtails tied with white and blue ribbons in matching colors for her cheerleader outfit. The shirt, if one can call it that, is not much bigger than a bra and ties in the front. I think it's called a halter top. Her small breasts pop on top, making them look twice as big. Her ribs, stomach, and lower belly are completely bare. The little skirt is low on her hips and flares when she walks. She has sneakers on instead of the expected heels she hates so much. We're both frozen in place. I'm painfully hard and need to adjust myself, but I can feel River watching me with an all-too-knowing smirk on her face.

"Down, boy."

She laughs at me.

I can see doubt in Skye's face.

"This is too much, right?"

She looks at me for confirmation but doesn't wait for an answer. Skye turns to River.

"I told you it was a bad idea."

I'm still frozen in place. If I move, it will be to bend Skye over the couch, pull that tiny skirt up, and fuck her until I pass out. Pretty sure neither of them would appreciate it.

I hear River laughing.

"Okay, I'll give you two a minute. I'll be in my room, checking on nothing."

She leaves toward the hall and I can't take it anymore. I have to adjust myself. Skye's eyes go big when she sees me doing just that. I stalk toward her.

"Are you trying to kill me?"

"What?"

"Have you seen yourself? Sweet mother of fuck. Can someone die from a hard-on?"

She looks down at herself and blushes. I can't hold back any longer. My hands find her waist and I pull her to me. My mouth is on hers before she has a chance to react. She melts into me, her lips opening and taking me in with a moan. She tastes like mint and Skye. I grab her hips and grind her into me, trying to get some relief, but all I accomplish is to get even more turned on.

Somewhere in the back of my mind, the sound of approaching steps registers. A sigh, a laugh, and the steps retreat. I have to stop myself.

Now.

Before we're both naked on the floor. With regret, I take a small step away from her and adjust myself again. Her eyes drop to my groin.

"I have a feeling I'll be adjusting myself a lot tonight."

"This is too much, right? I feel naked. I don't think I can do this."

"I have to be honest, Skye. A part of me wants to show you

off and the other part wants to lock you in my room and throw away the key."

"Which one is winning?"

Before I can answer her, River's voice comes down the hall.

"Are you guys decent in there? Can we get going or should I get the hose?"

She doesn't wait for a reply.

"Okay then. I got your jacket, Skye."

Skye turns around, and I notice her ass in that tiny little skirt.

"Please tell me you have shorts under that skirt."

They both laugh.

"Yes, we do."

River answers for Skye.

"Show him, Skye."

"Show me what?"

River laughs. Skye hesitates, then lifts the back of the skirt. And right across her ass, on the tiny shorts, the word *SCORE*.

Fuck.

Me.

CHAPTER TWENTY-SEVEN

Skye

THERE ARE PEOPLE EVERYWHERE, SPILLING OVER THE sidewalk, walking in and out of the frat house, leaning on cars and trees, and sitting on the curb. You'd think no one has classes tomorrow. We had to park two blocks away. Logan's arm at my back guides me around the side of the house and into the backyard. River is right behind us. More people gather around a fire pit, red cups in hand. Laughter and voices mingle with the music coming from inside the house and speakers around the yard. The amount of skin on display puts me at ease. Witches, nurses, pirates, and yes, cheerleaders, are everywhere. A lot of the guys are dressed up, and some, like Logan, took the easy way out and just put on a jersey.

Logan's arm goes around my shoulder, and he gestures to River to come in closer. He hugs both of us, and we lean in to hear him over the surrounding cacophony.

"I know I don't have to say this, but I'll say it anyway. Don't accept a drink from anyone but me. I'll get it for you. Pay attention to your surroundings. I'm not letting you out of my sight,

Skye. River, if you decide to walk around, let me know. You have your phone on you, right?"

"Yes, Dad."

River's response is sarcastic, but I can see gratitude in her face. She pats her phone, stuck inside her skirt. We have the same outfit, but in different colors. Mine is blue and River's bright pink. Logan suggested we leave our pocketbooks and jackets in the car. It would be a pain holding them all night, and if we left them anywhere here, odds are we would not find them again. I know it to be true from experience. Lost a favorite jacket freshman year this way.

Someone bumps into me, pushing me into Logan.

"Sorry," the guy apologizes.

"Oh, dude, you got two of them. Wanna share one with me? I'll take the brunette."

He's clearly drunk and not too steady on his feet. Logan's body goes rigid next to mine. I squeeze his arm to let him know it's okay. The last thing we need is to get into a fight five minutes into this party. Before Logan can say anything, River steps up to the guy and puts her hand on his shoulder. She leans closer to him and whispers something in his ear.

The guy is all smiles when he walks away.

The confusion on Logan's face is a reflection of mine.

"What did you do?" I ask.

"I told him to get us a couple of beers and to go wait for me in the bathroom on the third floor. Hide in the bathtub, and I would be up in ten minutes."

"What the fuck!"

Logan takes the words right out of my mouth.

"River!" I say.

River gives him a dirty look.

"I have no intention of going up there, but he'll get the

beers, go wait for me, get bored, drink them, and pass out in that bathtub. And tomorrow, if he remembers anything, he'll think it was a dream. Meanwhile, he's not bugging anyone else."

She points at Logan.

"And Mr. Handcuffs didn't have to badge up."

River turns and walk around the house to the backyard.

Logan looks at me and says, "How did your parents survive her?"

"I heard that!" she calls out.

LOGAN GETS US DRINKS, beer for him and River and a soda for me. I still don't like the bitter taste of beer. There are quite a few people I know here, and every time one of my male friends gets closer to say something, Logan's arm tightens around me. River stays near us, talking to her friends. Until Becca shows up.

"I'm going to hang out with Becca."

"Okay, be careful."

I don't understand her friendship with Becca. It seems so one-sided for me. Becca has let River down more times than I can remember, but River says Becca needs her friendship. She doesn't really share what Becca's deal is, but I get the feeling she has a lot of skeletons in her closet.

We've been around for a couple of hours, hanging out, talking, people watching, and making out a little when River comes back to where we're sitting by the fire pit. Logan is on a lawn chair, and I'm on his lap.

He's finally relaxed, and it has nothing to do with drinking. He had just the one beer when we got here and switched to water after. I think it's me sitting on his lap. The possessive way his hands are on my back and thigh are sending the message that

I'm taken, which puts him at ease. No guys are looking at me with interest. Logan's intense glaring at a couple of guys before made them get up and leave. It's mostly couples around the fire.

River comes around the circle of people and kneels on the grass next to us.

"Skye, I need to talk to you."

Logan is on alert, his body tensing under me.

"What is it? Did someone do anything to you?" he asks before I have a chance to.

"No, nothing like that. I just want to talk to Skye."

I can feel curious eyes on us, and so can Logan. He glances around and people turn away and go back to talking among themselves. He really has this intimidating look thing working for him.

I'm trying to read River's face and see what this is about.

"Give me a minute?"

Logan nods. I get up and walk a few yards with River but stay where he can see me. She doesn't waste any time.

"Blake is here."

"What?"

"Blake is here. I just saw him with a guy from the football team. I heard them talking. He transferred here last week."

"And he's here at this party right now?"

"Yes, he's inside. He didn't see me. I figured you'd want to know and maybe leave?"

"I don't want to see him. Especially when I'm dressed like this."

River winces. She remembers now.

"This fucking costume. Sorry, Skye. I forgot all about it. You were wearing it when he asked you out back in high school, right?"

"Yeah, that's okay, River. The clothes didn't make him the asshole he is."

"Oh, shit. You were wearing it when you met Jon too. Fuck. I'm really sorry. I'll burn it as soon as we get back home. This thing is cursed."

"I don't know. Logan seems to like it."

"What are we going to say to him?"

"The truth. I don't want to lie to Logan. Blake is in the past, and he doesn't matter. Hasn't mattered for years."

I look at the man in question and Logan is walking to us.

"Everything okay?" he asks, his fingers twisting around one of my pigtails, and not for the first time. He's been doing it all night.

"Hi."

I go on my tiptoes and kiss him.

"Can we leave?"

"Sure, we can go."

"I'm staying," River says.

"How are you going to get home?"

"I'm driving Becca to her dorm. She's drunk, and I want to get her out of here before she does something stupid. I have her car keys."

"You good to drive?"

Logan asks her, looking for the telltale signs of inebriation.

"Yes, I only had one beer, and I didn't even finish it."

After a prolonged examination, he's satisfied that she's sober.

"Okay, go get your friend. We'll wait and walk you to the car."

River looks back at the house and at me.

"No need. I'll just grab Becca and leave. I have my cell on me. I'll text Skye when we're in the car and then again when I get her into her room. I might crash there. I'll let you know."

Logan's eyes narrow on us. It doesn't take a trained cop to figure out we're hiding something.

"What's going on?"

I look at River.

"I'll tell you when we get home."

Logan doesn't push. His hand goes to the small of my back, and he guides me to the side of the house and out to the sidewalk where he stops to take his jersey off and pull it over my head.

"You're shivering."

It's colder now. I didn't feel it while sitting on his lap and by the fire pit, but now that I have neither heat source, the night chill is catching up with me. He has a white T-shirt on. I'm glad his body is not on display for any of the many girls I caught looking at him tonight. Okay, it's a little hypocritical, since my body has been on display for hours now. I know.

We make our way to the car in silence. We drove my car since it's a lot smaller than Logan's truck, and with the limited amount of space, it's easier to park. He opens the passenger door for me first and goes around to take the driver seat. We sit for a couple of minutes as the car warms up. The clock on the dashboard says it's nearly midnight. We've been out longer than I thought.

"Hungry?" he asks.

"I could eat."

Then I look at myself.

"Not exactly dressed for dinner."

"It's Halloween. No one will care, and my shirt goes nearly to your knees."

"True. Okay, then. Feed me, Seymour."

He laughs.

"I was thinking of something less *Little Shop of Horrors* and more like *Ratatouille*."

He brings me to a 24-hour diner near the campus. I don't stick out as much as I thought I would. The place is busy for being this late at night, and more than half of the occupants have costumes on. We're told to sit wherever we want, and Logan finds a corner booth away from most of the diners.

My phone buzzes against my belly. Like River, I had it stuck inside my skirt and forgot all about it. I pull it from under Logan's jersey.

River: Got Becca. Driving to her dorm now. Will spend the night with her.
Skye: Is she okay?
River: I don't know. I'll call you if anything changes.
Skye: Okay. Text me in the morning. I'll pick you up.

"It's River. She's okay. Driving Becca to her dorm."

The waitress comes, and without looking at the menu, Logan orders pancakes and coffee. I get the same.

He looks at me and waits. I love him for being so patient. This man who never pushes me and gives me the space I need, who puts me in control of every aspect of our relationship, not because he's a follower and can't make a decision but because he's a leader and knows that sometimes, the best way to lead is to let someone else take charge.

He gave me the confidence to take charge, to make choices, and in doing so, he gave me control not over him or our relationship, but over myself. I've always leaned on others. First my parents, then my sister. I leaned on Blake and he pushed me when I wasn't ready. Logan has never made feel like I didn't have a choice. He gave me something I had no idea I needed. Myself.

CHAPTER TWENTY-EIGHT

Logan

THE WAITRESS BRINGS US COFFEE AND LEAVES. SKYE IS sitting across the table from me. The high back on the fake red and white leather booth hides us from the rest of the diner. I purposely picked this spot. I have a feeling Skye won't want anyone else to hear her. I wait.

She adds sugar to her mug and stirs it before taking a sip of her coffee. I drink mine black. I welcome the bitterness. A few more minutes go by, and the waitress brings our pancakes and a jar of syrup. As if sensing we want to be left alone, she drops the check on the table and tells us we can pay on the way out. She doesn't ask if we want anything else, and I notice that when a group of people comes in, she steers them away from our section.

Skye picks up her fork and cuts through the stack of pancakes in front of her without adding any syrup to it. I add some of the sweet sticky stuff to my plate and hold the jar. She nods, and I pour some over hers as well.

"When River came to us and asked to talk, it was because

she saw someone we know at the party. Someone I didn't want to see again."

I take a bite and wait for her to continue. Skye plays with her food but doesn't eat.

"The person she saw is my ex, Blake. My high school boyfriend."

"I guess it didn't end well."

She laughs without humor.

I point at her plate.

"Take a bite. They're good."

She eats, and I do the same.

"No, it didn't end well at all."

She sighs and puts her fork down.

"Blake was my first real boyfriend. I had a crush on him for a couple of years, but I was always very shy and he never even looked at me. I mean, why would he? Blake was the captain of the football team and had all the girls after him. He could have any of them, and he had them all, if the talk in the girls' locker room was to be believed."

"Why wouldn't he notice you? You're beautiful, Skye."

She looks at me like she wants to believe the words I say but doesn't know how.

"I was the awkward, super-skinny book nerd with braces until the summer before senior year. Believe me, no boys looked at me like that. Especially not when River was around. She always had a huge circle of friends and boys asking her out."

"Did it bother you? That your sister got all the attention?"

"No, not really. I was glad. I wouldn't know what to do with the attention. And River didn't do it on purpose. People are just drawn to her. It's always been like that. And if you tell her that, she'll say you're crazy. She doesn't see it."

"Go on."

"So, senior year of high school, I finally shed the braces and grew some boobs."

She blushes. I smile, my eyes dipping to her chest, but my large jersey does a great job of hiding her body.

"River dragged me to a Halloween party, which just so happens was at Blake's house. And we had these same cheerleader outfits on."

She gestures at herself.

"Let me guess. This Blake kid noticed you."

Yeah, I call him a kid, because I already hate the guy and don't want to make him more than he is.

"Yes, he did. I later found out that he wanted River, but she was dating one of his teammates then. That's how she got into the party. Her boyfriend took her, and she took me. Blake didn't really socialize with the non-popular kids. As popular as River was, they never shared a class together, and Blake didn't notice her until that night. We only have one high school in our town, and it had well over a thousand students."

Skye takes a couple of bites of her pancakes and drinks her coffee. She has a distant look in her eyes, lost in the past.

"So Blake notices me for the first time. I was elated. We'd had a couple of classes together before, but of course, he didn't remember me. I never registered on his radar before. We started dating after that. River didn't trust him and told me so. Her boyfriend warned her about Blake. Said I should be careful with him. He'd heard stories."

"What kind of stories?"

"That he'd forced himself on other girls."

"What's his full name?"

She hesitates for a moment but answers.

"Blake James Scott."

I pull my iPhone from my pocket, unlock it, and open the Notes app.

"What's his birthday?"

Sky looks confused.

"May thirty. Why?"

"Year?"

I make a note of everything she's saying on the app.

"He's my age, so it has to be 1997?"

She answers it like a question.

"Which college is he going to?"

"He was going to UV, but River said she overheard a conversation and he's transferred over here. Why are you asking all these questions?"

I think about being evasive or not answering her, but she's been nothing but honest with me and she deserves the same from me.

"I just want to check on him. Make sure he doesn't have any felonies on him. Can't help it. I'm a cop."

I smile and finish my coffee. Most of the pancake is uneaten. I take a couple more bites to give her time to finish her story.

She mulls over what I said for a minute or two and continues.

"Where was I? Oh, yeah. River warned me away from him. I got mad at her. For the first time, I had a boy interested in me, and I told her she was jealous. Which, of course, she wasn't, but I was young and stupid and thought myself in love, and Blake was persuasive. He was manipulative. I can see it now. I couldn't back then. We dated for months. Whatever little confidence I gained by his attention, he'd tear down, little by little. It was never obvious or blatant. It was little comments here and there. He'd say something about what I was wearing or about my hair, about my lack of makeup. And I'd try to do and be what I thought he wanted because I needed him to like me. I was convinced if I did what he wanted, if I looked the part, he'd love me. He said as much. And in my naiveté, I believed him."

She takes a sip of her coffee. Both of our mugs are now empty. I wave at the waitress, who's keeping her distance but still paying attention to us, and she brings a carafe and refills our mugs.

When she leaves, Skye picks up where she stopped.

"Blake flirted with other girls in front of me and made jokes about my lack of experience. And I'm sure he was cheating from day one. I was a challenge, the innocent virgin girl he wanted just so he could say he did it and nothing more. With every passing month, he pressured me more and more to have sex. I wasn't ready. I was beginning to see that he was not what I thought. He would run hot and cold. River tried to make me see the truth, but it only made me want to prove her wrong more. In the end, I gave in. It was spring, before prom. I assumed we were going together. We'd been dating for six months, the longest he'd been with anyone. It just so happens that it was because I took the longest to give in. Two weeks before prom, he took me to his house. I'd been there before when his family was around. But they were away that week. His father was on a business trip and his mom went with him. His older sister was away at college. I hadn't realized we'd be alone. I can't say if I had known, I wouldn't have gone. I had my head in the clouds thinking about prom and imagining the perfect date. Naïve, remember?"

She laughs again, and the sound is bitter and filled with self-deprecation.

"So, anyway. Here we are, alone in his house, and he puts on a movie and brings me a wine cooler. I felt so mature, drinking alcohol with my boyfriend. I was tipsy before I finished the bottle. Next thing I know, I'm naked and he's on top of me."

Anger rises within me until it's burning a hole in my chest with the need to explode. I contain myself. I still my face and hold it all in. The last thing I want is for Skye to think this rage is directed at her. I wait another minute until I'm sure none of it will show in my voice. Skye doesn't look at me. I can feel her discomfort. I want to reach out to her and hold her tight, but I'm not sure this is what she needs right now.

"Do you think he drugged you?"

"No, I know he didn't. He gave me a sealed bottle. I opened it myself. I drank it of my own volition. I can't say he forced himself on me. As much as I'd like to blame someone else for that night, I did it to myself. I allowed it to happen. He kept going, and I never asked him to stop. I may not have been sober, but I was aware enough. I knew what was happening. He never asked if it was okay and I didn't ask him to stop. I just let it happen. Part of me was glad it would be over with. No longer a virgin. A bigger part of me wanted him to stop, but I said nothing. I can't blame him. It was as much my responsibility as it was his."

Knowing this now makes me really glad I never pushed Skye, not that I ever would, but our experience was the complete opposite of what she'd had with her asshole ex. I let her make the decisions and asked if she was sure every step of the way.

"I'm not sure I agree with you. Yes, you played a part in it, but he didn't want to stop, and I'm not sure he would have stopped if you'd asked him to. He knew what he was doing. He planned it."

She nods in agreement.

"It was . . . it was bad. It was painful and awkward. He didn't take his time. I think he was in a hurry to get it done with before I could come to my senses and ask him to stop. He told me to get dressed and drove me home after. He didn't even kiss me goodbye. Just dropped me at the door and drove away before I even got inside the house. I didn't see him the next day. He texted me and said he was busy with football and he'd call me later."

I tell myself to stick to the facts and leave emotions out of this. Stay focused.

"Please tell me he used a condom."

"He did the first time."

"What do you mean?"

"A couple of days later, he texted me and told me to meet him after class. I met him in the parking lot and we drove to his house again. We messed around, and I didn't have the excuse of a wine cooler this time, but I thought it's not like I'm a virgin anymore, so nothing to lose. I was so wrong."

Tears fill her eyes. I'm ready to hunt this asshole down and beat him within inches of his life.

"We went to his room this time. It was early, so his parents weren't home yet. I saw him grab a condom, I saw him tear the foil open, and I saw him put it on. But at some point, without my realizing it, he took it off. After, I went to the bathroom. I got scared. I thought the condom broke and told him. And he laughed. He said it didn't break. He took it off. I got angry. He said everyone was doing it and I should get over it. He called it *stealthing*. I'd never heard of it before. I asked him to take me home. He did. When we got home, I told him I needed some space. I needed a break. I wasn't okay with what he did. I told him maybe by the time prom came around, I'd be okay again. Stupid, I know. He laughed at me and said he had no intention of taking me to the prom, that I could take all the time I needed because I was a lousy lay and a prude. He told me to get out of his car and never call him again."

I HEARD ABOUT STEALTHING. It happens when a man removes the condom without his partner's knowledge, turning a consensual act into a non-consensual one. It's happening more and more. Forget about beating the shit out of the asshole. I want to kill him. With my bare hands.

"I held my tears until I got in the house. Luckily, my parents were busy with the farm and didn't see me when I got in, but River was home, and as soon as I saw her, the dam broke and the tears came. I told her everything that happened between sobs, and she somehow got me upstairs and in the bathroom. She helped me into the shower and washed me like a baby while I cried. She told me to cry all I wanted while in the shower and to wash every vestige of Blake off my body. But when I was done, that would be it. No more tears for that asshole. The next day was a Saturday, and she took me to a Planned Parenthood clinic two towns over. Luckily, I didn't get pregnant. They told me it just wasn't the right time in my cycle and that it was unlikely, but they gave me the plan B pills anyway and did a blood test. They told me what to look for and to come back in a month. I was lucky. He didn't give me any STIs, and I didn't get pregnant. But whatever little confidence I had, he shattered."

There's a catch in her voice, and I can tell how very difficult this is for her still.

"River wanted to kill him. Going back to school after the weekend was the hardest thing I ever did. I was afraid he'd say something or spread rumors. He didn't. He looked at me once in the cafeteria, turned away, and nearly ran out of it. No words from him, no gossip. People thought I broke up with him. I don't know how or what happened, but for the next six weeks, until we graduated, every time he saw me or River, he turned and walked the other way. I know River did something to shut him up, to make him so scared. He wouldn't even look at me. I have no idea what. She never told me. And knowing my sister, it could be anything."

"She's badass."

"That she is. I pity the guy who pisses her off."

I laugh.

"She told me she'd cut my balls off with a rusty, dull knife if I ever hurt you."

"No, she didn't!"

"Yes, she did. Her exact words were, *'If you ever hurt my sister, cop or no cop, I'll cut your balls off with a rusty, dull knife and feed them to you. Do we have an understanding?'*"

"Gosh, I'm sorry."

"Don't be. Like I said, badass. I'm glad you have her in your corner. Not everyone is lucky enough to have someone who cares."

"I'm glad too."

"Now, I'm really curious to know what she said to the asshole. You think she'll tell me if I ask nicely?"

CHAPTER TWENTY-NINE

Skye

LOGAN STAYED OVER. HE HELD ME ALL NIGHT, AND EVEN though I could feel how hard he was at my back, he didn't try to have sex. He just held me and told me to sleep. I think it's his way of telling me that what we have is more than sex. He's in my corner too.

I wake up to a text from River, saying all is well and she'll be home soon. I don't need to pick her up. I can hear Logan in the bathroom. He comes into my room a few minutes later, wearing boxer briefs and nothing else. I smile. He leans over me and kisses my forehead. I can smell my toothpaste on his breath. He's getting dressed.

"Hungry?" I ask him.

"Always."

"Give me a minute," I call to him as I make my way to the bathroom.

He waits for me, sitting on the bed. I walk to him and stand between his legs. Holding his face, I kiss him. He smiles into the kiss. His hands reach under the long enough to be a dress T-shirt I'm wearing and squeeze my ass. I don't feel the need to get dressed. I'm comfortable and at ease around Logan.

"Come, I'll make us breakfast."

"Did you hear from your sister?"

"Yes, she texted me. She's on her way home now."

Logan sits at the counter with a cup of coffee and watches me gather things to make us breakfast. The front door opens and River comes in. She's in sweats and a hoodie. I recognize Becca's clothing. They're small on River, as Becca is closer to my height and size than River's. She drops a bag and her heels on the floor as she walks into the kitchen.

"How's Becca?"

"Becca . . . you know how she gets. Becca is being extra Becca lately."

I don't really know how Becca gets. River is good at keeping secrets, her own and others'. What I do know of Becca is what I've witnessed and whatever gossip I heard by accident. Other people talking. Not River.

She sits at the counter next to Logan. Every so often, my old doubts show their ugly little heads. I give her a coffee and take a sip of my own.

"Hey, how's everything?"

She watches us, searching for signs of distress.

"Everything is good, River. We talked. I told Logan everything about what happened with Blake."

"Everything?"

"Everything. Except what you did to scare him off, because I still don't know what you did."

"Oh, that."

She takes a sip of her coffee and smirks over the cup. She's lost in thought.

"Yeah, that was kind of crazy. It was funny, though."

"What happened?"

Both Logan and I ask at the same time.

"You really want to know?"

"River! Tell me now. You've been holding out for years. There has to be a statute of limitations on secrets of revenge against a sister's exes."

"Okay." She sighs.

"That day, after everything that happened, you fell asleep. Before Mom and Dad came home, I called Doctor Taylor."

I interrupt River to explain to Logan what she meant. "Doctor Taylor is a vet. He cares for our animals and most of the farm animals around Apple Hill."

River picks up where she stopped.

"I asked Doctor Taylor if he'd have any geldings in the next couple of days. And luckily for me, he had a couple of colts to geld Monday morning at the Andersons'."

I look at Logan and explain.

"The Andersons are the next farm over. Their land abuts ours."

"Geldings?" Logan asks.

"Castrating," I clarify.

He winces.

River smirks at him before she goes on.

"They have a horse breeding farm and a stable where they do horse riding lessons, work with special needs kids, stuff like that. Some of their horses and ponies are gelded as to be more tame and easier for beginner riders."

She stops to take a sip of her coffee, and I grow impatient.

"So, I told Doctor Taylor I had this biology project and needed a couple of testicles for it and asked if I could tag along in the morning before I went to school."

She looks at me.

"You know Doctor Taylor always had a soft spot for me."

It's true. Doctor Taylor has three sons, and he always said River was the daughter he never had. He has high hopes one of his boys will catch River's eye. I wouldn't put my money on it.

"So, I got up way early that morning, met Doctor Taylor at the Andersons', and twenty minutes later, I got me a fresh pair of horse testicles in a plastic bag. Got back home before you were up and hid the evidence in my backpack."

Logan looks horrified and scoots his chair a little over and is facing her now. He looks ready to bolt.

"What the hell did you do, River?"

"Remember that old kitchen knife Mom likes to use to dig up weeds in the herb garden?"

"Yes, it's a huge rusty knife—holy shit!"

I look at Logan, remembering the warning she gave him about hurting him with a rusty knife. River laughs. Logan scoots over a little more and crosses his legs.

"So, after we got to school, I told you I had to go to the bathroom, remember?"

"Yes."

"I lied. I went back outside, into the parking lot. Blake always liked to hang out in his car listening to music and walk in just before the last bell. He liked to make an entrance."

Yeah, I remember it well. I was one of many hanging in the halls to catch a glimpse of him doing just that. Stupid teenage hormones.

"Yeah, that's true."

I look at Logan and he's hanging on her every word.

"I walked to his car and leaned my elbows on his open window. The asshole smirked at me and said that since he was done with you, I could have a ride on the Blake train next."

I gasp. I didn't know any of that.

"So, I very calmly told him he would keep his mouth shut and not say a word to anyone about you and that if anyone asked, he would say you broke up with him."

"What did he say to that?"

"He laughed. He said he'd do whatever the fuck he wanted. I pulled Mom's knife from my backpack and played with it. He stopped laughing then. I told him if he ever so much as looked at you again or opened his mouth to say anything about you or to you, I would cut his balls off. He didn't believe me.

So I stabbed the car seat, right between his legs, missing his junk by a couple of inches. It surprised me how easily that old knife cut through leather. It may have been old and rusty, but Mom kept it really sharp. He was stunned. He didn't even see when with my bare hands, I grabbed the colt's testicles from the plastic bag and dropped them on his lap. He looked at it and went white as a ghost. I wiped my hand on his shirt, smacked his face twice, grabbed the knife back, and pointed it at him and repeated, *Not a word.*"

Logan looks a little sick.

"What did he do?"

I can't believe River did this. She did this for me.

"Oh, it took him a second to realize what was happening. I think he thought it was his own balls at first. He was screaming and trying to open the door to get out of the car. When I looked back, he was kneeling on the ground, holding his crotch and puking all over himself. Stupid boy. He had no idea what horse testicles look like. Probably thinks I cut off someone's balls to this day."

CHAPTER THIRTY

Logan

I DON'T KNOW IF I SHOULD HIGH-FIVE RIVER OR RUN FOR cover. Then I'm laughing. Skye is laughing. River shrugs and smirks and goes on drinking her coffee.

"I hope I never piss you off, and I want to be proactive and apologize and beg for forgiveness ahead of time if I ever do."

I look at the counter, the egg carton and breakfast sausage forgotten.

"I don't know why, but suddenly, eggs and sausage for breakfast don't sound so appetizing."

Skye puts the sausage back in the fridge.

"How about a cheese omelet then?"

"I'm down for that," River replies.

"Yes. Feed me, Seymour."

With a wink at her, I repeat, Skye's words from last night.

RIVER SAID she needed a nap and is in her room. It's just Skye and me now. I'm worried about her ex. I'm worried he'll try something and I won't be around to protect her.

"What are you gonna do about this guy?" I ask.

"Blake?"

"Yeah."

"I have no idea. Pray I don't run into him?"

"It's not a huge campus, Skye. You will run into him, eventually."

"I know. Hopefully, he'll still remember River's threat and stay far away from me."

"And if he doesn't?"

"I'm not that naïve and scared little girl anymore. I think I can stand my ground and ignore whatever he throws at me."

"Guys like that, they don't really change. I knew my share of them back in high school and at Riggins."

"Yeah, but at least I know he's here, so it won't take me by surprise when I run into him. I'll be ready."

"I want you to tell me when you do. I want you to call me right away, and if he says or does anything to you, I need to know."

She looks at me with some hesitation.

"I mean it, Skye. I want to know. Not the next day. Not an hour later. Call me. No matter what."

"Okay, I will."

"Promise me, Skye?"

"Yes, I promise. Seal it with a kiss."

She leans into me and gives me a peck on my cheek.

"I think you can do better that."

"You do?"

She's flirting with me, a sexy smile playing on her lips.

"Uh-huh. Let's put it to the test."

I take her hand and tug her behind me and back to her bedroom.

CHAPTER THIRTY-ONE

Skye

I GUESS NO ONE WAS LISTENING TO MY PRAYERS BECAUSE IT didn't take long at all to run into Blake. As luck would have it, I didn't have to call Logan when it happened either, because he was right there with me.

We run into Blake on campus. Logan is picking me up after class for some Netflix and chill. AKA, pizza and mind-blowing sex. Whatever we have between us isn't just dating anymore. It's been over two months since we first met, and we're well established into couple territory. There was never a discussion of being exclusive, but we both fell into a routine that works around his erratic schedule and my classes, job, and studying. Living so close to each other helps.

He's parked on the curb and waiting for me outside the Austen building where I have all my English classes. The building is named after Jane Austen, one of my favorite authors.

I'm walking down the path, my eyes on Logan and his welcoming smile, admiring his long legs in a pair of faded jeans, crossed at the ankles as he leans against his truck, his arms crossed over his open jacket and a plain black T-shirt that's stretched tight across his wide chest, when I hear my name. I look over my shoulder and see Blake walking in my direction with another guy and a girl. It's been nearly four years since I last saw him. He's taller and bigger. More intimidating than I remember him. Riggins colors look wrong on him. I freeze on the spot. There's a smirk on his face. I guess he got over River's threat. Before he gets too close, Logan is at my side, his arm around my waist. He pulls me into his body and kisses the top of my head. I relax a little.

Blake stops a couple of feet away from us, flanked by his friends, and gives Logan a disinterested look, dismissing him on the spot. Logan's taller than Blake, but not as bulky. I wouldn't be surprised if Blake's muscles were created with the aid of some illegal substances. There were always rumors about it back in high school.

Blake's eyes find me again, and he smirks.

"Looking good, Skye."

I don't say anything. His smile falters for a second, but he backs it up with cockiness.

"What? You don't have a hug for your high school boyfriend? I know you missed me."

I snort at that. I actually snort at his words. The girl with him looks between us as if trying to figure the extent of our relationship. She seems uncomfortable with Blake's abrasiveness.

The guy on his right speaks up.

"Come on, Blake. Let's go."

"No, no. Don't be rude. Introductions are needed."

Blake points at the girl at his left.

"This is Brittany. She's in a couple of my classes. And this is Mark. He's on the football team with me."

He points at me with both hands.

"And this is Skye, and as I said before, my old high school girlfriend. We were together most of senior year."

The way he looks at me makes me want to take a shower. He nods at Logan.

"And who are you?"

Contempt in his tone.

Logan tenses next to me, and I reply to Blake before Logan can say or do anything.

"This is Logan, my boyfriend."

Neither makes an attempt to shake hands. I have a feeling if Logan lifts his hand, it will be to choke Blake.

Blake laughs. I'm familiar with that laugh. It always preceded something unpleasant.

"What do you know? Isn't that funny? The old boyfriend and the new one. I was her first, you know. Popped that cherry."

My face burns, but for once, it's not in embarrassment but in anger.

"Dude, not cool."

The guy next to him voices his opinion. The girl looks at Blake with disgust and takes a step to the side, putting some distance between them.

Logan smiles, and the coldness in his face gives me shivers.

"Yeah, I heard all about it. How you got her drunk on wine coolers and took advantage of her."

The girl gasps. The guy, Mark, shakes his head but says nothing. It's clear Blake hadn't expected me to talk about him.

"Is that what she told you? I remember it different—"

Logan cuts him off and lets go of me, taking a step closer to Blake. I find a small satisfaction in the fact Blake has to look up to keep eye contact with Logan.

"I know the truth about that night. I also know you got

kicked out UV for doing illegal enhancing drugs. And that you got caught with enough roofies on you to drug half a sorority house. I wonder how much your daddy had to shell out to clean up that mess."

The girl steps away from him and whispers, "I'm sorry" when she walks by me.

The other guy shakes his head and walks away too. It's just the three of us now.

Blake blanches, and his mouth opens and closes as if to deny it, but nothing comes out.

"And I also know about how you cried like the little bitch you are when River told you to leave Skye alone. Man, I wish I'd been there. It must have been epic."

Logan laughs and shakes his head. Then his posture goes from relaxed to steel rigid and the look in his eyes is deadly.

"But unlike River, I don't carry a rusty knife. I find it to be too . . . messy."

He puts his hands on his waist, which opens his jacket, and I can see a holster and his service gun. I know it to be a Glock 22. He told me about it. He keeps his gun under the driver seat of his truck when he's off duty and driving. I'm surprised to see it on him.

Blake takes notice and pales. I step closer to Logan and put my hand on his back.

"Babe, we gotta go."

He looks at me, and the coldness is his eyes is replaced with something warm and kind. He kisses my forehead. "Yeah, we do."

Logan's hand goes to my back, and as he guides me to his truck, he stops and turns to Blake.

"I'd hate to hear that you're running your mouth. And I'm sure River would too."

CHAPTER THIRTY-TWO

Logan

As soon as I saw that asshole, I knew who he was and grabbed my gun and put in the holster inside my jacket. I had no intention of using it, but I had a feeling this guy needed intimidation tactics. I recognized his face right away from the pictures revealed in my little investigation into him. Having access to police records helps. The guy is a punk. I can't believe what he said about taking Skye's virginity. I want to drive my fist through his skull, but I can't. Because next thing you know, I'd have assault charges against me. Skye is silent, and her eyes flit my way every so often. I'm pissed as hell. I'm pretty sure some of it is showing right now. She's nervous and embarrassed, even more so than the first time we met.

The few-minute drive is enough to cool me down. I pull into my driveway, put the truck in park, and turn off the ignition. Neither of us makes a move to leave the truck. I take my seatbelt off and turn to Skye. She does the same and looks at me. Her eyes are bright with unshed tears. I'm angry all over again.

"I'm sorry, I—"

"You have nothing to apologize for, Skye. You did nothing wrong."

She laughs without humor.

"I dated him."

"Yeah, years ago, and I've had my share of dating mistakes too. Some of them could make that asshole look like a saint."

I'm thinking of Amanda. I've never talked to Skye about Amanda. If I could take a pill and erase every memory of that woman from my mind, I would.

She smiles at me, but I can tell she thinks I'm joking. Fuck. This will happen. I guess this is as good a time as any.

"I'm not joking, Skye. I dated someone way longer than I should have, and it's one of my biggest regrets."

A silent "oh" leaves her lips and curiosity overcomes the sadness in her eyes.

In a flash, being inside this truck feels suffocating and the need to get out and breathe fresh air overwhelms me. This is not a new reaction. Every time I think of Amanda, I want to crawl out of my own skin. I'll tell her about Amanda, but not in here. I need to get out.

I run my fingers through the curls over her shoulders. Touching her calms me. If Amanda is poison, Skye is the antidote.

"Come on. I'll tell you about it."

I open my door, and Skye turns to open hers and is hopping out of the truck before I have a chance to come around and open it for her. I know she's perfectly capable of opening her own door and taking care of herself, but sometimes, I wish she'd let me do it for her.

We make our way inside my house and take our jackets and shoes off by the door. I realize I'm still wearing my gun and remove it, checking again that the safety is on. I walk to the kitchen to put it in its hiding place, the cabinet above the refrigerator. I grab two water bottles and go back to the living room. Skye is standing near the door, arms wrapped around herself. I hate to see her like this, so unsure of herself.

I put the water bottles on the coffee table and walk to her, put both of my hands on her face, and bring her mouth to mine. I kiss her gently, just a pass of lips, and keep kissing her until her hands grab at my shirt and I feel her relax into me.

Stepping back, I pull her behind me to sit on the couch. She pulls her feet up and sits with her legs crossed. I mimic her.

"I guess it's my turn to tell you about a terrible ex."

Her blue eyes are huge on her face and still shiny from unshed tears.

"Where to start?"

"You said you dated her far longer than you should."

She's confirming, not asking, but I hear the question anyway.

"Yes, for three years."

"Three years?"

The way she says it tells me it's longer than she thought.

"Yes, we started dating my first year at Riggins and broke up at the end of my junior year."

"That's a long time."

"In years, yeah, but not in actual time we spent together. Amanda went to Yale. We didn't see each other much during the school year. We got together on some weekends, breaks, and the summer, but not always. Amanda liked to travel. Her parents are divorced, and she often went to visit her mother in France. Or so I was led to believe."

"What do you mean?"

"It seems I was the only one who thought the relationship was exclusive."

Her eyes pop open, the clear blue catching the light from the sconces on the wall. A soft "oh" leaves her lips.

"Yeah, but that isn't even the worst of it."

"What can be worse than cheating?"

"Amanda is extremely high-maintenance. I never realized how much so until we broke up and I dated other women."

Her eyes narrow at me in confusion.

"I don't understand. You dated other girls before her, right?"

"Yes, I did. A lot, actually, but the girls, and later on, women, in my circle of friends were all very much like Amanda."

I loathe what I'm about to say next, but if I'm to be honest about myself and my life, this has to come out.

"Most people would say I was born with the proverbial silver spoon in my mouth. And they would be right. My family is wealthy. The families they relate to are wealthy. I attended private schools with kids who were rich and entitled. It was drilled into my brain from very early on that we were better than the rest of the world. I grew up among people who reinforced that idea. My grandparents, the ones who left me and my brother this house, tried to teach us otherwise and gave my brother and me a different perspective."

Skye listens intently. She's hanging on my every word. That's another opposite from Amanda. If the conversation was not about her, fashion, jewelry, or gossip about who did what, she was not interested. Looking back, I feel like an even bigger idiot.

"But it didn't really register until I moved here and started at Riggins. Being around so many people, with all different backgrounds, opened my eyes to all the hypocrisy my family and friends fed me."

I take a deep breath and run my fingers through my hair.

"I'm not making an excuse for having been an ass growing up. Not at all."

"You didn't know any different," she says.

"You are a product of your environment and the beliefs that were instilled in you."

My hands fist in my lap.

"Yeah, and add to that the way my father ran us all like a drill sergeant and my eagerness to please him and earn his love, and he had the perfect little puppet in his hands."

Fuck! I'd said too much. I didn't mean for it to come out. I glance back at Skye, unsure of what I'll find. I see no judgment, no pity. Thank God.

"No child should have to earn a parent's love. There should be no doubt of that love, ever."

"My grandparents gave me that love. We could be kids in this house. We felt loved and free over here. But we weren't around many kids our age. We spent a lot of time outdoors with our grandparents. Hiking, skiing, fishing, swimming, playing hockey, and running around like feral kids. It was the complete opposite of the kind of life we had back in Connecticut. My father didn't much care for our visiting our grandparents. He thought their lifestyle unfit, but now that I am older, I think it was more that he could not intimidate or control them and they had some kind of hold over him. What, I have no idea. And he traveled a lot too. Our mother usually accompanied him. Having our grandparents watch us solved the 'who will watch the kids' problem. I'm sure he would've been more than happy to hire a team of sitters, but like I said, my grandparents got us instead."

"I bet you loved that. Being able to spend all that time with them."

"I did. I loved it. My brother even more than me. Liam was

always in trouble with our father. He couldn't do anything right. I was always a rule follower, didn't question much. But once I moved out for college at eighteen, I really got to see the world through my own eyes and eventually be myself as well. I didn't like that version of me very much, and the further I tried to step away from it, the more my father tried to control me. I went along with his wishes for a while. Amanda was another extension of my father, but I didn't see it. I was a horny teenager with no clue about the real world and had this beautiful woman who claimed to love me."

"What do you mean by her being an extension of your father?"

"She kept tabs on me for him. She manipulated me on his behalf. Amanda is four years older than me. It flattered me. She knew just what to say and do."

"You're not the first teen led by his hormones. You were a kid, and she was an adult. You can't take the blame in this. If the gender roles were reversed, no one would blame the teen girl."

"That's true enough."

"I don't understand something. Why would she keep tabs on you?"

"Because her father and my father had plans, business plans that would make them millions of dollars, and I was part of it. They needed someone they could trust to run this company they had plans to develop. And they needed me to do it."

"Why not just tell you about it?"

"Because the plans they had, and the company, weren't exactly legal. Amanda was in on it. They needed someone they could control, someone to take the fall if shit went south. Someone they could claim they knew nothing about, because who would believe a father would set up his own son? And through my marriage with Amanda and the prenup they had planned, assets would be under her name and could not be touched if anything happened."

"Wow!"

"Wow doesn't begin to cover it. My father was pressuring me to propose to Amanda. He wanted us married before he started the new company. His bullshit reason was to have a solid foundation between the two families. The real reason was to have Amanda closer and able to manipulate me from the inside. She actually showed up one day with a huge rock on her finger and told me it was our engagement ring and she'd send me the bill. I later found out my father had paid for it."

"How did you figure it out?"

"It was summer before senior year. And I decided to go home and surprise her since I wouldn't be around during her birthday because I was taking summer classes that year. I went home but didn't tell anyone about it."

I have to stop and take a deep breath because the anger at them and at myself for being so blindly stupid still stings after all these years. Skye reaches out and grabs my hand, lacing our fingers together and holding them between both of her hands.

"When I got home, Amanda's car was in the driveway and I thought it would be perfect. I figured she was visiting with my parents and we could all have dinner together."

Skye squeezes my hand when I pause.

"I was so wrong. I parked my car beside hers and didn't bother to go through the front of the house. I walked around to the back instead. We have a huge patio outside the kitchen. I figured they'd be out. Mom liked having tea outside every after-noon if the weather was nice, and it was a beautiful day. But when I came around the back, no one was there. The patio door was open, though, and I just went inside. The house was silent.

Something in me, a voice in my head, told me to be quiet as well. I made my way into the house. There was no one in the kitchen, the living room, or the library. I checked my father's office too, but it was empty as well. I remember very clearly how my heart thundered. I didn't know what I was about to find out, but I knew it wouldn't be good."

Her eyes are on me, her breaths shallow in anticipation. Skye squeezes my hand again, encouraging me to go on. I squeeze it back and earn a small smile.

"I made my way upstairs. Unlike this house that creaks and complains when anyone walks around, my childhood home is built with a layer of soundproofing material between the floors. My father built that home that way years before I was born in anticipation of not having to listen to the sounds of children. He's a big proponent of the 'children should not be heard' idea. They never heard me. But I heard them. The bedroom door was wide-open. At first, I thought it might have been my father and my mother, but I knew it couldn't be as soon as the thought entered my mind. So I stood there, trying to get a grasp of what they were saying and what it meant."

Images fill my mind. Of all the places they could have fucked, why my bedroom?

"They were talking about me. My father and Amanda. And how very close I was to actually proposing to her. They had a wedding date picked, and they also talked about how easy it would be to feed me with false information on the new company. But that wasn't the worst of it. Between the bits of conversation, there were moans and the sounds of flesh slapping against flesh."

One of her hands leaves mine to cover her mouth, her eyes wide with disbelief.

"I was in shock. But I knew what I heard. Still, I had to see it with my own eyes. I couldn't leave that house without actually seeing it. I needed more proof. And I got it. I took the two steps I needed to stand in front of the open door. They didn't see me. They were facing away from me. And there they were. In my bedroom, on my bed, my father and my supposed fiancée and future wife, fucking."

"Oh my God."

"I don't know how long I stood there, paralyzed, my feet frozen in place."

That room, my bedroom, the only place that felt really mine. The one concession from the designer-decorated house. It still had posters of my favorite bands on the wall. It still had a cork board with pictures from vacations and all the places I visited with my grandparents. My high school trophies and medals next to my favorite books on the bookcase. A jersey draped over a chair from my last visit. And then all the things that didn't belong. Shoes that were not mine. A belt. A skirt and blouse. A black bra hanging off the side of the bed. Gray pants, a white dress shirt, a tie. All strewn across the blue carpet I used to lie on and do sit-ups and push-ups every morning when I woke up. That place, the only place that felt like mine in that house, was forever tainted.

There are tears in her eyes now. Tears for me. No one ever cried for me before. I wipe them with my free hand, running my thumb over her cheek.

"They just kept at it. Fucking and talking about their plans for me. And I stood there. I was a kid up to that moment. Still trying to earn my father's love and approval and living a life where most things were just handed to me." I shake my head as if I could get rid of those memories.

"The blinders fell off that day. I saw my father and Amanda for who they really are. I realized then I'd never be more than a pawn for my father. I left. They never even saw me. I drove back to Riggins. I was torn, and I realized I had no one I could talk to. I had dozens of friends and didn't trust a single one of them. They were party friends, good times friends. Even my teammates felt like strangers. The only two people who could understand me were unreachable. My brother, somewhere in the Middle East, and my grandma in Florida, still mourning Grandpa's death."

"What did you do?"

"Nothing. I stole my father's prized bottle of whiskey on the way out, but I didn't even get drunk. I didn't want to numb it with alcohol. I wanted to feel every ounce of pain and disappointment and have it burned into my memory so I'd never make the same mistake again."

Her eyes are full of pain. Skye's the first person I've told the full story. A part of me is still ashamed. How could I have been so stupid? How could I have never seen it? I've gone over it again and again. I analyzed every interaction with Amanda, with my father, and even my poor mother, who's just as under his thumb as I had been.

"A couple of days later, my mother called me to find out if I'd make it home for the weekend. I told her I couldn't make it, that I had tests I needed to prepare for. Which was true enough. Amanda called, and I ignored it. She texted me, and I ignored it. This went on for a couple of days. My father called then. I ignored him. Kept sending his calls to voice mail and deleting them without listening. It went on for a whole day. He'd never been one to text, but my lack of response must have pissed him off enough to text me. He berated me for not answering his and Amanda's calls. I was still staring at that message when my phone rang again. I answered him this time. Before I had a chance to say anything, he laid in on me. Called me all kinds of names and how dare I hurt my fiancée's feelings. I listened to the whole tirade in silence. He went on for minutes until he noticed my silence. Whenever I pissed him off, and it happened often enough, I'd be apologizing as he yelled at me. That was our MO, from the time I was a little kid. My silence finally got his attention, and he asked me if I had nothing to say for myself, and I said yes."

"What did you say?"

I can't help the smile on my face. Not a happy one, but a smile I know says more than words ever could.

"I said, 'Yes, I have something to say. I don't ever want to see you or that cheating bitch again. Fuck you both.' And then I hung up."

"I don't even know what to say. I'm so sorry, Logan."

"I'm not. I'm glad. I might have married her before I figured out what was happening and their plans for me."

"Jesus. I can't believe anyone could do something like this to anyone, much less their own child."

"He was never really a father. I don't think he's capable of love."

"Did they leave you alone after that?"

"Oh, no. Nothing is that easy. Amanda showed up a couple of hours later. She put on an act worthy of an Oscar. Denying it up and down, saying she loved me, that she'd never cheat on me, and that whoever told me she was cheating lied. She talked and talked and even managed some tears. I just sat right here on this couch and watched her performance. Didn't say a word. Then she tried to have sex. Stripped in the middle of the living room. I let her. When she was completely naked, I picked up all her clothes, walked to the front door, and tossed them all onto the porch. She was screaming then. I walked back to her, got a hold of her arm, and walked her outside and closed the door in her face."

Skye's hand covers her mouth and her expression is one between horrified and mirthful.

"She started banging on the door and threatening to call the police on me. Tell the cops I attacked her."

Skye's eyes never leave me.

"I opened the door again. She was still naked and tried to walk back into the house. I blocked her with my body. She switched from anger to tears again and asked why I didn't believe her."

"Didn't your father tell her you saw them?"

"I guess he didn't connect my calling her a cheater with my knowing about them."

The look on Amanda's face is still fresh in my memory, even after all this time.

"I said, 'I saw you. I saw you both fucking on my bed. Save your breath. There will be no wedding. There will be no new company. Find another guy to take the fall for you and my father. Never call me again. Never come here again. Never even think about me again. We're done.' Then I closed the door again. She kicked at it a few times, cursed, and I imagine gathered her clothes before she left since there was nothing left outside the next day."

"Why do I have a feeling there's more to this story?"

"Because there was. My father's threats came hours later. He demanded I go home. Then he demanded I get over it and get back to Amanda. He made threats against me. He made threats against my brother. He made threats against my mother. He tried everything he could think of. Tried to get me kicked out of school too. Said he wouldn't pay for my tuition. I expected that. But by then, my grandma had gotten wind of what had happened and intervened. Mrs. Iris next door knows everything that happens in the neighborhood. She heard Amanda and called Grandma. Grandma called, and I gave her the short and clean version of it. She sent a check to Riggins to cover the rest of my tuition until I graduated and also made a very generous donation in the name of my grandfather."

Grandpa had been a Riggins alumnus, and it was another reason I wanted to go there. All the stories he told me about Riggins when I was a kid. I just knew Riggins was it for me. I never even applied anywhere else.

"And that was it then? They gave up?"

"No, not for a long time. Both of them kept trying to make me change my mind. Amanda even tried to convince me she was pregnant. I knew it was a lie. And if she was pregnant, it sure as hell wouldn't be mine. We'd never had unprotected sex, and it had been weeks since we'd been together."

"What about your mother? Did you tell her?"

"Not at first. But there was enough going on that I'm sure she knew. My father traveled often, and I'm sure he had mistresses. They didn't share a bedroom. I didn't even know it was not normal for married couples to have separate bedrooms until I went over to a friend's house when I was five or six and realized his parents shared a bed."

"Why would your mom stay? Why not just take you and your brother and leave?"

"That's a question I've asked myself and her many times, and the answer was always that I wouldn't understand. But looking back, my mom is completely under his control. Mom never told me any of this, but my grandma did. My parents met when she was seventeen and a freshman in college. He's fifteen years older than her. But he was attractive and charming. She was young and naïve, far from home, and fell under his spell.

They got married a year later, and she was pregnant with me a few months into the marriage and dropped out of college. Mom was twenty when I was born. She was isolated from her family and her friends. My father controlled every aspect of her life. She was madly in love with him. I don't think he ever loved her back. I don't think he's capable of love. My grandparents tried to be a part of our life as much as they could. Living in different states made it harder, but they visited more often after I was born. My father tolerated their presence, and they tried to visit when he was away on business trips and my mother was left behind with Liam and me when we were babies. As we got older, my grandparents would take us back to Vermont to spend time with them. My father conceded. Not so much so that we could spend time with them, but because he didn't want to deal with two boys eager to get their father's attention."

"I don't know what to say. That's a terrible way to grow up."

"We really didn't know any different. Some of our friends went away to boarding school. We thought we were lucky to have two homes, one with our parents and one with our maternal grandparents. My father's parents died before I was born. Not until I was eleven or twelve did I begin to see all the ugly in my family, but I was a kid and still trying to win my father's affection. It was easy to ignore the ugly parts."

"Are your parents still together now, after all that?"

"As far as I know, they're still living in the same house. I never went back home. To be honest, I speak more often with Mary, our cook, than I ever did with my parents. She calls me every week, lets me know what's happening, and gives me news of my brother too. He keeps her up on what's happening with him when he can reach out."

"You're not close to your brother either?"

"We are, or were, very close growing up. But I left for

college and he was still in high school. And my father was always harder on him than me. Liam didn't conform as much. I expected him to join me at Riggins. That's something we'd always talked about, but he enlisted in the navy instead. I've only seen him a handful of times since he enlisted. He's a medic with the marines now and doesn't come home often."

"And I thought I had it bad with Blake. I wish I could do or say something to make it all go away."

I smile then, a real smile. I know exactly what she can do and say to get my mind off the past.

"You can say my name. Multiple times. While you're naked. Under me."

She does just that.

CHAPTER THIRTY-THREE

Skye

IT'S BEEN A WEEK SINCE THE DAY WE RAN INTO BLAKE AND Logan told me about his ex. I think about it often and thank God for the caring parents we have. River and I are so lucky to have parents who support and care for us. As crazy as Mom may be sometimes, and as many times as she's embarrassed me and River, I've never felt unloved by her.

Luckily, I haven't seen Blake since. I hope Logan's veiled threat is enough to keep him away from me and his mouth shut. River was so livid when I told her about it that she actually looked him up on the student directory to send him an email and remind him of her threat of cutting off his balls. I had to convince her it was best not to make any threats using school email since balls cutting is illegal and all.

That's River. My vigilant sister. I hope she doesn't run into him either. Dad hates when he has to wear his lawyer hat. And I didn't plan bail money into this month's budget.

Bruno is feeling left out since Logan's taking up all my free time. I don't want to be one of those girls who forgets her friends when she has a boyfriend. We still talk in class, but we haven't hung out in a while. Logan's working tonight, so it will be the perfect opportunity to do something together. I want to ask him about Sidney. They've been dating for a while now. He hasn't talked about his long-distance relationship recently, and I'm worried that not all is well with them. Bruno loves telling me all about Sidney, but he only does it when it's just the two of us, and we haven't had much one-on-one lately. I hope that's just it, but I have a gut feeling there may be more to Bruno's silence about it.

"Are you ready?"

River's voice brings me back to reality.

"Are you okay? You've been sitting there for the last five minutes holding that shoe but not putting it on."

I look at my hands and down at my feet, and sure enough, I have one pink and gray sneaker on but not the other. I put my shoe on and lace it.

"Yeah, I'm fine. Just thinking."

"Uh-oh. Everything okay with Logan? You didn't have a fight, did you?"

Just hearing his name puts a goofy smile on my face.

"No, not at all. We've never had a fight. Not even an argument. It's really easy being with him."

"Somebody's in *love*," River teases me.

"I think I am, River."

I stand up, and she stands next to me and pulls me into a hug.

"I'm so happy for you, Sis. Logan is a great guy, and you deserve to be with a great guy."

"Thank you. And you do too, River. Why aren't you dating anyone? You haven't talked about meeting any cute guys in months."

She steps away and turns to the door.

"Eh, nothing out there. I'm not interested in dating right now."

I can't see her face, but there's a strain in her voice. It's so brief and nonchalant that someone else may have never noticed it. But I know my sister and how very protective of her feelings she is. She hates showing any kind of weakness. I don't know what it will take to break through her walls. All I can do is keep trying.

"River?"

"We gotta get going if we want to be on time for the first class. Got everything you need?"

She's already opening the door, not looking at me. I follow her outside, and just as I'm about to try again, she beats me to it. River is a master of deflection.

"So, what were you thinking about before? You're so out of it. I called your name three times."

Had she? I hadn't heard her.

"Nothing, really. I was thinking about Bruno. Logan's working tonight, so Bruno's coming over for dinner at six. We're making pizza from scratch. Are you staying in?"

River goes to the passenger door of our car, unlocks it, and tosses the keys over. I usually drive us to Riggins in the morning. I always get lucky finding parking spots. It doesn't work if River is driving, only if I am.

"I have a study group tonight, but I should be back by nine-thirty, ten at the latest. Save me some?"

"Of course."

We could have walked. It's just about a ten-minute walk to campus, but it's November and cold. Never mind that I'm Vermont born and raised. The cold and I are not friends.

"So, what's the deal with you and Bruno?"

This again?

"You know the deal, River. He's a friend. Just a friend. Nothing more. Guys and girls can be platonic friends. When will you believe me?"

"I believe you, kind of. In my experience, guys and girls can try to be platonic friends, but one of them ends up wanting more. Every guy friend I've ever had, since seventh or eighth grade, has at some point made a pass at me. So maybe you have no interest in Bruno, but I find it hard to believe that with the amount of time you two spend together, there's nothing on his side."

We pull into the RU student parking lot.

"There's a spot right there."

River points to it.

"I know, but I think we can find one closer."

"At this time in the morning? There's no fuc—"

"Ha!"

Someone pulls out of a spot right on the first row.

"Told you!"

"Damn it! Every time! How the hell do you do it?"

I shrug.

"I use my woo-woo powers. Some people can find water in the desert. I can find open spots in a full parking lot."

I didn't forget what she said about Bruno. "Okay, first, you are gorgeous, so it's understandable that guys fall for you. Second, about Bruno. There's nothing there and never will be. Bruno is crazy in love with Sidney. We really are just friends."

She opens the door and grabs our bags before coming around to my side of the car.

"I've never seen this Sidney person. How do I even know she exists?"

"I've met Sidney, remember?"

"Okay, I'll take your word for it."

I look at my phone and we have seven minutes to get to class. I walk faster, but River, with her longer legs, just keeps at the same pace.

"And what about Logan?"

"What about him?"

"Has he ever said anything about you and Bruno?"

"No, why would he?"

"Because Logan's jealous of him."

"No, he's not."

"Yes, he is. You haven't noticed the way he acts when Bruno is around? Logan always pulls you to his side and puts himself between you and Bruno. And he watches how you two interact like a hawk."

I'm about to dismiss what she's saying, but as I run through my mind whatever interactions we've had together, I realize it's true. Logan always puts himself between me and Bruno. I stop and look up at her—this is my building, so we separate here—and her knowing smile tells me she can see I just figured it out.

She's walking backward now.

"Logan is jealous. He may not say anything, but he is."

CHAPTER THIRTY-FOUR

Logan

I'M GLAD I OPENED UP TO SKYE. I'VE NEVER SHARED ANY of my past with anyone. Liam knows some of it, but I spared him the uglier parts. He'd been deployed somewhere in the Middle East when it happened. Part of me is glad Liam is away from my father and his toxic influence, and part of me is terrified to have my baby brother in the middle of a war zone.

Logan: Hey, baby brother. Sorry, it's been a while since I talked to you.
Logan: I told her about the heartless bitch.
Logan: It feels like I dropped a thousand-pound weight.
Logan: I'm...I'm happy, Liam.
Logan: But I miss you like hell. When will it be over?
Logan: Come home.

Liam had just turned nineteen when I cut all ties with my father. He was just a kid. And a tender-hearted one at that. Liam is a nerd at heart. He doesn't look the part, though.

The one good thing our father passed on to us is his good

looks. I'm not being conceited. I have a mirror, and there were always legions of girls after Liam and me. I've been worrying a lot about my brother lately. I haven't heard from him in a long time. Last time we spoke, he said he was going in deep—whatever that means—and wouldn't be reachable for a while. It's been over six months now.

Liam is the smarter one between the two of us. He has zero interest in joining the family business. For as long as I can remember, all Liam wanted to do was to be a doctor. The kid read medical journals for fun. He watched every medical show on TV, be it fiction or not. He even joined our town's junior EMTs at fourteen. I didn't even know such a thing was possible. At fourteen, all I thought about was playing hockey.

Liam was always trying to rescue every critter he came across—baby birds, stray cats, lost dogs. If it had fur or feathers, he loved it. But we weren't allowed to have pets. My father believes that love makes people vulnerable and pets would make us weak.

Which I agree with, to an extent. It is true that love does make one vulnerable. But it doesn't have to be a bad thing. Right?

No one saw it coming when Liam joined the Navy. He didn't confide in me or anyone else. I wish Liam had reached out to me. I was away at Riggins and still don't know exactly what happened to make him feel that running away from home and enlisting was the only choice he had.

When I tried to pry information out of him, he didn't open up. He said what was done was done and talking about it wouldn't change anything.

I know our father had something to do with it. Of that, I'm certain.

One gets to do a lot of thinking sitting alone inside a squad car. I have to figure a way to reach Liam. Maybe Mary knows how.

The buzzing sound of my phone brings me back to reality. I glance at it sitting next to the squad laptop. *Skye.*

Just seeing her name on the screen makes me happy.

Skye: Hi.
Logan: Hey there.
Skye: Busy?
Logan: Just sitting here and waiting for someone to run a red light.
Skye: Or a yellow light . . .

I can't see her, but I know she's smiling.

Logan: You want to know a secret?
Skye: Yes!
Logan: I never pulled anyone over for running a yellow light unless it turns to red while they're doing it. And I didn't see you had a tail light out until I'd already stopped you.
Skye: But it didn't turn to red when I ran it. I went thru the light while it was green and then it turned yellow.
Logan: I know.
Skye: Then why did you go after me?
Logan: I have no idea. It was the end of my shift and I wasn't looking forward to doing any paperwork. But something just told me to go after you, and I did.
Skye: Wow!
Logan: Yeah, wow.

There were a few minutes of silence after that, and I could almost see the expression on her face as she thought it over. I have asked myself that same question many times. Why did I decide to go after that particular car when it had clearly crossed the intersection before the light turned yellow? I still don't have an answer.

Skye: If you hadn't . . .
Logan: I like to think we would have met anyway. We live practically on top of each other and we both go to Pat's.
Skye: Yes, but . . .

I can see the dots flowing on the screen. She's still typing.

Skye: We lived next to each other for three years and never met.
Logan: It was not the right time, I guess.
Skye: My mom would agree with you. She'd love you for saying that.

FROM THE FEW times we talked about her family, I got the impression that Serena, her mom, is a very spiritual person. I'm not religious and don't know much about any of it. Religion is another thing my father vetoed. But a lot of the guys at work are superstitious, and I have seen and heard enough to take heed and have a healthy respect for gut feelings.

Skye says her mom is a modern hippie. River calls their mother the Woo-Woo Lady. She doesn't seem to take it as seriously as Skye, but I might be wrong. River is really hard to read. As outspoken and sometimes abrasive with her no-holds-barred honesty as she is, I have a feeling she hides a lot. No proof. Just a . . . I laugh. Just a gut feeling.

Skye: How late are you working tonight?

Logan: Until midnight.

Skye: :(

Skye: I was hoping you'd be done early. Bruno is coming over and we're making pizza.

Fuck!

Fucking Bruno.

I hadn't seen or heard of him for over a week. I thought he'd gotten the hint and backed off. I guess not.

Now, I'm annoyed and jealous. Jealous of the time they spend together, jealous because I can't be there. Jealous of the three years they had together before we met. It's completely irrational, I know. I've never been the jealous type. And it's not that I don't trust Skye, because I do, even with all the crap I'm still carrying around since I found Amanda and my father fucking in my bed. It's that I don't trust Bruno. Or any guy, for that matter. But River should be there too, so at least there's that.

Logan: Sorry, I wish I could. Just the three of you then?

Skye: Three?

Skye: Oh, you mean River. No, just us two. River has a study group after school tonight and won't be home until later.

Red-hot, jealous anger takes a place in my chest and weighs me down into the seat. Jesus! I need to get ahold of myself. The need to bust into her little pizza dinner party for two is like a living, screaming thing inside me. And it's ugly.

I could stop at Pat's Cafe for a coffee. Nothing wrong with getting a cup of coffee during a late-night shift. It's expected, even. And if I take a short walk down the block . . . the ugly, screaming little beast inside me likes this plan and quiets down.

CHAPTER THIRTY-FIVE

Skye

"Dude! You'd better not eat everything, or River is going to be so mad at you."

"What?"

Bruno talks around a mouthful of pizza.

"There's a whole other pie waiting to be baked in the fridge."

I can't believe he can pack all that away, but then again, he is a big guy. He's already on his third slice to my one and only. I could never eat more than one slice of pizza, two if they are the thin crust kind.

"I'm saving that one for tomorrow, for Logan."

The oven timer dings, and I get up to check on the batch of peanut butter chocolate chip cookies I'm baking. There's a knock on the door as I'm pulling a cookie pan out of the oven. I glance at the clock on the microwave. It reads 8:12 p.m. Huh? Who could it be? River wouldn't knock.

"Can you get the door?"

I call out to Bruno, my back to him as I slide the parchment paper the cookies sit on onto the kitchen's granite countertop to cool.

"On it," he calls back.

I turn when the door opens and can't help the smile that takes over my face. I drop the hot cookie sheet in the sink and make a beeline to Logan. I throw myself at him, arms around his shoulders. He catches me, and his head buries into my neck a second later and he's inhaling me. His arms tightly wrapped around my back hold me flat against him. I want to wrap my legs around his waist, but police duty belt and the dozens of things hanging from it make that impossible. I settle for just hanging on to him, my feet dangling several inches off the floor.

He inhales me again and whispers against my skin.

"Hmm, orange blossom, pizza, and . . . is that cookies I smell too?"

I laugh. His cookie addiction cannot be denied. With one last squeeze, he sets me on the floor. I take him in. I love to see him in his uniform. I love it even more when he's out of it. *As in, naked.*

With no shoes and on my bare feet—or my socked feet, rather—the height difference between us is even more evident.

Logan reaches behind him and closes the door and looks over my head. I look back too and realize—with a little guilt—that I forgot Bruno was here. And now he's working on his fourth slice. I narrow my eyes at him and he smirks at me.

"What are you doing here? I thought you couldn't make it."

"That's because I'm not here. I'm at Pat's, getting a coffee. You haven't seen me tonight. Not at all."

Logan winks at me and I catch on.

"Too bad you're not here. If you were, you could have some homemade pizza and fresh-baked cookies."

"Oh, I think I'm also getting a slice of pizza and some cookies to go with that coffee from Pat's."

"Come on."

I tug at his hand.

He resists and glances back at Bruno sitting at the table and back at me, then pulls me into him again and kisses me. Not a hello kind of kiss. Not even a lingering hello kiss. Nope. With one arm around my waist and the other behind my head, Logan positions me against him and molds me to his body. This is a breath stealing, heart thundering, panty melting, fucking-my-mouth-with-his-mouth kind of kiss. The kind of kiss that promises so much more is on the way. The kind of kiss that gets burned into one's lips, skin, memory. If there were a Nobel Prize for kissing, this kiss would win it. By a landslide.

When Logan lets me go, I wobble a little on my feet. I'm drunk on lust. Logan steadies me, a smile on his face. His smile melts away the last few functioning brain cells I have. He looks over my head again. I turn back and remember Bruno. Damn it! I forgot all about him. Again.

Bruno's mouth is half-open, a bite of pizza hanging from it. And is he blushing? I've never seen Bruno blush. Ever. My face gets warm too, reaching the same heat level as the rest of my body.

I take a step away from Logan.

"Pizza?"

"I can't stay. I shouldn't even be here, but I had to see you."

"How about I get you a slice to go?"

"And some cookies too?"

His hopeful smile is that of a little boy. Gosh, he's melting my panties one minute and in the next, he's melting my heart.

"Come on, I'll pack it to go."

Logan sits at the table across from Bruno and nods at him.

Bruno, still looking uncomfortable, nods back.

I grab two slices of pizza and put them on a paper plate and cover it with another. That earns me a frown from Bruno.

"Oh, please. You're on your fourth slice. I don't know where you put all that."

Bruno flexes his biceps for me.

"Do you think these babies get this big all by themselves?"

I laugh.

"Uh-huh, I'm sure pizza is the building block of muscle."

I could swear Logan narrows his eyes at Bruno, but I'm still so flustered from that kiss I don't think my feet have touched the floor yet.

"Let me get you some cookies too."

I go back to the kitchen and grab some foil and wrap half a dozen cookies in it. They're still warm.

"Pizza and cookies. You're all set. Want a can of soda too?"

"No, thanks, babe. I'll stop at Pat's and get that coffee. She's my alibi."

He reaches for my hand.

"Walk me to the door?"

I trail after him to the door, and he pulls me into the hall, holding me with one hand and the food in the other.

When his head bends, his kiss is a lot sweeter and tender.

"I missed you."

My heart does a happy dance in my chest.

"I missed you too. I'm so happy you stopped by. Will you get in trouble?"

"If I do, it was worth it."

He gives me one last kiss, brushes his lips on my forehead, and leaves. I watch as he closes the outside door, staying in the hall for a full minute, enjoying the moment before I have to go back in and hear Bruno's commentary on that kiss.

The door opens again, and I smile, expecting him to come back, but it's River this time. I slump against the wall.

"Well, hello to you too!" Is her sarcastic remark.

"I thought you were Logan."

"I saw him walking to Pat's. Is he coming back?"

"No, he just left. He's working tonight."

We walk back into the apartment, and River kicks her shoes off by the door and drops her backpack and jacket on the couch.

"Touch that and die!"

I'm still in dreamland and jump at her words. She's walking to the table, and Bruno is frozen in place, a hand hovering over the last slice of pizza. River snatches the whole serving tray from right under his fingers and brings it to the kitchen with her, pausing to place it on the counter and wash and dry her hands before taking a huge bite of the last slice.

"You ate the whole pizza," she says accusingly.

"Me? No. Your sister ate some and Logan ate some."

She scoffs.

"We both know Skye only ate one slice. Logan's not here to defend himself, and I've seen you put away an entire pie. So don't go blaming everyone else. If you're man enough to eat a whole pie, you should be man enough to own up to it."

"I'll be man enough to own up that watching your sister make out with Logan five feet away from me gave me a chubby. Holy shit, I wish I'd thought to get my phone and video that kiss."

And now I'm blushing again. Heck, I wish he had it on video too. I want to see if it looked as hot as it felt.

"What?" River asks.

"Oh, it was just Logan marking his territory. I thought he was going to whip it out and piss a circle around Skye."

"No, he wasn't."

The need to defend Logan is greater than my embarrassment.

"Yes, he was. I bet you the only reason he stopped by was to check on us and make sure there's no funny business going on."

"Logan trusts me. And that's kind of hurtful and untrue. He stops by nearly every day."

"I'm sure he does, but it does not change the fact he's jealous and wanted to check in and make sure there was nothing going on that shouldn't be going on."

I look at River, trying to gauge her opinion on this, but she's leaning against the counter still, the last bite of pizza disappearing into her mouth. She grabs for a cookie next. She's watching the exchange with keen eyes, and I know she has an opinion on it and I also know she won't say anything in front of Bruno. Whatever she has to say is for my ears only. I never told either one of them what Logan said about his ex and his father. I can't help but think that maybe Bruno is right. That Logan's reason to visit had more to do with Bruno being here than stopping to see me. And it bothers me more than I can say. All the joy from seeing him evaporates. River's watching me closer now.

"I have another pizza in the fridge. We can put it in the oven for you."

"No, save it for tomorrow. They had snacks and I'm not that hungry."

"Why the nine degrees on my ass then?"

Bruno asks, still annoyed by River's dig on his pizza-eating habits.

"Because you should know better. You couldn't know if I ate before or not. I could be starving."

"We have a whole other pie!"

Bruno's voice is indignant.

"Besides the point."

River waves him off and walks to the bathroom. A minute later, we can hear the shower.

Bruno looks at me, his eyes narrow. He's always been good at reading me.

"I hurt your feelings. I'm sorry. I didn't mean to say the only reason Logan stopped by was to check on me. It's obvious he's very much into you and he feels threatened by my presence here with you alone."

"Maybe if I told him—"

"No. You promised me," he whispers and looks over his shoulder toward the hall. We can still hear the shower. There's no way River can hear this conversation.

"And I've never broken that promise. But don't you think it—"

"No. I have a plan and I'm sticking to it. I don't want to talk about it, Skye."

He stands up abruptly, gathering our paper plates and napkins.

"I should get going."

Bruno carries our dinner mess to the kitchen and tosses everything in the trash.

I'm standing in the same spot, hugging myself like I used to when I was a little kid whenever I was upset and my parents were busy at work and not around to cuddle me. *Hold it together, Skye.*

His eyes do not meet mine when he walks by, but he stops to kiss me on the cheek and squeeze my arm. This is a silent apology, I know. He grabs his jacket and is gone a moment later.

The door closes behind him with a dull thud.

CHAPTER THIRTY-SIX

Logan

THAT WAS A DICK MOVE, I KNOW. THAT KISS WAS MORE FOR Bruno's benefit than Skye's, and I feel like the asshole I am for doing it. Still, I don't regret it. I have no idea what the deal with Bruno is. Maybe he has no interest in Skye other than friendship. But he's a guy, and she's a sweet and sexy woman.

And biology is biology. A man does not have to be interested in a woman to fuck her. I have fucked my share of women whom I had little interest in. I've never led anyone to believe it was more than a simple fuck. She got off. I got off. We were even. End of story. Not that I'm proud of it.

I don't see myself as a player. I'm not playing games or putting marks on my bedpost. Just scratching the itch. But Skye is so much more than an itch. I want to know her. I want to know what makes her tick. What she hopes to do with her life. And how do I fit into it? It's so much more than lust and great sex. I enjoy her company, feel comfortable in her presence. Being near Skye is like being home. I can let my guard down. I don't have to be a cop, my father's son, or a Cole. I can just be me. Logan. And not just my last name or what is expected of me because of it.

I think I'm falling for Skye.

Fast.

Logan: I was a dick today, Liam.

Logan: I checked on my girl because I'm jealous of her friend.

Logan: Instead of trusting her like I should, I keep looking for clues that she's like Amanda.

Logan: There's a nasty voice in my head saying this is too good to be true and it sounds like Dad.

Logan: I'm falling for her.

Logan: And it's not fair for me to bring all this crap from my past and our family into our relationship.

Logan: What should I do?

The idea of being in love terrifies and fascinates me. Part of me is elated and so desperate to finally have someone love me for me. But it makes me feel weak and stupid and needy. I don't want to depend on someone's approval ever again. I don't want to need someone's love and try to fit into an impossible mold just to make them happy.

When I think of it, my first instinct is to run. I keep thinking this is too good to be true and waiting for the other shoe to drop. For her true colors to show. For Skye to be controlling like my father, or manipulative and cunning like Amanda, or aloof and detached like my mother. But she's none of these things. I keep reminding myself of that. Skye is not like them at all. Either that, or she's all of it and just much better at hiding it.

No.

I can't let myself go down that path. Nothing good can come from it. I have to learn to trust again. And if I can't trust her just yet, I can at least trust my gut. And it's telling me Skye is the real deal. I'd much rather go with that because it makes me happy in a way I've never experienced before.

CHAPTER THIRTY-SEVEN

Skye

"How long have you been dating Logan now?"

River's question takes me by surprise, and I have to think about it for a minute, but it's a welcome distraction from the class notes I have to study.

"Two months. Why?"

"It feels longer than that. You two got close really fast."

She folds another T-shirt. We have a pile of warm laundry between us on her bed. Folding laundry is one of the few house chores River does not hate. She finds it calming. The fresh, clean smell, the warm fabrics. It soothes her. Her words, not mine. Baking soothes me. I guess for the same reasons laundry does her. But a warm oven and baking scents instead.

I think about what she said. It does feel longer than two months. We've grown closer. Secrets have been shared. Logan makes me feel good about myself. He sees me and he's still here. He still cares.

"Has he said the L word yet?"

Her question brings me crashing down to reality. He hasn't. Not with words, anyway. But sometimes, I could swear he's on the verge of saying them but is holding back. Given his past, I can understand why.

"No."

I don't elaborate on it. What else can I say?

"Hmm."

The sound is loaded with meaning, yet I can't tell what she means by it.

"Hmm what?"

"I think he loves you."

"How so?"

I'm fishing, I know. But I want to see if someone else sees it too. I want to know it's not just me making up stories in my head.

"It's pretty clear in the way he talks to you and looks at you."

"Elaborate."

I wave my hand at her in a motion that says *keep going*.

River flattens a pair of jeans on the bed, wiping away any stubborn wrinkles, then folds it in half and adds it to the growing pile at the foot of the bed.

"His eyes are always following you. Like one of those weird paintings. Wherever you go, he tracks you. Kind of stalker-ish, really. It would be creepy if it wasn't so cute. And when you walk back into the room, his eyes light up like a kid's on Christmas morning."

That puts a smile on my face.

"And have you noticed he's always touching you? If you're within arm's reach, some part of his body will be touching yours. So, yeah, I'd say that boy is in love, and if he hasn't said the words yet, he will soon."

As River would say, my heart swells like Kanye West's head. I've noticed how Logan is always touching me. Holding my hand, brushing a lock of hair away from my face, the tender kisses when we're in public. And when we aren't together, he shows he's thinking of me with texts, phone calls, or pictures of something he saw in his day and thought I'd like. He cares. He may not have said the words, but it shows in his actions. And yet, I can't help but be a little disappointed too. I want to hear the words. And I'm too chicken to say them first.

"Have you said it to him?"

River asks me.

I shake my head.

"That's a negative, Ghost Rider."

"Why the hell not, Goose?"

River picks up on my *Top Gun* reference, one of our favorite eighties movies.

"Goose? I'm Goose?" I say.

"Please, we both know that if anyone is Maverick, that's me."

Damn it! She's right, and she knows it too.

"You do love him, right?" she asks again.

"I think I do. I think I'm halfway in love with him and just waiting for him to say the words so I can finish falling the rest of the way."

"I don't think you're halfway there. I think you bottomed out already. Kaput. Splat. Flat on the ground. You've fallen all the way."

I drop my notebook to the bed. There's no way I can concentrate on studying now. River is right. I'm in love with Logan. I've never felt this way. Whatever stupid infatuation I had for Blake back in high school has nothing on the way I feel about Logan. And yet I can't bring myself to say it to him.

I face-plant on the pillow next to me.

"Ugh. I am in love with him. What am I gonna do?"

My voice is muffled by the pillow, but River understands me all the same.

"Just tell him. One of you has to take the first step."

"What if I say it and he doesn't say it back? I'd be crushed. I don't think I could take it."

"I don't think he'd just leave you hanging and not say it back. I think he's over-thinking this like you are."

"You can't know that."

"Nope, not one hundred percent. Mom is the psychic in the family. We should call her."

I pick my head up off the pillow just high enough to give her the evil eye. She laughs at me. We'll have enough of Mom's psychic abilities when we go home for Thanksgiving next week. No need to start now.

"But you're a little psychic. You always have those gut feelings."

River huffs an inaudible response, folding the last T-shirt. The laundry's all organized in nice little piles, by type and color. She folds, and I put them away. That's the deal. I get up and put the neatly folded piles into their places in her drawers and closet first before doing my own.

"I'll think about it. I don't just want to blurt it out. Or say it during sex. I love you should not be said for the first time during sex. Or right after either. Too much room to confuse lust with love."

"You're such a planner, Skye. Just let it happen. Let it happen when it feels right. If it's during or after sex, who cares? You know you love him and it's not some hormone-induced blabber. This is not one of your romance books. You can't plot life. You're so busy plotting, you're forgetting to live."

CHAPTER THIRTY-EIGHT

Logan

THE CRACKLING SOUND COMING THROUGH THE RADIO asking for all officers in the vicinity of Riggins University to report to campus freezes me for a fraction of a second before training takes over and I turn the lights and sirens on. The sounds of my cruiser are soon joined by the same sounds coming from several others in the neighborhood, getting louder and louder the closer we get to campus.

My heart races in tempo with the cacophony of sirens. Police, ambulances, EMTs. More information comes through the radio. The thundering of my heart is so loud in my ears, I only hear fragments of the words—Riggins University . . . Jane Austen building . . . code 105 . . . active shooter . . . hostages . . . lockdown . . . caution . . . armed and dangerous—and between each word, along with the sound of sirens and my heart, another word on repeat.

Skye, Skye, Skye, Skye, Skye . . .

The five minutes it takes me to get to campus and the two more to navigate the throngs of students and staff running away from it feels like an eternity in hell. My eyes dart everywhere, looking for Skye and trying not to run anyone over. I come to a stop twenty yards away from the Jane Austen building, where I know Skye has half of her classes. Half a dozen other patrol cars are stopped in a haphazard semi-circle around it.

I was only eight years old when the Columbine attack happened, but it left such an impression on me. I watched it on TV and read about it on the newspapers my father left behind every morning. I was just a naïve kid back then and kept thinking if it was my school and I had a gun, I could have stopped it. Back then, I thought only bad guys and police officers had guns. I decided to be a cop on that day. For years, I nurtured that dream of stopping the bad guys. It faded as I grew up and my father molded me more and more to take over his company. But some of it lingered hidden still, because when I went to college, my major was Criminal Justice, which would be a nice segue into law school. But it never happened. My father and Amanda happened, and it gave me the final push to step from under his control and find my own way. And once I was out from under his domain, and faced with choices for what I wanted to do with my life, the first thing that came to my mind was my long-ago childhood dream of being one of the good guys with a gun. I never imagined that seventeen years later, I'd be facing the same kind of situation that made me want to be a cop in the first place.

The university is on lockdown. I remember the lockdown procedures from when I attended Riggins—close and barricade all doors. Stay away from the door and any windows. Hunker down until the eminent threat is eliminated and either a school authority or an officer tells you so.

Together with the other officers, I approach one of the entrances to the building. This one has four, aptly named North, South, East, and West. Each of the first-line officers on the scene pairs up and takes one of the entrances. We go South, and I hope this is not an omen for what's to come. We don't have enough guys for a diamond formation just yet, but backup is on the way, I'm sure. It used to be that the standard procedure was to wait and call in resources and ask for assistance or for a SWAT team to show up. In Vermont, we have TSU—a Tactical Services Unit that works pretty much like a SWAT team does. After so many schools and public place attacks over the last few years, the way law enforcement responds to this kind of situation has changed. The first-line officers on the scene need to aggressively step in and neutralize the threat. The more time the suspect has to walk around free, the more harm he can do.

I tamper down the urge to call or text Skye to make sure she's okay. If she's hiding somewhere, the last thing I want is for the sound of her phone ringing or buzzing to alert the shooter, whoever he is.

The guy I paired up with, Mike, takes the lead and I'm close behind him. The long, empty hallway leads to dozens of doors, each closed. The only sounds are our breaths and soft footsteps. The silence is deafening. We follow the protocol for checking and opening doors, taking turns, staying behind the door, ducking under and catching the door with a foot, and entering the room with our weapons raised. Each room we check is empty. Papers and books lie abandoned on desks and the floor, water bottles and laptops left behind. We signal to the other officers and clear the first floor. This guy is either gone or upstairs. I know Skye's classes are on the third floor of this building. Dread's icy fingers run down my spine. We're approaching the wide stairs at the center of the building now when I hear *Pop-pop-pop.*

Three rapid-fire shots. Screams. No. Not screams. Shouts.

The whole group takes the stairs now, stopping on the first landing to listen. More sounds come from upstairs. Three of us take the lead, and we're running up the stairs now. Another six guys are behind us for cover and to protect our rear. We still don't know if this is a lone shooter or if there's more than one. When we get to the second floor, I can make out what he's saying. He's calling someone. And he's a floor above us. The third floor. The floor where I hope Skye isn't. My rapidly beating heart seems to stop with the realization that she could be in harm's way before resuming an adrenaline-infused gallop.

"You think you can leave me and take everything?"

The shout echoes in the empty hallway.

"Answer me, goddammit! Where are you, Regina?"

The sound comes from our right, but when we spy around the top of the stairs, we can't see him. He must be in one of the side corridors from the main one.

"If you don't come out here, I'm going to kill all these kids you love so much."

He follows the threat with another round of shots. The situation is escalating. We look at each other, and everyone is thinking the same thing. We have to take this guy down now. He's losing his grip on reality fast.

Without saying a word, we fall into two diamond formations. I take the front—I'm the point man—and two other officers flank me, Mike on my right, Steven on my left. And a fourth takes the rear to cover the three of us ahead of him. This formation originated in the military. The idea is that officers will have overlapping fields of vision and shooting ranges. The most difficult thing in this scenario is what we call sympathetic shooting, a trigger reflex when we hear gunfire, which is emphasized in the chaos of confronting an active shooter. But that's where training comes into play.

We don't see any victims as we make our way closer to the shooter. That's one of the hardest parts of confronting an active shooter. We can't stop to help the victims until the danger is neutralized. Stopping the shooter from hurting anyone else is our first priority.

Our steps are careful and soft. We want to keep the element of surprise as long as possible, even though this guy, whoever he is, must know cops will be closing on him sooner or later. Situations like this never end well.

We close in on the corner, and now I can tell he's in the corridor away from me.

Steven signals and we close in behind him. He looks around the corner and calls out.

"Drop your weapon and get on the ground!"

The suspect whirls around and looks at me and Steven, raising his gun in our direction. We both take cover behind the wall, which is not an ideal situation since only two of us can look at him and take cover at the same time. As expected, he shoots at us. We duck behind the wall again. The gunshots are much louder now that we're so close to him. Four more shots. The sound echoes in the empty hallway. Plaster rains on the ground as a cloud of dust settles around us. The acrid smell of gunpowder fills the air and coats my throat with a sharp and pungent metallic flavor. We wait and listen for his footsteps. Nothing. I'm holding my breath in a futile attempt to slow down my heart, but the adrenaline coursing through my veins won't allow it. We're going to have to take this guy down before he hurts someone. I've been lucky as a cop. I've never had to shoot at anyone before, and I don't want to now. Steven looks at me and must read the hesitation in my face. This is not the place or time to second-guess myself. I think of Skye and the armed suspect who's putting her life at risk and keeping me from getting to her. Coldness like I've never felt before washes over me. I would kill him with my bare hands, rip him to shreds to keep Skye safe. The realization shocks me, but I don't have time to dwell on it right now. Steven is still watching me, and whatever he sees now must satisfy him because he nods at me to take position. The other guys fall into place as well. Steven calls out again.

"Last chance to drop your weapon. You don't want to do this. They're just kids—"

"I don't want to hurt the kids. I just want my wife. She won't talk to me."

"Okay, we can get her for you," Steven bluffs.

"Just put the gun down, and we'll make sure to get her. What's her name?"

"No!" he screams.

"I need my gun. This is the only way. I know she'll come if she thinks I'll hurt her students."

"I'm Steven. What's your name?"

Steven asks in a friendly tone, like they just met and are sharing a beer.

There's hesitation. We can hear him shuffling.

"Just your first name and your wife's, so we can get her for you," Steven goes on.

There's perspiration around his temples, and I realize that cold sweat is running down my spine.

"My name is Joe and my wife's name is Regina."

Steven signals for one of the guys in the back, and he goes out to get more information on the teacher. There's only silence over my earpiece. We stay quiet as not to alert the shooter of what's happening on our side of the wall. It feels like hours, but it's been only minutes.

"Joe? We're sending one of the guys to get Regina. Why

don't you put the gun down, so you can talk to her when she gets here?"

"No. Get me her first, and then I'll put the gun down."

"Now, Joe, you know we can't do that. For everyone's safety, you have to put the gun down first."

"No. If I put it down, she won't talk to me."

I hear quiet steps behind me. We have backup now, and one of them has an iPad with a live feed from the security cameras in the hallway. We can see the suspect—Joe—in the grainy black and white video. He's pacing, a rifle in his hand, a duffel bag on the floor near him, and I bet it has more guns and ammo inside. Vermont gun laws are very lax. Visitors and residents can openly carry firearms or conceal them without a permit, and they can buy rifles and shotguns as easily as a can of soda. Handguns take a little more work as they have to be shipped through a federal firearms seller. There could be anything inside that bag, and knowing this terrifies me. The newcomers signal for us to pay attention to the communication from our earpieces.

"The suspect is one Joseph James Orcher, forty-seven, married to Regina Ann Orcher. It seems that they are going through an ugly divorce and he's none too happy about it. They have one kid, twelve years old, same name as the father."

I hold my breath for what I know is coming.

"The wife is on this floor, room 307, and her roster has twenty-seven students in it. We can't confirm if all students in her classroom are in attendance."

I should be thinking of the task at hand, but all I can think about is Skye. Her name pounds into me with each frantic beat of my heart.

Steven resumes negotiations.

"Hey, Joe? We talked to Regina. She said she'll come out

and talk to you, but you have to put the gun down. We can't let her come in here if you are still armed."

"No. You're lying. It's a trick, I just know it. She's in one of these rooms. I just need to find out which one."

We watch the video feed. He's pacing frantically now, trying to look into the small windows of the two classrooms closest to him. I look the opposite way down the corridor he's in, noting the numbers above the doors.

Jesus Christ.

His wife is in one of those rooms he's closest to.

"It's not a trick, Joe. Think of your kid. How scared would he be if something happened to his mom or you? He needs his parents. Don't do something you'll regret."

"It's too late, too late, too late," he screams.

We watch the video on the iPad. He's walking our way, his voice getting louder with each step, the rifle raised. We've run out of time and options.

CHAPTER THIRTY-NINE

Skye

THE SHOUTS OUTSIDE GET LOUDER AND LOUDER AND THEN lower as the man in the hallway seems to pass the door to our classroom. We're all huddled in the back, some of us inside a closet, but it can't fit all of us in. Tables and chairs offer a weak barricade against the crazy man outside these walls. I think of River and whether she knows what's happening or not. And of Logan. He must know. I'm sure the police got dozens of calls, if not hundreds. My phone is in my bag, in the front of the classroom. I can't call Logan or my sister. But even if I had my phone, we're all too afraid to make a sound. We stay as quiet as we can, but muted whimpers and low cries mingle between our tightly compressed bodies. Safety in numbers feels like a lie. I don't feel safe in the least. I feel like a fish in a barrel, waiting to be shot.

Bruno squeezes my hand. I know he's as scared as I am, but he's putting a brave face on. He offers me his phone and I shake my head. If River doesn't know what's happening—and she might not know yet, since she's on the other side of campus—I don't want to worry her.

Mrs. Orcher, our teacher, wanted to go out there and talk to him. We stopped her. We convinced her if he knew where she was, he might kill us all. She cried and apologized over and over again—she mouths the words soundlessly—but her pain and regret hit me with the force of a sonic boom. It explodes in my chest and washes over me until her pain is my pain and I feel the weight of it, so heavy I don't think I could have moved if I tried.

Shots.

Pop-pop-pop

On repeat.

Pop-pop-pop

Again and again.

Screams.

Shouts.

Voices, heavy steps on tiled floors.

Silence.

I clamp both hands over my mouth.

I want to scream.

I am screaming inside my head.

Screaming so loudly, my throat burns.

Burns with silence.

Burns with unshed tears.

Burns because I know.

I know Logan is outside the locked door, and I have no idea what I'll find when we get out.

If we get out.

The other students move around me, our faces reflecting each other's fears and unanswered questions.

Is this it?

Is it over?

Are we safe now?

We stay quiet and listen.

Steps running outside the door.

Voices. Snippets of words.

"Single shooter . . ."

"Suspect neutralized . . ."

"Officer down, officer down . . ."

"Check other rooms . . ."

People begin to move around but stay in the back of the room. Whispered questions wondering if it's over go unanswered.

Mrs. Orcher is crying openly now, no longer able to hold in her pain. Sobs wrack her body every few seconds, her shoulders hunched over as if she's trying to cave in on herself and disappear. There's guilt and sorrow written all over her face. She aged twenty years in a matter of minutes. I reach for her and squeeze her hand. She looks at me with gratitude in her watery eyes before turning away again and stepping to the side, away from the twenty-something students in her classroom. She's my favorite teacher. Something tells me I won't see her in this classroom again. Some people are texting furiously, letting their loved ones know they're okay. I look at my bag in the front of the room. I dare not walk to it. In horror movies, this is when the blond heroine does something stupid and dies. I'm staying right here. Bruno has his arms around me. I could ask for his phone, but . . . what if it's not over? What if I text River or Logan and something else happens? My mind is in turmoil. I can't think straight. My body feels heavy and my head too light.

We wait for what seems an eternity. The muffled sounds outside seem to multiply. More footsteps, more indistinguishable voices travel through the walls. New sounds have us all looking at the door. It opens a moment later, with a loud bang against the wall. I jump.

The room fills with men in body armor holding guns pointed at us, and there are screams all around me as people retreat and look for cover. I stay rooted on the spot. My eyes are frantically searching the faces behind the guns until I find him . . . just before everything goes black.

CHAPTER FORTY

Logan

THE AIR IS THICK WITH GUN SMOKE AND THE METALLIC smell of blood. So much blood, I can taste it. The suspect is down. He was cuffed and his body checked for more weapons. But he's not going anywhere. He's dead. We still have to wait for a medic to come in and pronounce him, but that will have to wait until the whole building is cleared and declared safe. As suspected, the duffel bag is full of ammo and more guns. Everyone in the building is very lucky he wanted to bargain with his wife first. I don't want to think of the outcome if he didn't.

His wife may be better off without him, but now his son has to live the rest of his life knowing what his father did. I feel sorry for the kid.

Dozens of officers are here now. The TSU team has arrived and taken over. They have to secure the area, check all classrooms, make sure this was a solo act. Three police officers were shot, including Mike. Flesh wound to the right thigh. He took that bullet instead of me when he stepped in my way. He and the other two guys were moved to a staging area outside the building. They're probably on their way to the hospital. Now that the TSU is here, most of the guys moved outside to secure the perimeter. But I'm not going anywhere until I make sure Skye is safe. Steven is hanging behind with me. He's reading me again, and I'm sure he can see how worried I am.

Processing the scene will take hours. Pictures have to be taken and everything documented before the scene is released to detectives, crime scene investigators, and forensics.

TSU is clearing the classrooms farthest away from the body. A tent was set up to keep the gore hidden from curious eyes. The last thing we need is cell phone pictures and videos. The media coverage will be crazy enough without the addition of any photos or videos to fuel it. Everyone is being taken outside. Their faces show shock and disbelief. Some have to be helped by their friends. As far as I can tell, this is one man going on an angry rampage because he couldn't deal with his wife leaving him.

I still don't know where Skye is. I paid attention as each of the other classrooms were evacuated and she wasn't in any of them. My gut tells me she's in room 307, with the suspect's wife.

Jesus! Had the suspect known which room his wife was teaching in, the wife and every single student in that classroom could have been killed. Skye included. The thought makes me sick to my stomach. If I puke now, everyone will think it's because of the horrible scene at our feet. Everyone looks as if they're on the verge of getting sick too. The coroner's crew has arrived. TSU is going into 307 now. I follow them in even though I know I'm breaking protocol.

Room 307 is the last occupied room. They wanted to make sure that Mrs. Orcher didn't have a chance to look at what's left of her husband before they tented the area around his body.

TSU moves in. I follow and pray this classroom will be a repeat of all the other ones we evacuated and no one is harmed.

Five TSU officers sweep into the room, guns raised, looking for anything other than the students and the teacher. A few of the kids scream and shuffle to the back before they realize we're the good guys. My eyes search for Skye everywhere. I'm vaguely aware of the students being evacuated. I'm so frantic and filled with dread, I miss her the first time I glance over the left side of the room. Then I find her. Her blue eyes—huge on her pale face—lock on mine, her lips tremble, and her legs give out. Bruno is behind Skye and catches her just before she hits the tiled floor. I get to them a second too late. I'm both grateful he kept her from getting hurt and angry he has his hands on her, that he was here when I couldn't be.

I take Skye from him and pick her up, burying my face into her neck. I breathe her in. I'm so overcome with relief, I can feel tears stinging my eyes. I can't remember the last time I cried. *When I was a kid, maybe.*

It registers that I'm on my knees when I feel a hand on my shoulder. I look up and Steven has positioned himself between me and the other cops and discreetly hands me my gun. Fuck! I don't even remember dropping it. He covered for me. I can't work my throat just yet, so I nod my thanks and holster the Glock, making sure the safety is engaged.

"You know her."

Steven's voice is low. For my ears only. It's not a question.

I nod again and find words this time.

"My girlfriend."

"Holy shit, man. Did you know she was here?"

"Not for sure, but I suspected."

"You were pretty cool under pressure out there."

"I feel like I need a vacation."

Steven laughs, but the sound lacks humor.

"Me too, bro. Me too."

One of the TSU guys approaches, and Steven takes him to the side, explaining why I'm on the floor holding a passed-out girl in my arms, I'm sure.

We're all relieved. This could have been so much worse. No innocent people died today. Just the asshole who thought it was a good idea to bring guns to the university to convince his wife not to divorce him.

I look around when a woman with an EMT uniform kneels next to us. The room is empty except for the five of us. Mrs. Orcher and the other students were quickly evacuated. Bruno lingers a few feet back, but Steven takes him out. It's just me, Skye, and the EMT lady now.

She checks Skye's vitals and asks questions I answer the best I can.

When Skye starts to come around, she whimpers, and the first word she says, even before she opens her eyes, is my name.

CHAPTER FORTY-ONE

Skye

"Logan?"

"I'm here, baby. I got you. You're safe. It's over."

I try to reach for Logan, but my arm is trapped in someone's hand. I find a woman holding my hand, a stethoscope on my wrist and a blood pressure cuff on my upper arm.

I look at it. Logan reads the confusion in my face.

"You passed out. We're just making sure you're okay."

"Her blood pressure is a little low, but I think she's okay," the woman says to Logan.

She looks at me.

"How do you feel, honey? Do you want to go to the hospital?"

I shake my head.

"No hospital, thank you. I just feel a little dizzy. I've never fainted before."

"That happens sometimes when someone is under a lot of stress. Just take it easy for the next couple of days."

"I got her," I hear Logan say, and the EMT lady packs her things and leaves.

Just the two of us left in here now.

"Are you okay? Where's everyone? Is anyone hurt? What happened? Is he . . . dead?"

Questions tumble out of my mouth, one after the other, so fast that Logan doesn't have a chance to answer me.

He pulls me into his chest and holds me tight. His Kevlar vest digs into me, but I don't complain.

I'm sitting on the floor, between his knees, and he's completely wrapped around me. The heat from his body, his scent, his chest expanding as he breathes me in, his lips pressed on my forehead . . . it all calms me down, makes me feel safe.

I hold on to him.

I hold on, and I'm never letting go.

CHAPTER FORTY-TWO

Logan

I HOLD ON TO SKYE AND BREATHE IN HER ORANGE blossom scent. I hold on to her as relief floods me. The weight of worry and not knowing where she was has been lifted off my shoulders, but the stress of it has made me so tired, I could fall asleep right now, like this, kneeling on the cold, hard floor with her in my arms.

We stay in that empty room for a long time as commotion slows and quiets outside the door.

I move her away from me, just enough that I can see her.

My eyes flit all over her face, drinking her in. Her blue eyes are bright with unshed tears. There's so much love in them. So much want.

"Skye . . ."

I kiss her then.

Gentle at first.

Just a brush of lips.

A taste.

A lick.

A nibble.

I try to hold back. I do.

But the fear I felt before, the desperation when I didn't know where she was, takes over and breaks free.

I kiss Skye as if my life depends on it.

I kiss her to make sure this is real, and she's here in my arms and unharmed.

I kiss her because I cannot *not* kiss her.

And she kisses me back with the same intensity, with the same desperation and need.

Skye kisses me back as if her life also depends on it.

When we break apart, her lips are red and swollen. My own feel the same.

"Skye—God—this is not how I imagined saying this. Not at all, but I can't wait any longer. I can't hold it in for one more second."

My thumbs graze her cheeks as I hold her face up to mine.

"I love you. I'm crazy in love with you, Skye. And I was so scared something would happen to you and you wouldn't know. You wouldn't know how much I love you. How important you are to me. How big a part of my life you are."

Her eyes fill with tears and spill over. I catch them with my lips. I kiss her tears away.

"Shh, don't cry, don't be upset."

"I'm not upset. It's not sadness spilling out of me. It's love. Love for you. I love you too, Logan. I'm crazy in love with you."

She repeats the words I said to her, back to me. They form around a watery smile, and I catch them with my mouth. I taste love and tears in her lips. This might be the absolute worst place and time for a love declaration, but if anything, this horrible situation serves to show me time is precious and short.

Love should never be held back, contained, or denied. Love is a wild animal. It does not belong in captivity. It needs to be freely given to grow and thrive.

I'm done holding back. It's time to let go and trust.

"I'm all in, Skye. I'm all in."

CHAPTER FORTY-THREE

Skye

W FINALLY MAKE IT OUTSIDE AFTER LOGAN TELLS ME NOT to look at whatever they're doing in the hallway. No worries there. I have no intention of seeing anything. I've heard enough, and my imagination is filling in whatever I didn't see. Logan doesn't say, but I know the guy is dead.

There's some kind of tent blocking part of the hall, and someone made a pathway with a long tarp along the wall. Logan said it was to evacuate the students and staff as fast as possible and not contaminate the crime scene. The little I saw reminded me of a movie. Lots of people wearing gloves, taking pictures, the little yellow number thingies—whatever they call them—all over the floor.

We walk quickly, and now that I'm free of the building, I want to find River. I dig through my bag to find my cell phone when I hear my name. The whole area around the building is closed off. Metal barriers and yellow tape. Cops everywhere. It takes me a few seconds to locate River. She ducks under a stretch of tape and runs across the street. A cop tries to stop her, but Logan waves him off and I'm already on my feet, running to my sister. We collide in a hug and tears.

We don't say anything for long minutes, just hold each other and sob. The other cop is saying we have to move. I can feel Logan nearby. His arms come around me and River, and he hugs both of us for a few seconds before gently guiding us to the side.

"Are you okay?"

River's words are filled with worry and love.

"Yes, I'm fine. Just tired, so tired."

"I was so worried. I must have sent you a dozen texts. You didn't answer me."

"I didn't have my phone with me, and I was afraid to let you know what was happening."

"Word got out fast. The whole campus went on lockdown, and when we heard it was the Jane Austen building . . . gosh, Skye. I thought I was going to have a heart attack. You should have texted me."

"I almost did, but then I pictured you running into the building and trying to take the guy down with your bare hands and I couldn't do it. I couldn't risk it."

"I'd probably try to do it, too."

Logan's hand goes around my waist.

"I hate to do this, but I have to get back in there. And it will probably be hours before I can leave."

I disengage from River and throw myself at Logan. His arms hold me tight.

"Thank you. Thank you for saving me."

He kisses the top of my head.

"I'm just glad it's over."

Logan looks at River.

"Can you take her home? Make sure she rests? Stay with her?"

"Yes, of course. All classes have been canceled today and tomorrow."

His hands cup my face.

"I'll come to you as soon as I can. I love you."

"I love you too."

He kisses me then, restrained but full of promise. Then he turns away and walks back into the building.

River is looking from me to him, pointing back and forth between me and the building Logan just walked into.

"When did this happen?"

"Come on, let's go home. I'll tell you everything. And I have to call Mom and Dad too."

"I called them already. Bruno texted me and said you were okay and Logan was with you. I told Mom you'd call as soon as we get back home."

A pang of guilt hits me. I forgot all about Bruno. My best friend. The guy who tried to comfort me when we were trapped in that classroom. As soon as I saw Logan, everything else fell away. I have to talk to him too. But first, I need to go home. I desperately want to take a hot shower. My skin feels grimy, as if what happened today made me dirty somehow. I just want it off me.

River has her arm around me as we walk through the parking lot and find the car. She opens the passenger door and I get in.

I guess I'm not driving today. I know she has questions, but I don't want to talk right now. All I want is to close my eyes and forget what happened today. Well, everything but Logan telling me he loves me. That, I'll remember forever.

CHAPTER FORTY-FOUR

Logan

MINUTES TICK LIKE HOURS AND HOURS TICK LIKE YEARS.
It took another seven hours to process the scene, file reports,
and clear the building.

Logan: Liam . . . I don't know how you do it every day.
Logan: I died a thousand deaths today.

I desperately want to go to Skye, but I make my way home
first to shower and change. I need to wash this day away, and I
stay in the hot shower longer than I normally would. I'm tired,
hungry, and something else I can't identify. I dry off and dress
in sweatpants and an old T-shirt, clothes I wouldn't normally go
out in, but they're comfortable and I need that right now.

I grab my jacket and make my way to Skye. I hope she's
awake. I texted her hours ago, letting her know it would take all
day to process the scene and I still had to work my full shift
anyway.

The door opens before I have a chance to knock and Skye
wraps herself around me. Her small body presses into mine, her

cheek flat on my chest. She hugs me like she's trying to get under my skin. I hug her back, tuck her head under my chin, one hand into her hair, the other across her back. I feel like I can breathe again. I felt uneasy for the entire day after I let her go. I had no choice in the matter. I had to go back to work. I can relax now.

That something I couldn't identify before? I know what it is now. This is it. Skye in my arms. I missed her, but it was more than that. Having to let her go right after such a traumatic experience took a part of me away.

Today, I learned that my need to be in control and follow the rules does not guarantee safety. The illusion of safety was shattered by the shooter. Life can change in a second. All we have is this moment. Right now. I make a decision, a decision I now realize has been in the making for a while.

I can't move forward while holding onto the past.

I have to let go of my anger. I have to let go of my need to control. I have to allow myself to trust, be open, take risks, and allow life to unfold itself. Trust it will take me where I need to go rather than try to force my way into it. And I have to forgive my parents. Not forget. But forgive. It doesn't mean I have to comply with my father's wishes. I can forgive him and still be me and not the person he tried to make me into.

We stay locked with each other until River comes to the door and gets our attention.

"That's cute and all, but my skinny ass is freezing. So maybe come in and close that door?"

You can always count on River to add a good dose of reality. We walk in, and Skye tugs me to the kitchen and motions for me to sit in one of the stools by the counter.

"I cooked. And baked. I do that when I get stressed. I hope you're hungry."

"I'm starving, actually. Haven't had a chance to eat anything since this morning."

We don't need to go into details of why I didn't eat. But River is not letting that go. She sits next to me as Skye moves about the kitchen and grabs a plate and silverware.

"So, the bastard is dead. What now?"

"River! I told you not to ask him anything."

"And I didn't listen. You got lucky, Skye. You got so lucky today. And thank God I called Mom and Dad so they found out what happened from me and not the news. I can only imagine how they would've been if they happened to be home and with the TV on this morning."

Skye turns, an apologetic expression on her face.

"I'm not sure I have much more to say in addition to what you've already seen on TV or heard from Riggins," Logan adds.

River looks pensive.

"The university contacted me. Offered counseling. Said there will be several counselors available to anyone who wants to talk to one. I'm still processing everything that happened. Not sure what they could say that would make a difference," Skye says.

"Talking to someone can help, Skye. Even if you don't think you'll get anything out of it. Sometimes, just venting, letting it all out with a stranger helps. Even more so than talking to someone you know."

River's voice is softer when she replies to Skye.

"I really think you should go. It can't hurt."

"I'll think about it."

Skye places a plate in front of me and a glass of water. This is what one would call a man's meal. Beef stew, potatoes, carrots, and . . .

"Is that homemade bread?"

"Yeah. I couldn't help myself."

I dunk a chunk of the bread into the rich wine-colored sauce on my plate and moan with the first bite.

"This is amazing. Thank you."

River is silent, but I can tell she wants to talk. Skye is glaring at her in an obvious *keep quiet* warning.

I take three huge bites before turning to River.

"Spill it. What do you want to know?"

"I don't want any of the gory details," she says, and I let out a breath of relief. I wouldn't say anything anyway, but I'm glad that's not what she's after.

"What I want to know is, what can someone in this situation do to make sure they survive it? We're all very lucky this guy only wanted his wife and shot no one he crossed paths with. I heard from several people that he walked into the building with a gun in his hand. He could have—"

Her voice falters.

"He could have killed a dozen people if he wanted."

I take a deep breath and answer her.

"In training, they say you should run, hide, fight. In that order. If you can run, do it. If you can't make it to a door and you're in a room with windows, lock the door and try to get out of a window if you can. Don't waste time. Don't go back for anything."

"And if I can't run?"

"Then you hide. Lock the door and turn off the lights. Push anything you can against the door. Stay out of sight and stay quiet. Turn your phone to silent mode and turn off vibrate. You want to stay as quiet as possible and hope the shooter thinks the room is empty and bypasses it."

She looks at me and waits for the next step. *Fight.*

"If you're trapped and can't run or hide and the shooter is

coming into the space or room you're at, find something to fight back with. Anything you can put your hands on and use as a weapon. Be it a chair, a keyboard, anything. You fight back."

"How come no one ever told us that before?" She looks at Skye.

"Probably because it's the kind of thing no one wants to believe could happen to them. There are videos on YouTube. Search *how to survive an active shooter.*"

"There are? I gotta check this out."

River leaves to go look for videos.

IT'S JUST Skye and me now. I finish my plate in silence. We look at each other. The silence is heavy and loaded with unsaid words.

I drink the water, push the plate and glass away, turn away from the counter, and stand up. I take Skye's hand and walk to her bedroom, and she closes the door behind us.

We're both exhausted. We shed our clothes in silence, words unnecessary. I pull the blanket back and get in the bed first. I open my arms and Skye comes to me. Her small body fits perfectly into mine. Her back to my front, we fold into each other like matching pieces of a puzzle. A perfect fit. A better picture together than separated.

Our bodies tell a story, our touches the narrative of what's to come. I nuzzle into her neck and hair, inhaling her into my lungs, my skin, the very center of my being. Skye melts into me, molding herself to the shape of me. I'm the vessel and she's water.

CHAPTER FORTY-FIVE

Skye

WE DIDN'T HAVE SEX LAST NIGHT. AND YET, BEING together like that was more intimate than anything we've ever done. The walls have crumbled. Whatever reason Logan had to hold back is gone now. Whether it was the words we finally said out loud—I love you—or the scare we both went through, although from different perspectives, the last barrier, the last vestige of the fear of giving in 100 percent is gone now.

There's a new level of comfort and understanding between us, even though we haven't discussed it out loud. We both know it's different now. Up to this point, we held back a little. We enjoyed each other's company and had tons of fun together, and we knew of each other's affections, but I can't say we were all in.

That has changed. I can see in the way Logan looks at me, in the way he touches me, kisses me, holds me. There's a new level of tenderness and vulnerability. Our chests are open, hearts exposed. And there's no fear.

Opening yourself to someone, letting down your guard, being vulnerable—this right here is pure and undiluted trust. I've earned his, and Logan has earned mine. And it's beautiful.

Who would've guessed that out of something so scary and ugly, we'd find something so beautiful?

He looks like a little boy in his sleep, the intensity and tension I so often see in him nonexistent in this moment. I love watching Logan sleep. I rarely get to watch him for more than a couple of minutes. Somehow, he always knows when I'm watching him like a creep. But not today. I've been watching for some thirty minutes and he's yet to open his eyes and catch me. I relish this unguarded moment. I memorize every feature, every nuance, each breath he takes. The way his lips part on the exhale and how his long lashes cast shadows on his face. The strong jaw and the hint of whiskers. How his hair falls over his forehead. My hands itch to brush it away and touch him, but I dare not.

"You're watching me again."

His voice is no more than a whisper and his eyes are still closed.

How does he do it?

I blush at being caught.

"And now you're blushing too. God, I love the way the pink spreads down from your face to your body."

His eyes are still closed and there's a hint of a smile on his lips. I consider staying silent and try to fool him into thinking I'm sleeping, but I know I can't get away with it. He's using his cop mojo on me. He always knows everything.

"Yeah, you caught me. I'm being creep-tastic again."

"Is that a new word, Miss English major?"

He unleashes a full smile on me now. The parts of my body covered by the sheets wake up and pay attention.

"Yes. In fact, it is. It means being extra-creepy. In the dictionary, my picture sits right next to it. No need to look it up. Take my word for it. "

His eyes open and flit all over my face and bare shoulders peeking from under the covers. I'm lost in blue.

"I'll take anything and everything you have to offer, Skye."

CHAPTER FORTY-SIX

Logan

"And I'll give it to you."

God, her voice is like melted chocolate.

If I hadn't already woken up with morning wood, her voice and her words alone would have done the job.

I don't make a move to touch to her. I just watch and relish her presence. Skye watches me back.

We're lost in each other's gaze, and just as I'm about to pull Skye into me and kiss her, the door opens and River comes in.

She doesn't bother to knock.

Hair in a mess of waves, sweats, and a tank top she clearly slept in.

"Oh, glad you two are awake and not doing the nasty. Nobody needs that visual."

That visual is actually very appealing, but I don't say it out loud.

"Jesus, River! Ever heard of knocking? There's a reason that door was closed."

River ignores Skye and lifts the cover next to her, scooting under it.

"If you really wanted to keep me out, you would've locked the door. You didn't. That means I can come in."

River tugs at the covers.

I pull Skye's body closer in an attempt to use her as a shield against her sister.

"We *are* naked under the blanket, you know?"

Maybe she'll leave if I make her uncomfortable.

"I do *now.* Thanks a bunch, Officer TMI."

So much for that. River's not moving.

Time to ante up the stakes.

"My DNA could be all over this bed. Doesn't that bother you?"

"Nope. I know for a fact you two didn't bump uglies last night, and Skye changed the bedding yesterday morning. So the sheets are clean."

"And how would you know?"

She rolls her eyes at me as if the answer is obvious and I'm dumb for asking.

"Dude, you two are not exactly quiet. I always know when you're doing the deed. People three zip codes away know when you're doing the horizontal mambo."

Skye is blushing, and I'm blushing.

"Aww, cute. Look at the two of you. Pink and Pinker. *So* adorable. Too bad adorable does not fill bellies. I'm hungry. One of you has to feed me."

I see what she's doing and I'm grateful for it. River is trying to make today as normal as possible and get Skye's mind and my own away from what happened yesterday.

Skye speaks up.

"Seriously? Is that why you came in here? Because you're hungry? Well, go feed yourself. There's plenty of food in the fridge and pantry."

"But I want a breakfast burrito. And you know I'm a terrible cook. I'd make an attempt, but all I'd accomplish is wasting good food and making a mess."

My stomach growls in agreement with River. A breakfast burrito sounds fantastic right about now.

Skye looks at me and I nod. Hopefully, not too eagerly. I'm starving too.

"Okay. I'll make breakfast. Now go, so we can get up and get dressed."

River gets up, a bounce in her step. When she gets to the door, she turns back to Skye.

"Sheesh. So grumpy. Maybe you should eat something. You'll feel better."

Skye tosses a pillow at her, but she's too late. The door closes and the pillow lands on the floor with a dull thump.

CHAPTER FORTY-SEVEN

Skye

AT LEAST RIVER SET UP ALL THE INGREDIENTS ON THE kitchen counter. For someone who claims not to know how to cook, she sure knows everything that goes into a breakfast burrito. I narrow my eyes at her and she returns my gaze, all innocent-like.

Tomatoes, onions, cilantro, avocado, eggs, salt, pepper, tortillas, cheese, and frozen hash browns. All set and ready to go.

"Okay, you guys get to chopping and I'll start with the potatoes."

With the three of us working together, breakfast is ready in no time. I layer the warm tortillas with the scrambled eggs, potatoes, cheese, and all the cooked chopped veggies, add several slices of avocado on top, and roll them like a pro. This is not my first burrito.

River sets the table and Logan gets us orange juice and coffee.

There's a collective moan when we take the first bite. This is so good, I slow myself down to make it last longer. Logan already ate half of his and is eyeing mine. I scoot away from him.

"Don't even think about it, buddy."

He pouts. I laugh. River rolls her eyes at us.

"You two are disgustingly cute."

She makes a fake gagging motion.

"I can't wait to see you fall in love, River."

She scoffs, takes another bite, and looks away. And that shadow of something I can never figure out crosses her face for a split second again. I wish she opened up. But that has never been River's style. She's like Fort Knox with her secrets.

When we're done eating, River takes our plates and brings back the coffee pot. She refills all of our mugs and sits down.

"How are you guys, really? On the surface, you two look okay, but I can't imagine that either of you could shake off what happened so easily."

I take a deep breath and glance at Logan. He's looking down at his mug and doesn't say anything.

River waits. As much as she keeps all her feelings locked up tight and hates talking about herself, she's superb at getting others to open up. After a long minute, Logan looks up and opens his mouth, but no words are said. He holds the mug with both hands as if drawing strength from it. His shoulders are tense and there's a slight shake of his head. The internal debate is clear. I don't want him to feel like he has to do this, and I'm about to speak up when words spill out of him in a murmur. I play the sounds over in my head again to make out what he said.

"I was terrified."

He looks at me then. He's answering River, but his eyes never leave mine. The blue is somehow more intense. I see fear in them. And love. It's an odd combination, but I understand it all too well. In that moment, in that building, I feared for Logan too.

"I was terrified something would happen to you. I knew you were in the building. I was sure of it. Everything in me told me you were there and your life was at risk. When the call came over the radio about an active shooter at Riggins, God, I thought I was going to have a heart attack. I don't even remember the ride there."

His eyes close and his hands tremble around the mug. I reach out to him and wrap a hand around his wrist.

"When I got to the building, it took everything in me not to rush the place screaming for you. If it wasn't for all the training I got and my years as a cop, I think I would have done just that."

Logan laces his fingers with mine and turns to completely face me.

"When I heard the first gunshots, I think I died a little. I ran up to the third floor with the other cops. For a brief moment, I thought we'd be able to deescalate the situation. He seemed to listen to us, but then he just started shooting and we had to return fire and stop him. A man died yesterday, and I don't know if it was my gun that killed him. Another man took a bullet that was intended for me when he stepped in my way. I've never had to shoot at anyone before."

I can feel my chest constrict.

"I don't know how or what I should feel right now. Part of me is sick someone had to die and for the role I played in it and that maybe . . . maybe I'm the one who delivered the fatal shot. Maybe I'm the one who killed him. But the other part, the bigger part knows if I had to do it over, I would. If I thought someone was trying to hurt you, Skye, I'd rip him to shreds, limb by limb with my bare hands. And knowing this scares the shit out of me."

I stand up, step between his knees, and pull him into me. His head finds the curve of my neck and his arms bring me in closer to him, and we're pressed together when the first muffled sound of a sob breaks the silence that follows his confession.

I look at River over his head. Quiet as a ghost, she leaves the room.

CHAPTER FORTY-EIGHT

Logan

I don't know what the hell is going on with me. This. Breaking down like this. Being this open about how I feel is not normal behavior for me.

My head is buried in Skye's neck and her citrus scent soothes me. The way she smells, the way she feels, does something to me. She's the cure for a disease I didn't know I had. And I sound like a fucking pussy for even thinking this. My father would slap me if he ever heard me voice my thoughts. But he's not here, and I no longer give a fuck about what he thinks. If anything, doing the opposite of what he thinks is a great motivator. But years of conditioning still reach me, and even if I recognize my father's reach, sometimes, it's hard to turn it off.

"Logan, you can't think like that. Even if it was your gun that killed that man, you had no choice. If you and the other cops hadn't stopped him, he could have hurt dozens of people."

It's true, I know. That duffel bag he had with him had enough ammo to take down dozens of people. Still. Knowing it, acting on it, and reconciling it with the knowledge that a human being is dead, and I had a part in it, still bothers me.

I pull away, just enough so I can see her eyes. I need the reassurance they will give me. And I find it. Love, trust, concern for me. It's all there in Skye's clear blue gaze.

"I know. I know you're right, Skye. That guy was FTD the moment he walked into that building loaded with weapons."

"FTD?"

"Fixed to die," I explain. "Cop lingo."

A small smile tugs at my lips.

"What about you? Are you okay? How are you holding it together?"

Her hands run through my hair, and I fight the urge to close my eyes and lean into her touch like a puppy.

"I was scared. Terrified. But not for myself. I was sure I'd be okay. I was afraid for you. I knew you had to be around. I just knew that as soon as someone called the cops, you'd be near, and I was terrified that whoever was out there was going to hurt you."

"Oh, the irony. You were afraid for me and I was afraid for you. And neither one of us was concerned for our own safety."

"A side effect of loving someone. You put their wellbeing before your own."

I recognize the truth in her words even though I've never experienced it before. Certainly not from my parents. My grandparents, maybe. But thankfully, they never had to make that choice.

I think about it and how little I know about love. I loved my grandparents, but I only got to see them on breaks from school. And I love my brother, who I haven't seen in a year. I have no idea where he is or what he's up to. I wish he had come to find me when our father forced his hand instead of enlisting when he was eighteen.

I come from a family that always looked perfect on the outside. And I didn't realize how broken and unhealthy my family dynamic was and is until I was in high school. I look at Skye and River and how they talk about their parents and the way they grew up, and it's so alien to me. I can't imagine having that kind of upbringing.

Of course, I've seen loving families in movies, but it always felt like fiction. The way I grew up, the friends I had growing up, all reinforced the sterile way in which my brother Liam and I were raised. We were never kids. We were projects. Investments for the future of the family business.

It's a miracle I can even relate to Skye at all. She fills a need in me I never knew I had. I can only hope to fill her empty spaces in the same way.

CHAPTER FORTY-NINE

Skye

A WEEK AFTER THE SHOOTING, WE MAKE IT HOME FOR Thanksgiving. Logan drives us in the Escalade he rarely uses. It sits in the garage most of the time. He prefers to drive the truck. But this is a much more comfortable ride than his old truck or my little Honda Civic, I have to say.

As soon as we walk up the veranda, the door opens and Mom throws herself at Logan in a tight hug.

"Thank you for saving my baby. Thank you for keeping her safe."

He's too stunned to react at first, but his arms find her and hug her back. Not as tightly as she hugs him, though. I come around to Mom's side, and Logan's eyes find me over Mom's head. He's shocked and speechless.

"Mom, you're going to scare him off. And how about saving some of that love for the baby in question?"

She hugs me just as tightly. Dad comes out then. Logan gives him a hand to shake, but Dad pulls him in for a hug as well. A manly one, with lots of backslapping.

Dad hugs me next while Mom grabs River.

"We are a hugging family," I say after everyone has been hugged.

"Better get used to it."

Mom ushers us into the house, and Dad grabs River's and my luggage. We don't carry much. We have a lot of our stuff here anyway.

The smells of my childhood hit my lungs with a flood of memories. Apple pie, wood floor polish, and some kind of roast. One might think all those scents fight each other, but for me, it smells like home. Like bare feet on grass and cool nights reading by the wood-burning fireplace. It smells like laughs, tight hugs, and movie nights. It smells like family. It doesn't matter that I came home just a couple of months ago. Every time we're back, I'm reminded of how much I'm loved.

It's easy to forget and take for granted those we care most about in the middle of the demands of life. This past week, with all that happened, being back home tugs at my heartstrings a little harder.

Logan looks a little bewildered by my family. I take his hand and he gives me a grateful smile.

"Logan, we're so glad to finally meet you. The pictures don't do you justice."

I look at Mom.

"What pictures?"

"Oh, you know."

Mom waves her hand like I do know. I have no clue what she's talking about.

"The pictures River sent me. She's right. You got yourself a Hot Cop, indeed."

Logan blushes, and I sputter, trying to say Mom and River at the same time, and what comes out is something that sounds like *Miver*.

"Awe, look at her, Logan. You got her all tongue-tied."

Mom pats his face. Mom pats my boyfriend's face. A six-foot-two grown man who towers over her, since like me, she's just five-foot-three. She winks at him and then looks at me.

"All the best ones do. Leave your tongue tied, you know?"

Well, I can't yell at my mom, so I find the next best thing. River.

"What?"

she says, like she had no hand in any of this, and the three of them walk away, leaving Logan and me behind.

"Gotta check that pot roast," Mom says as she walks to the kitchen.

"Skye, you can put Logan in the room next to yours. It will make it easier to sneak in the middle of the night. But you'd better do it in your bed. The guest one is very squeaky."

Logan's wide eyes find me, and his face is frozen between embarrassment and a laugh.

"Now I know where River gets it from."

Ugh.

"You have no idea."

CHAPTER FIFTY

Logan

WE'LL BE LEAVING IN A FEW HOURS. TOMORROW IS Monday and I'm back to work. The girls have school. Hopefully, things will be back to normal at Riggins.

I spent every night in Skye's bed as per her mom's suggestion. I still can't believe she said that. I tried to be very discreet about it, but she had a knowing smirk on her face every morning. Skye is sleeping next to me, blond hair spread across the pillow and over her shoulders. She looks so peaceful. Just looking at her centers me and calms all the turmoil inside me. She has a quiet power about her and she doesn't even know it.

The whole family has a strength about them I've never encountered before. They're so completely different from mine. I had no idea there could be such love and trust. I mean, rationally, I know it. But to see it at work, it's something I've never been exposed to.

Skye is more like her father. He has a quiet aura about him, but I'm not foolish enough to think it means he's a pushover. The love he has for Serena, his wife, and the girls is clear in his every word and gesture. Time and again, I catch myself wishing my father could have been more like David. But my father loves power, not people.

Skye stirs, her eyes flutter, and she catches me watching her. A smile tugs at her lips.

"Good morning, Sunshine."

The smile gets bigger.

As corny as it sounds, she is like sunshine. My life up to the moment I met Skye was rules, order, laws, gray. But on a cold September night, she decided to go out in tiny shorts and pink bunny slippers, and it was like seeing colors for the first time. She surprised me. I wasn't ready for her. I thought I had my life all lined up. I never realized how much under my father's influence I still was. Not until Skye showed me differently, and I can't even pinpoint how. She just does. She just is. No reasons, no explanations, no justifications needed.

"Have you been awake long?"

Her voice is husky with sleep, and it makes my morning wood jump and move the sheet, which does not go unnoticed. Her eyes pop up and glance back at my face.

"Do it again?"

I indulge her and contract my stomach muscles, making my dick jump.

She reaches over and brushes her fingertips over me through the sheet with the lightest of touches, and my dick moves again.

"It's alive!"

Skye says in a maniacal voice a la Doctor Frankenstein.

She giggles. The giggles turn into laughs. I can't help but laugh with her.

"Nothing is that funny at seven-thirty in the morning." River's voice floats to us through the locked door. Learned my lesson. Lock the door and triple-check it.

Skye and I look at each other and laugh even louder now until we both have tears streaming down our faces.

In this moment, the full strength of my love for this girl hits me so hard, it takes my breath away. I've never been happier, never felt this accepted and loved. It might be just eleven weeks since that cold September night we met, but I can say with certainty that Skye is it for me.

I've found my one and only.

CHAPTER FIFTY-ONE

Skye

IT'S BEEN A MONTH SINCE THE SHOOTING. SINCE LOGAN said he loved me. The trip home for Thanksgiving solidified something in our relationship. We spend every free minute together. We sleep in each other's houses, and River has learned not to barge in through closed doors.

But not before catching us in the shower. That damn bathroom lock was always tricky. My fault for not triple-checking like Logan does. Yep. River got an eyeful. She says she's scarred for life now, but when Logan wasn't around, she confided in me that she thinks he has an amazing ass. He does.

We didn't see much of each other for the last three days since Logan is taking a lot of shifts this week. But the good news is that he got a whole week off for Christmas and New Year's and he's coming home with us again. Tonight is his last full night shift, and after tomorrow, he switches to day shift until the end of the week and then we can go home for the holiday break.

River is at a Christmas party with Becca and it's just me at home tonight, watching *Miracle on 34th Street*—the original one in black and white—and drinking hot chocolate. The perfect companion for the snow that began falling at the same time the movie started playing.

My phone buzzes. I expect it to be Logan, but it's Bruno.

Bruno: Hey, are you home?
Me: Yes.
Bruno: Is Logan or River there?
Me: No, just me. Why?
Bruno: Can I come over?
Me: Sure, is everything okay?

A second later, the doorbell rings.

Bruno: It's me. I'm outside.

This is odd. Bruno is supposed to be out of town with Sidney, having an early Christmas celebration since he has to spend the actual holiday with his family.

I rush to the door to let him in and one look at him tells me something is very wrong. Bruno walks right past me and into the living room. He takes off his sneakers and jacket and puts them in the closet by the front door, a habit he's always had. His mom hates clutter in the house. Shoes and jackets have to always be hidden in a closet somewhere. He walks straight to the couch and drops into it like the weight of the world is pushing down on him.

I close and lock the door and sit next to him, both feet folded under me. I wait.

His eyes are red and his face blotchy, like he's been crying for hours.

"Sidney broke up with me."

My heart sinks. They've been together for over four years. Sidney and Bruno began dating senior year of high school. Sidney goes to a different college a couple of hours away, and Bruno goes away to visit as much as he can. They've kept this relationship alive and thriving for all this time. Seeing my best friend this broken brings tears to my eyes.

"What happened?"

"Apparently, I'm not committed to our relationship enough."

"What?"

"Sidney gave me an ultimatum. Now or never."

"I thought you were supposed to wait until graduation."

"So did I. We agreed to it. Right after graduation, but—"

A sob escapes him and he crumbles. My best friend is falling apart right in front of me and there's nothing I can say or do to make it better. I do the only thing I can. I scoot closer to him, wrap my arms around his trembling shoulders, and wait until the sobs diminish.

Bruno looks at me, and his face is a mask of pain, anger, and despair.

"Five months, damn it. Five fucking months. Is that too much to ask for?"

"No," I say. "Not when it's been almost five years."

"That's what I said. What kind of love is this? Five months is not too much to ask for. And I'm the one who's not committed enough?"

I don't say anything because I know that's not what he wants from me.

"I drove up there almost every weekend, every break, every chance I had. And that's what I get? A big fucking ultimatum? Do or die? I couldn't do it. I walked away. I had to leave before I said something stupid and hurtful."

"Do you want me to call h—"

"No."

Bruno cuts me off before I have a chance to ask. He's proud, and he's hurt.

My phone buzzes again. River this time.

River: Do we have any dinner leftovers? I'm hungry and it's snowing harder. I don't want to stop to get anything.

Me: Yes, we have leftovers.

River: Ok, will be there in ten. Party is boring, I just dropped Becca off. See you soon.

I show my phone to Bruno.

"River will be home in ten minutes."

He gets up.

"I gotta go."

"No, you're in no condition to drive. Stay."

"I don't want her to see me like this."

"It's snowing harder now. You already drove for hours. Your eyes are nearly swollen shut. Just go into my room, close the door, and wait there. Once River goes to bed, you can leave. Just give yourself a chance to calm down, okay?"

IT'S BEEN over two hours since River came home and she's still up. She ate and watched a movie. I stayed with her, as she has the habit of coming into my room if I go to bed before her. An old routine from when we were kids and shared a room. I was afraid of the dark, and River always stayed until I fell asleep. Knowing she was watching over me made me feel safe. I outgrew my fear of the dark, but River still watches over me, still checks on me on nights Logan doesn't stay over.

"I'm going to bed," she says in a yawn, the sound of her voice distorted by it.

"Good night, Sis. I'm going soon too. Just want to check a couple of emails."

I wave my phone at her for good measure and hope she buys the white lie. River waves at me over her shoulder and walks down the hall. I can hear her in the bathroom, and a couple of minutes later, her bedroom door closes. I wait five minutes and then go to the bathroom myself, brush my teeth, and change into my favorite tank top and pajama pants.

It's quiet across the hall. I tiptoe to my room. The lamp next to my bedside is on and Bruno is fast asleep, curled into a fetal position on the edge of my bed. I check the storm outside my window, the streetlight showing that several more inches have fallen. I don't want to wake him up. I tug the blackout curtains into place, grab a throw blanket, and cover Bruno. I'll wake him before River is up in the morning. Tomorrow is Saturday, and she likes to sleep in. The township is good about cleaning the streets, and the roads should be clean by early morning. With a sigh, I get under the covers and turn the lamp off. My heart is breaking for my best friend. I'm glad he fell asleep. He can't hurt in his sleep.

CHAPTER FIFTY-TWO

Logan

THIS WAS THE LONGEST NIGHT OF MY LIFE. YOU'D THINK being in Vermont, people would be used to the snow by now, but there's always one guy who thinks he can drive through the white stuff piling up on the roads at normal speed. I had to help rescue three different cars from ditches. Thankfully, no one was seriously hurt. Just egos and bumpers got damaged on my watch tonight.

I miss Skye and can't wait to see her. Having opened to each other crumbled the last wall I had in place. It's freeing not having to keep my guard up. It's freeing being able to just be me without the fear of being betrayed or hurt by someone I love.

As soon as I'm done with my shift, I make my way to her house, stopping at Pat's first to get breakfast for the girls.

I know it's early, not even 7:00 a.m. yet, and it's Saturday, so they're sleeping for sure, but I don't want to wait. I don't even change into civilian clothes.

A while back, Skye gave me the code for the outer door, and I let myself into the hall. I knock on the door lightly and hope someone will hear me. I wait a minute, and I'm about to knock again when River opens the door. Her eyes are barely open and her hair is a wild mess of curls. She's wearing a knee-length purple T-shirt and socks with unicorns all over them. I hold back a laugh. One sister with bunny slippers and the other with unicorn socks.

"Logan, it's too early for a booty call. You're lucky I was going to the bathroom or no one would have heard you."

I smirk at her and present the cardboard tray with the three coffee cups in it.

"I come bearing gifts."

She takes one of the coffees and I hand her a bag.

"Got you a muffin too."

"In that case, please come in, just keep the moaning and grunting down. I'm going back to sleep."

"No promises."

She grumbles as she walks away, and it sounds like she's saying, *damn horny people.*

THE ROOM IS STILL DARK, thanks to the blackout curtains Skye is so found of. I put the coffee tray and a pastry bag on the night table and sit on the side of the bed. I can barely make out the small shape of her body under the blankets. My fingers are less patient than me and find their way to Skye's face, brushing the hair over her shoulder. Skin on skin, but for the thin strap of her tank top. She's warm, and my fingers are cold from just having come inside. Skye stirs and looks at me, groggy from sleep still. Her eyes blink open a few times, fighting to stay open and losing the battle. A smile appears next and tells me she's awake. She sighs a content sound when my hand drifts under the covers and slides down her back and grabs a handful of that ass I'm obsessed with.

"Logan."

My name is but a whisper.

"You're done with work? What time is it?"

The bed shifts, but it's not Skye who's moving. For a confused second, I wonder if River somehow snuck in the bed and I missed it, or maybe she got a dog overnight and didn't tell me. But the form lying behind Skye in the dark room is much larger than River. Or a dog.

My brain fights my eyes for what it's seeing. My brain is screaming no, no, no, not Skye. Not again. My eyes confirm what my brain is trying to run from. I jump out of the bed and turn the lights on, blinking several times as I adjust to the sudden brightness. My heart stops. My brain can no longer deny what my eyes see. But my heart? My heart feels as if it just exploded into a million pieces.

My heart is no more.

Both of them are holding their hands over their eyes, momentarily blinded by the lights. Skye is looking at me with confusion in her eyes. But I can't look at her. All I can see is Bruno in bed with her. He's frozen in place.

"Logan?"

Her voice reaches me as if coming from miles away. Miles is what I feel between us. Ten seconds ago, the closeness we shared was the most important thing in my life. Now, there's an abyss in the three feet of space between us.

Bruno's eyes are fixed on me as he gets out of the bed dressed only in boxers. Skye's face blanches when she looks over her shoulder and her eyes widen in surprise. My hand opens and clenches next to my gun. Bruno looks away when he picks his clothes off the floor and then gets dressed, avoiding eye contact.

The look of surprise on Skye's face turns into horror.

"No, no, no. This is not what it looks like. Nothing happened. I swear."

She's one hell of an actress.

I can't move. If I move a muscle, I'll do something I'll regret for the rest of my life. I'm in uniform still. I could barely wait for my shift to end to come and see her. As much as I want to beat the living shit out of Bruno, I already know I won't. So I stand here, my eyes going from one to the other. So much for good intentions. Like my father always said, good intentions will only get you fucked. In the ass. Hard and dry.

Skye gets up on her knees now and reaches out. She is speaking, I know she is because I can see her lips moving, but I'm not registering anything she's saying. This cannot be happening again. Old memories come rushing back. Amanda and my father. But this, this is so much worse than finding Amanda and my father fucking in my bed. I never loved Amanda. It was easy to walk away.

But this?

How can I stay?

How can I walk away?

Skye turns to Bruno. He's zipping his pants.

"Say something! Tell him what happened. Tell him why you're here!"

But Bruno just shakes his head.

"I can't."

He looks terrified, and that makes it even worse than it already is. Little wimpy son of a bitch can't even stand up for himself and say anything at all. Fucking coward.

She looks him up and down.

"What happened? What happened to your clothes? Why did you take them off?"

"I got hot. You were too warm."

Wrong fucking thing to say, pal!

I take two steps forward, and even though he's on the other side of the queen-sized bed, he flinches. His arms go up and over his head in a defensive manner and he turns his back halfway. It makes me hesitate, but it's the crisscrossing of scars on his back, thin pink lines paler than his skin, that stop me.

This is the kind of reaction I've seen on victims of abuse and domestic violence. The scars are forgotten in my anger. He's a big fucking grown man and has to have a good twenty pounds of muscle on me. Even if he sucks at fighting, a guy his size should be able to hold his own.

But that reaction alone is what saves his ass, and mine too, for that matter, because I'd be in a world of trouble if I gave this guy the beating I want.

My attention is back on Skye and her pajama pants and tank top. The same tank top she was wearing the day I pulled her over. I refocus my anger on her. Bruno may have been a willing participant, but he owes me no loyalty. She's the one I'm dating. She's my girlfriend, and she's the one who claimed there has never been anything sexual between her and Bruno, but she was lying before and she's lying now. Her sister herself had said they were fuck buddies, and even if nothing happened today, it's obvious in the way they're so comfortable with each other, in the way she shared her bed with him, that something is going on between them.

Maybe he's cheating on his out-of-town girlfriend. He's always around during the week, but every weekend, he goes away to meet this mysterious person. That's what Skye always says. But he was supposed to be away today, and he's here. So something happened. Maybe the girlfriend found out he's cheating and kicked him out, or maybe they could not get together and he went back to his old fuck buddy—my girlfriend.

Either way, I'm done.

This is done.

Skye is done.

It's all going to hell in a fucking hand basket because there's no way I'll go along with whatever Skye's saying. I can't believe a word coming out that pretty mouth, and fuck me if I still don't want to kiss her! I have to get out of here.

"Just tell him. Tell him the truth."

Skye's crying and yelling at Bruno to tell me that nothing happened. He shakes his head and doesn't even look at her. Fucking asshole is not man enough to either own up to what he did or lie for his so-called best friend.

I take two steps back and Skye tries to come to me. I raise my hands and she stops. I turn and see River by the door. I don't know how long she's been there. Watching. She doesn't say a word. I guess she had no idea her sister had a guy in her bed or she wouldn't have let me in. River's eyes look as startled as mine probably did when I first realized there was someone in the bed with Skye.

Bruno finally finds a pair and speaks up.

"I'm leaving, and you two can talk."

He looks at Skye and shakes his head, a plea in the way he looks at her.

"I'm sorry," he whispers. "I can't. I just can't. And you promised. You promised me."

It's just too much.

Too much.

Too much all over again, too much.

"Don't fucking bother. I'm the one leaving."

I look at Skye then. I don't know if I'm trying to memorize

her face or completely forget it. Because I know. I just know I'll never look at her again.

I will never speak to her or hear her voice again.

I will never kiss her mouth, taste her skin, or feel her body trembling under mine.

I will never hear her giggle when I tickle her or hear her laugh when she finds something to be funny.

I will never see that smile again.

I will never love anyone else again.

Never.

Again.

I leave, the three of them watching me. Skye's calling my name between sobs. Bruno's frozen in place.

There's no going back.

CHAPTER FIFTY-THREE

Skye

HE LEFT.

He just left.

Logan just left me.

The door closing behind him without a sound speaks louder than banging it would.

I can barely see through my tears.

"What just happened?" I ask no one.

There's no answer. Immense silence fills the space where Logan stood before.

My legs give out and I drop to my knees, bracing myself as if it could contain the pain inside. How can there be so much silence when my heart is shattering to pieces?

Heartbreak should have a sound.

A ripping.

A crash.

A wail.

But there's nothing. Not even the sounds of my own sobs or ragged breaths reach my ears. It's just me and the empty space Logan left behind.

A hand covers my shoulder. Bruno. I shake it off and wipe my face with trembling hands, the anger at him halting the tears. I can't look at him.

"Leave."

I feel him hesitate before his feet disappear through my bedroom door. More emptiness.

River kneels next to me and rubs my back, and the touch anchors me. All I want to do is run and escape this pain ripping my chest open and clawing at me. But there's no escape. Wherever I go, I'll take my broken heart with me.

Why wouldn't he listen to me? *You know why*, a voice in my head tells me.

"Skye?"

I hear my name as if she's calling me from far, far away and not kneeling right next to me.

"What happened?"

"He left. Logan left me."

River pulls me into her arms. She asks no more questions and just holds me. Her kindness breaks the last barrier and the tears come back unbidden. I cry until there's nothing left. I cry until I'm numb inside and my eyes are swollen shut.

Crumpled tissues litter the floor around me like clumps of snow, a sad witness to my agony.

River pulls me to my feet and guides me back to my bed. Like a puppet, I comply with her ministrations. My body aches. My head is pounding. I don't know how long I've been on the floor. It could have been minutes or hours.

My mind is trapped in a loop, a bad movie playing again and again. Logan's pained face and hurtful words on repeat. I'm both the villain and the victim, stuck in a role I didn't choose to play.

I'm vaguely aware of River pulling the covers around me.

She turns the light off and the room drops into darkness. I curl myself into the smallest version of me possible, as if I could dispel the pain by hiding from it. The bed dips as she sits next to me, her fingers running through my hair like Mom did when we were kids and didn't feel good. River rubs my back and tells me to sleep. Exhaustion takes over and I feel myself drifting off into welcoming nothingness.

Everything will be better when I wake up, she says.

She lied.

CHAPTER FIFTY-FOUR

Logan

"Fuck."

My head is ringing and pounding. I struggle to open my eyes. The first thing I'm aware of is the dry and bitter taste in my mouth. Then the memory of what happened this morning. The first thing I see when I actually manage to open my eyes is the nearly empty bottle of Brora. The twenty-six-year-old single malt whiskey I stole from my father when I saw him with Amanda. Stealing his prized fifteen-hundred-dollar bottle soothed some of the anger I felt then, even if it embarrassed me later on. It's only fitting that I drain that bottle to celebrate the occasion. Stole it because of one cheater. Drank it because of another.

The ringing and pounding is outside my head now. *What the fuck?*

The banging on the door and the bell ringing shatters the contented numbness my friend Brora put me under. If there's one positive thing I can say about my father, it's that the bastard knows how to pick his whiskey. I drank enough to pass out and yet I suffer none of the side effects of a hangover. Maybe I'm still drunk. I get up and walk to the door.

"Calm the fuck down. If the house isn't on fire, stop this fucking racket!"

The silence that follows my harsh words makes me hesitate. It had better not be Skye. Or that fucker, Bruno. I'm off the clock now, and this is my property. He won't leave it in one piece.

I yank the door open and River is on the other side, arms crossed over her chest and a furious expression on her face. I look over her head, hoping to see Skye even though I just told myself I don't want to see her. Anger at myself is renewed tenfold. Even after she cheated on me, I'm hoping to see her. *What the fuck is wrong with me?*

River walks right in and shoulders me out of the way. I stumble back a step.

"By all means, come in. It's not like I'm pissed off or anything."

Sarcasm does not faze River one bit. She invented the damn thing.

"What do you want?"

There are limits to my patience, and the excellent scotch I drank may have extended it, but my anger is burning through it at light speed.

"I want to know what happened."

"What? Skye didn't tell you?"

Saying her name hurts, and I raise my voice to cover the pain.

"Don't you raise your voice at me! I'm not one of your perps or whatever the hell you call them. I want to know what happened."

Her voice softens with the last few words.

I run a hand through my hair and realize I'm still in uniform. But no belt and no gun. *Where the fuck is it?*

I look around the room and find it on the floor next to the empty bottle.

"What happened is that your sister cheated on me with her fuck buddy, Bruno."

River snorts. She actually snorts at me.

"Skye would never cheat on you. And Bruno was never her fuck buddy. I just liked to say that to get under her skin."

"Well, you must be psychic then, because that's exactly what he is."

"You're drunk."

"Yes, I am. But that does not change the fact I caught them in bed this morning."

She blanches.

"What?"

All the anger evaporates, and what is left is an emptiness so vast it feels as if I'm free falling into an abyss. Didn't she see him nearly naked? Maybe she came after he was dressed.

"I saw them, River."

My voice is shaky, my eyes burn, and there's a boulder in my throat.

"I saw them," I whisper as if the hushed words could somehow diminish the pain of saying them.

She's shaking her head as if denying it would make it less true.

"I don't know what you saw, but what I do know is Skye loves you. She's crazy in love with you, and she would never, could never do that. She doesn't have it in her to cheat on some-one. She never even cheated on board games or a test in school."

"He was in her bed, and all he had on was his boxers."

Saying this, having the images come back to my mind, pushes the boulder in my throat down into my chest and it weighs a thousand pounds. My heart squeezes under its pressure.

"It's not possible."

"Did she send you here? To try to convince me to forgive her and take her back?"

"No, she didn't. She doesn't know I'm here. She cried until she passed out from exhaustion."

I flinch at her words. Why is it that knowing that Skye is suffering hurts me more than my own pain? *Because you love her, you idiot.*

"Talk to your sister. I'm not the one in the wrong here. I know what I saw. And he didn't deny it."

I walk back to the door and open it wide, a clear sign that this conversation is over.

River's shoulders drop, and she shuffles to the door and steps out. She turns and pleads.

"Just hear her out."

"I don't think I can."

I close the door and lock it. The symbolism does not escape me.

CHAPTER FIFTY-FIVE

Skye

I WAKE UP WITH A START. YOU KNOW THAT FEELING WHEN you wake up and think you're late for work or school? That's how I come to, wondering which day and what time it is. But the blissful moment of confusion evaporates with the first memory of what happened. Pain squeezes my chest. Can heartbreak cause a heart attack? I step out of my bed on unstable feet and pull open the curtains.

I don't know how long I slept, but the sun is low in the sky. Last night's snow glints in the late afternoon light in big piles on the side of the road. The street is clear and life goes on outside the window.

Did I sleep the entire day?

Did all of it really happen?

My eyes fall to the small trash can in the corner. It's full to the top with crumpled and balled-up tissues. If pain could be measured on a scale of tissue boxes, how many boxes would I need to measure mine? I grab my phone from the night table and check it. No messages, no missed calls. I didn't expect to hear from Logan, but Bruno's silence annoys me. He still has nothing to say. After all the years we've been friends and all the secrets I've kept for him, all he had to do was say a single word and Logan would believe me, but he didn't. He refused. And I couldn't break my promise to him, not even to right a wrong, not even for Logan. My loyalty to both of them wars inside me. I'm angry at Bruno for not coming clean. I'm angry at myself for not speaking up. But above all, I'm angry at Logan for believing what he thinks he saw instead of me.

The voice of doubt rears its ugly little head again. It had been a long time since the little monster made itself known, but she's here now. Loud and clear.

He never really loved you. What did you expect?
You don't deserve him. You picked Bruno over Logan. What kind of love is that you claim to have?
You're nothing. You're not good enough for him. Blake was right.

My hands cover my ears to stop the voice.

"Shut up, shut up, shut up."

I feel dirty. I want out of my skin. That's not possible, so I settle for ripping the sheets off my bed and taking a shower.

River comes into the hall as I'm walking to the small laundry room behind the kitchen.

"Hey."

"Hi."

"What are you doing?"

"Getting rid of his smell. The sheets smell like Bruno's cologne."

Her eyes go wide.

"Did you—you didn't . . ."

River is studying me, looking for something, but I'm empty except for the pain.

"Did you sleep with Bruno?"

The question makes me want to laugh into hysterics.

"He slept in my bed, but I didn't have sex with him, if that's what you're asking."

I can see her visibly relax.

"Why did Bruno sleep in your bed?"

I suck in a deep breath, hoping the extra air will shift the pressure in my chest. It doesn't work.

"Sidney broke up with him. He was a mess. You were coming home, and he didn't want you to see him like that. It was snowing so hard and I didn't want him to drive in it. I told him to go hide in my room until you went to bed." The words come out of me in a monotone. Empty of any feelings or emotions. The anger from before evaporates. I'm no longer angry at Bruno for putting me in this situation. No longer angry at Logan for not giving me a chance to speak. No longer angry at myself for keeping secrets that destroyed the best thing that had ever happened to me. I feel nothing. I am nothing. It's all empty space. I can't take this anymore. I drop the bundle of sheets to the floor.

"I'll do this later. I need a shower."

"Skye?" I don't make it far.

"Aren't you going to call Logan?"

I answer her, but I don't turn around. "He won't listen."

"You have to try. Make him listen to you."

"I don't think I can."

"He said the same thing."

"What?" I didn't quite hear what River said. Her voice was low.

"Nothing. I said nothing, thinking out loud."

I stay in the shower until it runs cold and I'm shivering. I try hard to remember all the happy times I shared with Logan, but all of them have been replaced with images of this morning. Logan would forgive anything except cheating. Not after what happened with his ex and his father. He'll never listen to me. And I was never good at speaking up and defending myself, anyway. Even if I'm innocent, guilt still hits me hard. I had two loyalties, and I picked Bruno over Logan. What does that say about me? I don't deserve him. He needs someone who will always take his side, someone stronger, someone who'll stand up for him.

I'm not that person.

CHAPTER FIFTY-SIX

Logan

I'VE BEEN STARING AT MY PHONE FOR HOURS SINCE RIVER left, willing it to ring, willing for an apology message or call, hoping she'll beg for forgiveness, and angry at myself because of it.

If she calls, I'll break down and take her back. And I'll be a bigger fool than I was when I was dating Amanda and under my father's thumb. I don't want to be that blind again. I won't allow anyone that much power over me ever again. I can't let Skye do this to me too.

I text Liam. I know he won't see this, but I need to say the words so I believe them myself.

Logan: It's over, baby brother.

Then, I find her contact on my phone and block her. I disable the Facebook account I rarely use as well. My finger hovers over the *Pictures* icon. I tap it and browse through the dozens and dozens of pictures I took of her, of us together, of places we've been. I can't delete them. Not yet.

I'll keep the pictures as a reminder of how easily she fooled me so I'll never fall for it again.

I almost believe myself.

The phone rings, and I jump, nearly dropping it.

It's not Skye. I know it's not her. I just blocked her number, but part of me still hopes some tech glitch allows her call to get through to me anyway.

The text message is from my captain, asking if I can do a couple of overtime shifts before I go on my Christmas vacation. There will be no Christmas vacation. This will be just another Christmas I spend alone. No family. No friends. No Skye. But I don't tell him that.

Yes. Yes, I can work overtime.

Staying busy will get my mind off her.

I'll do anything to get my mind off Skye.

CHAPTER FIFTY-SEVEN

Skye

NIGHT HAS FALLEN, AND THE HOUSE IS QUIET BUT FOR the sounds of the heat kicking in every so often. River is asleep in her room. She wanted to stay with me, but I said no. I missed classes and slept most of the day again today. I know I'll be up all night. Almost forty-eight hours since I last saw Logan.

The lights are out, but the full moon shining on the snow outside reflects onto the walls through the open curtains and lends enough light to create shadows everywhere in my room. It's oddly comforting.

My stomach grumbles, reminding me I ate nothing today. My eyes fall to the night table. The long-cold coffee and bakery bag still sit on it. Logan's parting gift. River tried to throw it away, but I didn't let her. It's the last physical reminder that Logan was here.

I imagine what would have happened if Sidney hadn't broken up with Bruno. He would've never come over. Logan would've never found him in my bed, and we'd be wrapped in each other and talking, as we often did in the middle of the night.

I look at my phone. I've been holding it for hours, but it stays stubbornly silent.

Five percent battery life left.

I should plug it in, go get something to eat, and try to sleep. I don't do either of those things.

Instead, I text Logan.

Me: I miss you.
Me: Nothing happened. You have to believe me.
Me: There's a reason

I hesitate. I don't want to bring Bruno's name up. But I have to. It's so much easier to be brave over a text message. I stare at my phone for long minutes, tapping it every time the screen dims before it goes dark. How long have I stared at the unsent message? I heave a heavy breath.

Me: There's a reason for what you saw Saturday morning. Just give me a chance to explain.
Me: Please?
Me: I love you. You know I do.

My phone goes dark. Dead. Is this an omen?

CHAPTER FIFTY-EIGHT

Skye

DAY THREE WITHOUT HIM. IT'S THE LAST WEEK OF SCHOOL before winter break. The kids at my daycare job are restless and eager to go on break. Later this week, I have my last two finals this semester. My mind isn't in the right place, but I force myself to get up, shower, and get dressed in leggings and a *Star Wars* hoodie. It's "wear your favorite movie" day at the daycare, and all the kids seem to love *Star Wars*. River went to Pat's to get us coffee and some pastries. She thinks the sugar will make me feel better. I barely ate since that morning and only did it while she was hovering over me like a mother hen and practically force-feeding me.

The silence is broken by River's hurried footsteps into the living room. She comes to the kitchen and just looks at me. She's white as a ghost and breathing so fast, she's hyperventilating.

"What? What is it?"

"Skye."

All she says is my name, but it scares me.

I take a step closer to her.

"What happened?"

I don't even know what's going on and my eyes are already misting.

"I'm so sorry. I'm so sorry."

River's crying now. River never cries, and I'm terrified. My heart contracts with fear and races as if trying to escape my chest. I don't blame it. If I could escape myself, I'd run too.

"You're scaring me. What happened?"

A thousand thoughts assault me in unison.

Another shooting at Riggins?

Someone hurt River?

Mom?

Dad?

LOGAN!

My head is shaking, and I step back as if retreating and denying whatever River is about to say would make it any less real.

"It's Logan. Something happened. I'm so sorry, Skye. He's been shot."

SHE'S SPEAKING. I can see her lips moving, but I hear no sounds other than the pounding of my heart in my ears. River tries to hold me, but I slap her hands away and turn my back to her. Something takes over me, possesses my body, and I'm no longer me. Raw, burning pain claws at my chest and steals my breath away. I'm heaving and feel sick to my stomach, but it's empty and there's nothing to expel. Her arms come around me and I fight her. I fight my sister because I can't fight the hurt. I push her away.

A part of me watches it all from the outside. Looking in, I see myself fall apart, lose control, become rage and pain, trapped in the body of a twenty-one-year-old woman. The other me watches with curiosity and detachment. She watches me as I break down.

A stinging burn on my left cheek brings me back from the abyss I fell into. A voice reaches me. Low, very low at first, and then it grows.

"Skye!"

"Skye, listen to me."

Firm hands grasp my upper arms and shake me.

My eyes find River. She's crying, her eyes are red, her hair in disarray.

"He's alive, Skye. He's in surgery. That's all I know."

Air, glorious air, reaches my lungs, and I suck in one breath after the other, no longer drowning. River's words are a lifesaver. I hold on to them with everything I have.

I have to blink several times until I can see her face clearly. My cheek still stings.

"He's alive?"

"Yes, he is, but it's bad, Skye. We have to go. Let's go to the hospital."

Some of the numbness eases off.

"Did you slap me?"

"Yes. I'm sorry, but I had to. You're hysterical, and I didn't know what else to do. Come on, put some shoes and a jacket on and let's go. I'll drive us to the hospital."

ON THE WAY to the hospital, River tells me what she knows. She went to Pat's to get us breakfast and Pat told her. Pat's sister is a nurse at the hospital, and she was working when Logan was admitted. Logan was shot while trying to arrest a guy high on drugs and alcohol, and he's in surgery. That's all the information Pat's sister could provide. They're both friends with Logan's grandparents and saw him grow up. I know Pat is fond of Logan, but I never realized how close they were. River doesn't know when it happened.

We walk up to the information desk in the ER. The lady behind the desk moves at molasses speed. I can barely contain myself. River holds my hand and squeezes it.

"Excuse me, we want to check on the status of a patient." River is all business and authority. The lady takes us in and shuffles closer. The nametag on her scrubs says *Joanne*.

"Yes, how can I help you?"

"We need to know about a patient who was brought in today or last night. His name is Logan Cole."

"Are you family?" she asks.

I freeze, but River just goes on.

"Yes, she's his girlfriend."

I flinch at the word. I'm not. I'm no longer his girlfriend, but if a lie will get me information on him, I'll be his grandma, for all I care.

The lady looks nervous all of a sudden and looks behind us at where a few people are seated in the small waiting room.

She whispers, "I'm sorry, did you say girlfriend?"

"Yes," River and I reply at the same time.

She presses her lips together as if trying to figure what to say next. She continues in a low voice, intended only for us.

"I'm sorry, but information can be released to family members only, but the people in the waiting room behind you are related to the patient. His parents, and"—she takes a deep breath—"and his fiancée."

"What?" River's voice sounds loud in the quiet space.

I look over my shoulder, seeing the faces this time. An older couple, the lady in her forties, the man late fifties, and a woman in her late twenties. The woman is breathtakingly beautiful. And she looks at me like I'm something she wants to scrape off the bottom of her very expensive shoes.

I whisper back to River while the lady behind the desk watches us.

"That's his ex. They broke up over four years ago."

"You know her?"

"I know of her."

I turn to the nurse. "Can you just tell me if he's okay? Please?"

She hesitates and then looks at her computer, tapping a few keys. I hold on to hope as if my own life depends on it.

Just as she looks up, the ex-fiancée stands next to us. She looks me up and down and glares at Joanne behind the desk.

"Were you about to give information to a non-family member?"

"No, ma'am."

She turns her attention to me now.

"I heard you mention my fiancé's name. Who are you?"

Her voice is loud enough to call Logan's parents' attention. Joanne shifts behind her desk. River stiffens. I can feel her gearing up for a fight, and that's the last thing we need. I just want to know about Logan. I don't care how or who I get the information from. I grab River's arm, and she receives my silent message.

There are other people waiting for the information desk now. I step around the ex and walk the few feet to the waiting area.

I make eye contact. Logan's father is a handsome man, and it's easy to see where Logan got his looks from. He's dressed in a suit that looks like it costs more than my entire closet put together. But he lacks the warmth and openness Logan has. His mother is a beautiful woman, but petite and timid-looking. There's curiosity in her eyes, while his father's only hold coldness. She looks friendly. So while I look at both of them, I address the question to her.

"Hi, my name is Skye. I just heard what happened. Can you please tell me how he's doing?"

A sad smile touches her lips but disappears as soon as Logan's father opens his mouth. He does not respond to my question but interrogates me instead. He stands and towers over me. I recognize the intimidating gesture for what it is. The few times Logan talked about his father come to mind. Controlling, intimidating, cold. Yes, he's all that and more. I can't help but compare this cold man standing in front of me to my always happy and loving father.

"Who are you? How do you know my son?" He snaps the question at me as if the hospital belongs to him and I'm breaking in.

River cracks her knuckles behind me, a gesture I'm well accustomed to—a clear sign that she's about to release fury out into the world. Our father nicknamed her *The Kraken* when we were kids because her tantrums were that scary. She's about to have a throwdown with Logan's father and I can't let that happen. I catch her eyes and send her a silent plea. She nods at me, but I know she's a hair-trigger away from teaching this guy a few new curse words he's never heard before.

"As I said before." I take a deep breath to steady myself. "My name is Skye, and I'm a friend of Logan's."

"Never heard of you." His disdain is clear. The ex stands next to him, hands on tilted hips. Face fierce, perfect hair, perfect makeup. She looks like she's posing for a magazine cover, dressed in caramel-colored soft wool pants, four-inch heels, and a cream silk blouse. Jewelry sparkles on her wrist and . . . the left ring finger.

"Funny, I heard a lot about you." I let my eyes glance at the ex, and his face loses the haughtiness for the briefest of moments, but the composure is back just as fast.

The ex—Amanda is her name, if I remember correctly—speaks up. "A friend? Or a girlfriend? Are you lying now, or were you lying before? I heard what you said to the receptionist." She waves her hand as she speaks, the intent to show off the garish diamond ring on her finger clear. She's staking a claim and I have nothing to hold on to. Logan is no longer mine.

"I'm not lying."

She looks me up and down, and I'm painfully aware of my limp hair, lack of makeup, the black leggings, an old pair of Uggs I've had since high school, and my oversized hoodie with Yoda on the front and the famous quote, *Do or do not. There is no try.*

She laughs a fake laugh, and it's as annoying as her voice, nasally, whiny, and sharp at the same time.

"Oh, you poor little thing. Did you think he actually cared about you? You're a bed warmer and nothing more. I told him to have his fun while we're not married. We laugh about it when he calls me. The poor little girl who thinks she got herself a big fish."

A fake laugh follows the cruel words. It's a lie. I know it is. She's trying to hurt me and make me leave.

But is it? Is it a lie?

How do you know?

Blake thought you were just a challenge. Jon just wanted to use you.

Why would Logan be any different?

The voice of doubt whispers in my head, but it may as well

be screaming. I stand there, paralyzed by fear, hurt, and doubt. River shifts to my side and squeezes my shoulder.

"Let me, please let me," she begs.

I just shake my head and turn away from them when I see cops walking down the hall in the direction of the waiting room. One of them looks familiar. He stops the other two and says something to them, and they continue to walk my way, except for the familiar one. He nods at me to follow him and I do, River trailing several feet behind me and giving us space to talk.

I meet him away from the waiting area where we can't be seen by Logan's family.

"You're Skye, right? Logan's girlfriend?"

I lie again. "Yes. Can you tell me anything?"

"I thought so. I didn't want to say anything in front of his family. It's no wonder Logan never spends any time with them."

"I heard Logan was shot. Please, do you know anything?"

"Yes, he was shot, and the info we have is that it's not life-threatening."

A flood of relief nearly knocks me on my knees.

"How did it happen?" I have to know.

"I'll tell you what I know, but you can't repeat it."

I nod in agreement.

"Here's what we pieced together. Logan was following a driver who seemed to be driving under the influence and he pulled him over. He informed dispatch and proceeded to check on the driver. Up to this point, everything was going by the book. But it went down south pretty fast from there. As soon as he got to the driver's window, Logan could tell the guy was flying high on some heavy-duty drugs. He told the guy to stay in the car and called for backup. At some point, the suspect exited the car and went after Logan."

The officer shakes his head. I look at him willing the memory of how I know him to come. It clicks.

"You were at Riggins. You were there with Logan that day." No need to clarify which day I'm talking about.

"Yes, I was, and that's how I knew who you are the moment I saw you."

I nod and he continues.

"Logan tasered the suspect, but he just kept coming at him. There was a scuffle, but this guy was so high, it would have taken half a dozen of us to stop him. We have an eyewitness who said the suspect picked Logan up like he weighed nothing and tossed him to the middle of the street. The suspect pulled a gun from his waistband, and while standing over Logan, he shot him several times. By then, other officers had arrived on scene and they opened fire. This guy was raging. He was so high that even after being shot, he kept going after them. They finally managed to get him down by shooting at both of his legs. It took six officers to restrain and cuff him."

"Oh my God."

I'm shaking.

River steps closer and pulls me to her side.

"We think the suspect was high on PCP, Flakka, or bath salts. It's known to make people go insane and it gives them superhuman strength."

"Thank you so much, Officer."

We go back to the waiting room.

River sits to my right and glares at Logan's family. The mom looks at me, and the corner of her mouth lifts as if trying to smile, but she doesn't know how. She casts her eyes down. Amanda sits next to Logan's dad, her body inclined toward him, and I notice how he speaks to her in a low hush but never speaks to or even glances at his wife on the other side of him.

The secret Logan shared with me comes to the front of my mind, and it makes me sick. If I had anything in my stomach, I'd puke at their feet. How could they? And after all that, it's obvious they're still carrying on with the affair. I glance at the mom again and wonder if she knows. She has to. No one can be that oblivious. And if she knows, how can she put up with it?

"Is it me," River whispers, "or is there something going on with Logan's dad and his ex?"

I close my eyes, ready to deny it. It's Logan's secret and not mine to tell, but anyone with eyes can see what's happening right in front of us. And I'm tired of being the keeper of everyone's secrets.

"It's not you. I see it too."

"Sick."

"If you only knew."

River looks at me sharply, and she's about to interrogate me when a doctor comes into the waiting area. We all jump to our feet. The three officers step behind River and me—it feels as if they took sides and picked us.

"Mr. and Mrs. Cole?"

"Yes." His father takes the lead, his imposing figure filling the space.

"He's okay."

I sag against River, and her arms come around me and hold me up. His mother visibly relaxes. His father has no outward reaction and the ex just looks bored.

"He's still sedated and will be waking up soon, but we need to give his body a chance to heal and fight back. He'll be in the ICU, and someone will come to get you once he's prepped and comfortable. You can see him, two at a time, and just for a few minutes. He really needs to avoid stress and rest."

"Do you have any questions for me?"

His father says no, and as the doctor is turning to leave, I step up.

"I do. Have questions, that is."

The doctor looks between us and glances back at Joanne behind her desk. I guess he's been made aware of the situation.

"Yes, miss?" His tone is dry.

I want to scream. *Can't you see I'm the only one who cares? The one who loves him?*

"What's the nature of his injuries?"

I can feel Amanda staring daggers at the back of my head, but I ignore her.

"He was shot five times, one bullet through his left arm and the other grazed his neck. He was very lucky as both bullets missed bones and arteries and he has no major damage from them. But he also suffered a contusion. He dislocated a shoulder and broke his left arm in three places. My guess is that when he was thrown, he used the left arm to brace himself. We had to reset and pin the bones. Our biggest concern right now is the head trauma as he stayed unconscious for a long time. We are keeping a very close watch."

I gasp and my hands go my mouth. *Hold it in, Skye. You can fall apart later. Hold it in.*

"I don't understand. You said five shots."

The doctor's voice is somber.

"He was wearing a Kevlar vest. There were three other bullets on it. That vest saved his life."

I nod and hold my hand up, asking him for a moment while I blink several times to keep the tears at bay.

"Is there a risk of brain damage?"

My voice is shaky.

"There's always risk any time someone suffers any kind of

head trauma, but the likelihood of any permanent damage is minimal."

"And what about his other injuries? Will he make a full recovery?"

"He's young and strong. The next twenty-four hours will be telling, but I think we have a good chance of full recovery. He might need some physical therapy for the arm, but his chances are good."

"Thank you. Thank you for saving his life."

The doctor nods and looks back at Logan's family, who are sitting back with a displeased look about them. Well, not his mother. She has silent tears streaming down her face.

The doctor walks away but stops after a few steps and looks directly at me.

"If you have any more questions, have the front desk page Doctor Marcus."

And without another glance toward the other side of the waiting room, he leaves.

I sit back with River. The officers huddle in a corner, their voices too low for me to make out what they're saying. Logan's father and the ex turn to each other, whispering. His mom holds my stare and mouths a *thank you*.

CHAPTER FIFTY-NINE

Logan

THE WORST PART OF BEING SHOT ISN'T THE ACTUAL shooting. It's being trapped in this bed and not being able to get up and walk away when my father came into the recovery room with Amanda late yesterday after they finally moved me out of ICU. My mother trailed a few feet behind them, like the second thought she's always been to my father. One look at the both of them and I can tell they're still carrying on with their affair. Fucking sick.

Thankfully, they left in fewer than twenty minutes. Dr. Marcus kicked them out. If anyone missed the anger on my face when they came in, the loud and erratic beeping on the monitors attached to my chest made it very clear.

When I first woke up three days ago, I wasn't aware of what was going on. I have fragmented images, more like a dream than a memory, a result of my concussion.

I remember following a driver who was swerving in and out of his lane. I remember putting the lights on the cruiser and pulling the driver over and telling him to stay in the car. He was high on some fucked up shit . . . then a huge guy tackling me, falling down, the sound of cracking bones, pain, loud pops so close it hurt my ears, the taste of blood, and getting dizzy. Sirens, someone telling me to hold on, then nothing.

The chief visited while I was in ICU and filled me in on what's missing from my memory based on what the other guys told him. The suspect got out of his car and attacked me, knocked me down. I hit the ground hard enough to break my arm and nearly crack my head open. He had a handgun, luckily for me, a small-caliber one. He was able to squeeze off a few rounds. Two hit me, and the Kevlar vest took the rest and saved my life. I can go home tomorrow. I have to take it easy for a while, look into some physical therapy for my arm, but I'll make a full recovery. The perp survived the shots he took. He'll go to trial for attempted murder, among other felonies.

I haven't seen Steven or any of the other cops I usually work with. Being in the ICU has kept them out—the hospital can't have every cop in town trying to visit. They usually have a chain of command setup. One or two guys come in and pass information along. In our station, the chief is the one who does the rounds. But now that I'm in a private room, I expect they'll come once visiting hours start later this morning.

I wasn't supposed to be working that night. If I hadn't caught Skye cheating on me, I would have been in her bed, safe in her arms. Instead, I'm stuck in a hospital and my father thinks he can start right where we left off. I'd rather get shot again than go anywhere near my father and Amanda.

I don't blame Skye, even as part of me rationalizes all the steps that brought me to this moment and loop back to Skye cheating on me. I have to take responsibility for the part I played. I was hungover, tired, and distracted. I didn't follow protocol. I put myself in danger. It's all on me.

I have to tell the hospital I don't want them coming back to see me. My father didn't even ask how I felt. He didn't ask me anything at all. He just went on and on about the business and that as soon as I was released, we'd go back to Connecticut and leave the playing at cop foolishness behind. I feel bad for my mom, though. She's just a puppet in his hands. I don't understand why she stays with him. I'm getting tired again, and my eyes close.

The hustle of feet by the door drags me back from the claws of sleep. It's too early to be a visitor and the nurse just left. I keep my eyes closed, ignoring whoever is in the room now. I'm hurting, but the physical discomfort is nothing compared to the pain of betrayal. My mind got a break for a few days. Getting shot will do that to you. An occupational hazard, you could say. But now that I'm out of the woods and the doctors guarantee I'll be fully recovered and able to get back to work in a few months, my OCD brain goes back to obsessing over Skye and Bruno.

The squeaky sound of sneakers on cheap linoleum comes closer and stops at the foot of my bed. I keep my eyes closed in the hope that whoever this is, they'll go away. I'm in no mood to see or talk to anyone.

"She didn't cheat on you."

What?

The.

Actual.

Fuck.

Is this for real?

My drugged-up brain must be playing a trick on my ears, but that voice, the voice I just heard, the words, it sounds just like Fuck Buddy. And if it's him standing right here, right now, well, it's probably a good thing we're in a hospital because he'll need it.

312

I open my eyes.

It is him.

My jaw locks so tight, my teeth hurt.

"Get out," I growl at him.

"She didn't cheat on you. You must know that. Skye does not have it in her to ever cheat on anyone. Much less you. She loves you."

"She has a funny way of showing it."

"She didn't. You have to believe it—"

"I believe what I saw with my own eyes. The two of you were sleeping together in her bed, nearly naked."

"Nothing happened."

"No, I'm sure it didn't. Did she send you here to try to convince me you two have not been fucking behind my back all along?"

"No, she has no idea I'm here. River called me yesterday. I didn't know about what happened to you. I was giving Skye a little space and time to stop hating me. Nothing happened that night or any other time before. We really are just good friends."

"Good friends who sleep together. Oh, wait, there is a name for that—fuck buddies. Save it and get the hell out of here before I fuck you up."

The asshole laughs. He actually laughs.

"Oh, the irony. I'd take you up on that offer, but I'm in a relationship and Skye would be none too happy. Well, at least I was until that night. We broke up."

"You're not making any sense, kid."

"I was dating someone for a few years. I got dumped. That's why I was over at her place that night. I was upset and needed to talk. Skye is my best friend, and I needed her."

"Couldn't be that upset if the first thing you do is go fuck your *best friend*."

"You're not getting it, are you?"

"Oh, I get it, all right. Skye sent you over here to try to persuade me to take her back. It's not going to happen. I could have forgiven her anything, except this."

"I didn't fuck Skye. Not that night, not ever. In fact, I've never fucked a girl. A couple of boys, yes, but no girls. Ever."

"What?"

The painkillers must be playing games with my ears. Did I hear him right? No girl? Ever?

"I'm gay, stupid! That's what I've been trying to say. I'm gay, queer, I play for the other team. I'm a fag, get it?"

Something akin to hope dares flash in my chest, but I shut it down. I can't trust it. I can't believe it.

"You're just saying that to try to convince me to forgive her."

"Jesus! What do I have to do to prove it to you? Bend over your hospital bed and have someone fuck me in the ass?"

"That might do it," I sneer at him.

"Well, I can't because my boyfriend got tired of waiting on me and gave me an ultimatum. Either come out of the closet or break up. I couldn't come clean. Not yet. It's . . . complicated."

His voice trembles, and he breaks eye contact for the first time. There's a flash of pain and despair in his eyes, but it's gone a moment later.

"If that is true, why wouldn't Skye tell me so herself?"

"Because she made a promise she'd never tell a soul, and she's loyal to a fault. Not even River knows I'm gay."

His eyes drop to the floor, and he closes them for a long moment. When he looks back at me, the sheen of unshed tears shines in them.

"I'm a coward, and because of it, I lost the man I love and Skye lost hers. It might be too late for me. Sidney won't wait for me. He made it clear, but it's not too late for you and Skye. What you two have is special. Everybody can see it. Don't make the same mistake I did."

"I didn't make a mistake. I didn't cheat. If she cares so much, where is she now? Why didn't she come to see me?"

"She did. Skye has been here every day since she first heard about you. She spent hours in the waiting room. She almost missed her finals to be near you. River had to drag her to class to take the tests and back home to shower and eat, and then she's right back here again. You were in the ICU until now, and your father said family only and prohibited them from letting her near you. He threatened to sue the hospital if anyone talked to her."

My fucking father. It sounds like something he'd do, all right. I'm still not ready to give in.

"I don't remember being related to you, and here we are."

"It's a lot harder to get into the ICU. But here, they're a lot more relaxed. My name is not on the blackout list. Pat's sister helped me, and technically, I'm visiting the napping little old lady next door."

Anger and hope war in my chest. I can feel my heart picking up speed. Bruno glances at the monitor next to my bed.

"And she couldn't get Skye in? Why should I believe anything you say? If she wanted to see me so badly, she'd be here and not send you to make up stories about being gay."

"How many times do I have to say this? Skye has been here every day, but after meeting your fiancée, the one you forgot to tell her about, she kept out of sight. It seems you failed to mention that to Skye. Imagine her surprise when she met the future Mrs. Logan Cole."

"What the fuck are you talking about?"

I ask, but I already know what he will say. *Had Skye run into my parents and Amanda?*

"Oh, you know. The other blond, blue-eyed girl you're fucking. Does the name Amanda ring a bell at all?"

"She's not my fiancée. She was my girlfriend, but we broke up four years ago."

"Well, that's not the impression Amanda gave. And that was a nice big rock on her finger. Didn't strike me as your taste, though. It was a little garish."

"She's not my fiancée," I repeat.

"When Skye came in with River, the day you got shot, your parents were here with *your fiancée,* and Amanda made it very clear that Skye was just a little plaything and she knew about your little affair with Skye and that it was okay. She gave you permission to play around until you two get married."

"Fuck!"

"I told Skye I did not believe a word of it, but I was not there to witness it, and it seems your parents corroborated the story. Skye is devastated, but she didn't leave. She stayed in the waiting room."

"Jesus, I had no idea. No one told me anything."

I have no words for this mess. I feel responsible. If I had waited and heard Skye out. If I was paying more attention and not distracted by my anger. If I had not taken the extra shift. All those ifs could have resulted in a different outcome.

"Let's just say that not too many people here are very fond of your family and fiancée."

"Would you stop saying that? She's not my fiancée. She never was. We dated for a long time and one day, she showed up with a ring and said she was sending me the bill for her engagement ring. I went along with it. And yes, I feel really stupid. I was young and under a lot of pressure. That is my only excuse."

"Someone should give her an Oscar then, because the woman can be very convincing."

"Skye would never believe her."

Not after all I told her about Amanda and my father.

"Yeah, what makes you so sure?"

I open my mouth to speak, but nothing comes out. How can I be so sure? I didn't believe Skye, so what basis do I have to expect her to believe me over anything Amanda may have said and my father confirmed?

There's a knock on the door, and Bruno disappears into the bathroom at lightning speed. I guess he really is trying to sneak in unseen.

I close my eyes and try to slow down my breath, faking sleep. I don't want to see anyone, and maybe if they think I'm sleeping, they'll go away and I can hear what else Bruno has to say. I want to believe him with every fiber of my being. I need to believe him. Part of me still denies what he said. Could it be? Could he really be gay?

I listen carefully but hear nothing. I give it another thirty seconds to be sure whoever came in has left and open my eyes.

And she's here. Skye is standing at the foot of the bed, almost unrecognizable. She's wearing a Riggins baseball cap and a large hoodie that swallows her and hides her face and body. She looks like a teen boy in the shapeless and masculine clothes. But I'd recognize her small frame anywhere. She looks at me and pulls the hoodie down. The beautiful golden hair is tucked under the cap and hidden. Her blue eyes are huge on her pale face. And like the first time I saw her, there's not an ounce of makeup on her face. Not even the shimmer of lip gloss. And yet, she's the most beautiful thing I've ever seen.

So many emotions cross her delicate face. Relief, grief, hurt, hope, anger, love. I drink her in and send a silent *thank you* up into the universe that I survived and was granted a second chance to see her again.

I brace myself on the bed and push my body up with a wince as the sharp pain reminds me I was shot just three days ago.

I open my mouth to speak, not knowing what I'll say, but she lifts a hand and silences me.

CHAPTER SIXTY

Skye

HE'S OKAY.

He's okay. I knew this.

Pat stayed in touch with her sister at the hospital and passed along all the information to me. But still, to hear about it and see it—see him with my own eyes—makes a world of difference. The weight of worry drifts off my shoulders and makes me feel ten feet tall. Good. I will need it.

"I have a few things to say to you, Logan, and you will listen."

My voice wavers, but I push on.

"I tried to imagine what it was like for you to come into my room and see what you saw. I looked at it from your point of view, and I have to say if the roles were reversed, I don't know that I'd react any differently than you did."

I wait to make sure he's awake enough to understand me. He nods.

"All I have is my word as proof that nothing happened between Bruno and me. Not that night, not ever. And it never will. There's a reason Bruno was in my bed that night. He had a

319

fight with his b—with Sidney. They broke up, and he was upset. I didn't want him to drive in that bad weather when he was so upset. There's more to it, but it's not my story to tell and I made a promise I have no intention of breaking. Just like I made a promise to you, even though you don't know it."

His head tilts in curiosity, but he stays silent. I'm grateful for it.

"I made a silent promise to you I'd never be like the people in your family or like your ex. I'd never pressure you into being someone you're not or doing something you don't want to. And I intend to stick to that promise. But I can't let things stand as they are right now. I can't allow you to think I'd cheat on you or hurt you like that. You don't have to believe me, and honestly? I don't expect you to. God knows, I'd have one heck of a time believing you if I found you in bed with another woman."

I swallow the lump in my throat. This is it. This might be the last time I have a chance to see him, talk to him. I don't expect to run into him in our neighborhood. We lived on the same street for three years and never met. Once the spring semester begins, I'll be so busy with classes and applications for jobs that there won't be much free time. There will be no more surprise visits on campus and sneaking away for lunch and make-out sessions between classes.

"That's all I have to say. I wish you well. I hope you recover fast, and I hope—"

My voice breaks, and I have to take several breaths before I can speak again. "I hope that one day, you'll allow yourself to love again and that she'll love you as much as I do."

His eyes widen as my words sink in. As he understands that this is my goodbye.

"You deserve to be happy. You deserve to be loved for you and only you. And I wish you that."

I suck in another breath.

"Thank you. Thank you for seeing me. I will always have this, and I'm grateful for it."

THERE'S a commotion outside the door that has us both looking at it. The door opens with a bang as it smashes against the wall. And in its frame stands the ex. Amanda. Perfectly dressed, as always. I don't need this. I was about to leave. Couldn't I have ten more seconds, God? Is that too much to ask for?

"What is this?" Her voice sounds like nails on a chalkboard.

She looks outside and yells at the nurses and whoever else is around.

"Didn't we give explicit instructions to keep her away from him?" She points at me, the ugly rock shining on her ring finger.

People scurry outside.

"Larry? Larry!"

Who the hell is Larry? Logan's father appears at the door. Oh, I guess that's Larry. How did I not know his father's name?

They both walk in, and Amanda is making such a circus about my being in the room that I expect elephants and clowns to parade in at any second now.

The movie playing in my mind, combined with the stress of the last few days and the relief of seeing Logan, has the strangest effect on me, and I giggle. The giggles turn into laughs. The kind of laugh you can't stop and takes your breath away. A door opens, and Bruno comes out of the bathroom. Was he there this whole time? This strikes me as even funnier, and the laughs grow. They all stare at me, different reactions painted on their faces. Anger on Amanda's face, annoyance on Logan's father's,

Bruno looks worried, and Logan . . . Logan looks like he's in shock. Amanda's screeching brings more people into the room. Two nurses stand just inside the door, and a visitor from another room spies from the hall.

Tears are streaming down my face, and my cheeks hurt from all the laughing. I lift one hand, fanning my face, place the other on my chest, and take a few deep breaths. Silence fills the room.

I cross my arms over my chest and face them, and as I do, I realize I'm no longer the same insecure and scared girl from months ago. I'm no longer the same girl who fell for Logan so hard and didn't think she was good enough for him, or anyone else, for that matter. In that moment of hysterical laughter, when everything seemed to be falling apart around me, something else cracked. My biggest fears have all come to pass and I'm still standing. Fear of loving someone who didn't love me. Fear of losing that love if it was ever returned. Fear of rejection. Fear of never being good enough.

Fear that kept me in the shadows because God forbid, someone actually saw me and saw all of my flaws and insecurities. But here I am. Exposed. To Logan, the man I love. Bruno, the best friend I never confessed my fears to. Logan's father, a powerful and intimidating man. Amanda, a beautiful and confident woman and the representation of everything I can never be. And let's not forget all these strangers. People I never saw before but who are sure judging me right now. And how much do you want to bet that, now that I've made a fool of myself, I'll be running into them every other day?

All eyes are on me. I've always wondered how River managed all the attention she gets. What would River do in this situation? It's so surreal. No scenario I played in my head as I decided to come here today prepared me for this. It was supposed to be a stealth operation. I was supposed to be a ninja this morning. Go in, say my piece, get out. Job done. Not quite, it appears.

Amanda sneers at me.

"Who do you think you are? How dare you come here and try to steal my fiancé?"

I roll my eyes. Is this how River feels all the time? This cool and aloof and in control?

"Please. You are not, nor have you ever been, his fiancée. He dumped your skinny cheating ass years ago. Buying yourself an ugly ring does not a fiancée make. When will you give up the farce? Don't you have somebody else's daddy to fuck? I saw a bunch of old men outside. I think one or twelve of them would do."

She goes pale and then red.

"How dare you!"

"No, the question is, how dare you fuck your boyfriend's father? Did you go after the uncles too? Any other rich and powerful men in your little black book? Do your legs automatically fall open at the sight of power and money?"

There's murmuring all around the room.

"What? You thought no one knew you were cheating on your boyfriend with his own father?"

Shit! Did I just say that out loud in a room full of people? Oh my God. I can't believe I exposed Logan like this. All my old fears and insecurities come rushing in. I look at him, expecting to see anger, regret, and disappointment. He surprises me with a smirk, his hand holding his chest as it heaves in silent laughter. I'm reminded of all I lost and the metaphoric wind goes out of my sails.

A small smile touches my lips. I did what I set out to do and a little more. It's time for me to go and learn to be the new me. A little more than the old Skye, but maybe not as much River. *Jesus!* The world is not ready for that.

I take a step toward the door, and the people in the room part for me. His father and Amanda just stare, mouths open. Bruno grins like the Cheshire cat. It's a little creepy. I make my way out of the hospital and don't look back.

I feel like I just shed a thousand-pound armor.

CHAPTER SIXTY-ONE

Logan

It's been seventeen days since I last saw Skye. Sixteen days since I got released from the hospital. One day since my last doctor visit and clearance to drive. Short distances, he said. Short is relative, right? A two-hour drive through Vermont's countryside is not stressful. It's relaxing. My left arm will be in a cast for a few weeks more, but the pain from the gunshot wounds is gone and what I'm left with are ugly scars and numbness. The spots feel a little tender and numb, but not painful. The headaches are less intense and less frequent. I'll have to wait until the cast is off before I can start physical therapy and regain some of the strength in my arm. I have a medical leave from work, and once I'm cleared to go back, I'll ask for a regular shift. I'm no longer the guy who will fill in for everyone else. The truck window is open an inch or so, despite the cold January day. The skies are clear, the air crisp. I'll never take another breath for granted again. I fill my lungs with the cool, clean air. I love Vermont and how green it smells.

I spent Christmas and New Year's alone. Haven't heard from Skye since she came to the hospital.

I have since unblocked her number. I did a lot of thinking and re-thinking. I had nothing else to do but think and heal.

After Skye left, Doctor Marcus came in and kicked everyone out of my room—everyone except Bruno. He hid in the bathroom again. He came out when all was quiet, unlocked his phone, and handed it over. The photo app was open. I didn't have to see the dozens and dozens of pictures of him and another dude—hugging, kissing, holding each other—to believe him. They looked good together. I already believed him. The moment Skye came into my room and looked at me, I knew they both spoke the truth. But I wasn't ready to accept that just yet.

I made sure to put my parents and Amanda on the persona non grata list and take Skye off it. But she never came back. The only visitors were other cops.

And now, I find myself driving to her house. I could have waited until next week and seen her when she's back at Riggins for her new job and her master's—the spring semester always starts on the second week of January—but I can't wait a moment longer. I'll face her at home, where she'll be surrounded by her family.

No one knows I'm coming. I don't know what to expect. Her father might finish the job the asshole who shot me started. I made this trip once before, for Thanksgiving, and we had planned on coming back for Christmas, but it never happened. Skye's gift sits unopened in a drawer at home.

I open the window all the way as I turn into the long driveway that goes up to the house. Gravel crunches under the tires of my truck. The blue sky betrays the scent of impending snow. They called for several inches later tonight. I packed a bag. If she doesn't want to listen to me today, I'll stay in a motel in town and come back tomorrow. I'll come back every day until she forgives me. I can only hope she gives me a chance. The chance I never gave her.

I park in front of the house and turn off the engine but don't leave the truck just yet. A flood of memories of us together here comes unbidden. In this house, I got to see what a family is meant to be. They took me in as if I were one of their own. I felt more at home here than I ever felt in the house I grew up in.

"It took you long enough."

I nearly jump out of my skin. River stands outside my door, her head barely visible above the sill. I close the window all the way up and open the door. Grass meets my feet.

"River." I nod.

"Logan." She smirks at me.

We don't say anything for a while.

"Are you here to apologize and grovel? Because if you're not, you can get back into that truck and turn right back around."

"I am, but I'm a little afraid your dad might shoot me before I have a chance to talk to her."

"You're in luck. They're out of town. Went to visit some friends. Won't be back until tomorrow."

"Can I go in?" I nod at the house.

"You could, but she's not in the house. She's out back, by her favorite tree."

I WALK around the house and along the fence that houses one of the horse enclosures. I can see the weeping willow tree several yards away. The long, thin branches, now naked, graze the ground. A little over a month ago, the yellowing leaves were so dense, you could hide behind them. Skye's favorite place in the world, she told me. Her own little green universe sat at the base of that tree. It was the place she went to disappear, to think, to read, to just be. I wonder which of those things draws her to it now. At the base, a red and blue quilt cocoons Skye. I can't see any part of her, but I know she's in there with a book. She's facing away from me, and my steps are silent, muted by the yellowed winter grass. I stop three feet away from her. All I can see now is the top of her blond head. Her hands in blue fingerless gloves hold a Kindle.

I hope whatever she's reading makes her happy. She deserves a happily ever after, even if it's just fiction.

As if sensing someone, her eyes lift from the book and find me. And for the first time, I understand what she means by this tree being her own little universe. When we lock eyes, everything else vanishes. Birds stop singing, the air around us stills, and we're frozen in the moment, but I didn't come all the way here to just stare at her.

"Can I sit?"

She doesn't respond but unwraps the quilt and pulls it to the side, making enough room for me to sit next to her. I do and pull the quilt around me and over her with my good hand, enclosing us into the nest she created for herself. I leave a couple of inches between us. The quilt is big enough to cover us both. I turn so I can face her. The heat from her body reaches me, and I fight the urge to just kiss her. Hopefully, there will be plenty of time for that after she hears me out. Her sunshine and orange blossom smell fill my lungs, and it's like breathing for the first time in weeks. Blue eyes wait on me.

"I missed you."

I didn't plan on starting with that, but it's the truth. I did miss her. Like I've never missed anything else in my life before. No response. She's not going to make it any easier for me.

"I believe you."

Still nothing, but her eyes never leave mine.

"I'm sorry I didn't believe you before. I'm sorry my actions hurt you. I'm sorry it took me so long to get here. I could use the excuse of not being able to drive until now, but we both know if I really wanted to be here, I would have found a way around it."

She flinches.

"It's not that I didn't want to see you, it's that I wasn't ready to. Not in the state of mind I was in."

It's hard to be this close to her, her breath touching my lips, openness clear in her eyes, and not just let my body take over. She wouldn't stop me, I know, but that's not what I want. I need more than that.

"There's tremendous strength and courage in vulnerability, in opening yourself to someone and risking getting hurt. I thought I was the stronger one in our relationship. I thought that because I was on guard and not giving you all of me, I was in control. I was a fool. You're so much braver than I could ever be. I don't want to be that person anymore. I don't want to hold back when I know you gave me all of you."

Another silence falls between us, and a breeze stirs the thin branches, as if urging me to go on.

"It took me all this time to get my head out of my own ass." There's a faint shadow of a smile then.

"I needed to be *me* first. The whole me. Not the watered-down version I gave you. I want to make sure I can give you what you need. You deserve someone who will be there for you one hundred percent, and I know I wasn't it. Not really. It may have looked like it, but a big part of me was waiting for something to go wrong. When I saw you and Bruno together in your bed, I got the validation I was expecting and looking for. I felt I was right all along and that trusting you, trusting anyone, would backfire. And I fed on it like a frenzied shark in a sea full of chum. I reveled in that anger. It fueled me. It made me feel righteous."

She nods at me, the first real sign she's listening, understanding.

"But even then, I was lying to myself. I blocked your name on my phone, but the whole time, I hoped that somehow, a call would get through or that you'd come to me. But you didn't come to me, and I'm glad you didn't."

She flinches again.

"I'm glad you didn't because I would have taken you back, but I would have kept you out. I would have taken you back, but I wouldn't trust you. I would have taken you back just so no one else could have you, but I would withhold my love."

Her eyes mist over.

"You deserve so much more than someone who isn't willing to give you his all, and I was that man."

My hands ache to touch her, but I hold back.

"I don't want to be that man anymore. I want to be the man you deserve, whole and committed to you. Committed to us. I don't want to hold back anymore. I don't want to be with you and not be one hundred percent invested in us. I'm not perfect, but I love you. I love you with everything I am, with every cell in my body, with every breath in my lungs. I love you and I need you in my life. I don't know how to be me without you. I miss you, and I miss the man I am when I'm with you. The man I know I can be."

The scent of snow and orange blossoms hangs in the space between us, at odds with each other and yet so perfect together.

"Please forgive me. I never want to hurt you again."

Her fingers curl around the edge of the quilt as if they, too, ache to touch me.

"I'm a work in progress, Skye."

The breeze picks up and swirls around us. Tendrils of golden hair brush my face, as if parts of her are already reaching to touch me. I dare to hope.

CHAPTER SIXTY-TWO

Skye

"I LOVE YOU," HE SAYS. I KNOW HE DOES. THE TRUTH OF his words shines in his eyes.

"Please, Skye, say something."

I'm not the same person I was before I met Logan or the same person I was before he broke up with me or got shot. All these versions of me broke away with each strike and revealed a new me, tender and tentative, but lighter, more self-assured.

I had so many fears, imagined and real. So many things that held me back. I was comfortable in my complacency. Safe in the small space I created for myself.

Until I wasn't.

Until I no longer felt comfortable or safe and was forced to step out.

Funny thing about stepping from under the protection of living in fear—once I got out from under fear's cover, I found that the confidence I never thought I had was right outside of it. I learned a lot about myself in the weeks since what I call *The Bruno Incident* and Logan's shooting. Once all the things I feared most happened, there was nothing else to be afraid of. I wore my fear like a shield. River wears snark and sarcasm. Logan hides behind control. We all wear shields. Some of us are just better at it than others and choose shields that go unnoticed until something cracks them. And then we're left to decide.

Mend the shield or throw it away? Mine was shredded to pieces. I had no choice but to face life and myself without its protection, and once I did, I liked what I saw. I'm not perfect. The urge to retreat, to build a new shield, is there. But I'm working on it, fighting it instead of fighting myself and learning to see my own beauty and worth and value it. I am me and no one else. There's no one outside of me I can compare to, *not even my sister.* I can only compare the today version of me to the yesterday version of me and work to make it better.

"Logan?"

"Yeah?" His lips are so close to mine, I can taste him in my inhale.

"I'm a work in progress too."

"Maybe we can be a work in progress together."

"I'd like that."

His hand cups my face and his fingers tremble against my skin.

"Can I kiss you now?"

"I love you, Logan." My lips graze his.

"I know."

CHAPTER SIXTY-THREE

River

I CAN'T HELP THE HUGE SMILE ON MY FACE OR THE TEARS that spill over without permission.

I'm not a crier. I hate crying or getting all sappy.

Yes, I'm spying on my sister and Logan. I'm making sure I don't have to step in and kick his ass.

I'm not close enough to hear anything they're saying, but I have a great view of them from Skye's bedroom window.

I don't need super-hearing abilities to tell they're making amends and promises to each other. I can see it in their faces through the bare branches of the willow tree. Had this been any other time of the year, they would have been hidden by the leaves. So I take it as an invitation to watch. If the universe didn't want me to be a witness, it would not have placed that tree right outside the window and it wouldn't have been winter.

I love the way they hold each other and kiss with such urgency.

Oh.

Okay, then.

Time to stop watching.

It looks like Skye's fantasy of making love under her willow tree is about to come true.

All right, moving on.

I step away from the window with one last glance before going to my own room across the hall.

My heart aches, both with happiness for Skye and Logan and with dread for myself.

My heart aches and constricts in my chest, making all that I lost so much more real when I see my sister in love. My heart aches for what I know I'll never have.

I think of all the boys I met and dated, and was friends with. I search all the memories and find nothing that compares. And I think of that night, months ago, wishing yet again that it had been different. But instead, I have nothing—just a big black hole where knowing should be.

Whether it's a curse or a blessing is yet to be decided.

EPILOGUE

Logan

FOUR YEARS LATER.

FAMILY.

Family is what matters most.

Skye taught me the true meaning of the word.

I look at all the happy faces around me.

River, Skye's parents, David and Serena, who are more of a father and mother to me than my own ever were, and my baby brother, Liam. I'm surrounded by the people I love most.

Love may be an abstract thing, without shape, form, or color. But it's not intangible.

You can feel love.

You can see love in actions and deeds.

You can taste love in a home-cooked meal or the kiss of a beautiful and timid pixie of a girl.

You can hear love in words, in songs, and promises never spoken out loud.

And you can touch and hold love in your hands.

One might argue that last one. But no one can dispute the proof of love I hold in my arms right now.

All five pounds, nine ounces of him. He is undeniable proof that love can be held.

Times two.

Skye is next to me, holding his twin. Six pounds even.

They have our blue eyes and Skye's fair skin. And a lifetime of unconditional love and support ahead of them.

Our boys are just three hours old, and they have already taught me more about love than I ever imagined possible.

After being with Skye for over four years, I thought I knew what love was—and I do. But holding my sons for the first time has expanded that love to immeasurable proportions, and just when I thought I couldn't love Skye any more than I already do, I found I was wrong.

Love multiplies. Infinity times infinity times infinity.

"I love you," I say to Skye just before I lean in and kiss the downy head of one of our newborns in her arms.

She smiles. No words needed.

"Here, you can put this back on."

I put the wedding ring she'd had to remove when she'd gone in for the C-section back on her finger. The diamond surrounded by sapphires sparkles on her hand. A promise of forever.

"I love you too," she says.

Indigo and Rebel, our twins, coo in agreement.

"I still think you should name them River Two and River Three," the owner of said name pipes in again.

There are laughs all around the room.

We are a family.

A happy and crazy family.

My family.

A NOTE FROM THE AUTHOR

Dear reader:

I want to thank you for coming along on this ride. I hope you enjoyed reading Sky and Logan's story.

I would love to read your thoughts on it. Please consider leaving a brief review in one or more of the following:

Amazon
GoodReads
BookBub

Would you like to read a bonus scene for Because of Logan? Go to:

https://www.authorericaalexander.com/because-of-logan-bonus-scene

ACKNOWLEDGMENTS

Throughout this journey, from day one I have had many author friends treading the same path as I. One of them stands out a little more than the others.

She gets to see what I write first, with all the typos and unfinished ideas. Her input and suggestions have always been on point.

So, thank you Kata Čuić, for all the support, suggestions, and hours spent digging through a raw manuscript and above all, thank you for the honest feedback and friendship.

Thank you to my good friend and book buddy, Giseli Vargas—you have been with me since the beginning and I'm so glad we found each other.

Thank you beta readers, the first ones to lay eyes on this book: Giseli, Lisa Salvucci Codianne and Melissa Jones.

I also need to thank my fellow authors in the Do Not Disturb Book Club. You guys have been a great source of knowledge and support. Dear reader, if you are not in our club, you need to join us. We have loads of fun every day.

Next, I want to send a shout out to the Ninjas. You know who you are. I can't wait to see your books on Amazon.

To my very patient husband and kids. My three boys put up with a messy house, laundry undone, and dinners forgotten while I spent hours upon hours on the computer. I love the three of you more than words can express. Thank you for making my life beautiful.

And last, but not least, I want to say thanks to you, reading these words right now. Your support allows me to make a reality out of the stories.

Thank you for the kindness, for telling me the words I've written has touched you. You have no idea how meaningful it is to me that something I created has touched you. Because above all, as human beings, what we crave is connection. And words are a beautiful bridge between us.

Much love,
Erica.

ALSO BY ERICA ALEXANDER

Riggins U Series

Because of Logan (Book 1)
Because of Liam (Book 2)
Because of Dylan (Book 3)

Seventeen Wishes

Would you like a signed paperback?
Find them at:

https://www.authorericaalexander.com/signed-paperbacks

ABOUT THE AUTHOR

Erica Alexander has been a storyteller her entire life. If she's not writing stories, she's daydreaming them. Which has gotten her in trouble once or twice. She has an inclination to use sarcasm and she can make anything that comes out of her mouth, sound dirty. It's a gift.

Erica's life goals are: to make sure her family is happy and healthy, bring to life all the stories in her head, visit Australia, and jump off a plane. Preferably with a parachute.

Erica has degrees in Communications and Computer Science and she loves history, all things Native American, and anything that's off the beaten path and weird.

You can find Erica at:
http://www.authorericaalexander.com

Sign up for her newsletter:
http://eepurl.com/b6p0zP

Join Erica's Reader Group
https://www.facebook.com/groups/EricasHEA/

facebook.com/AuthorEricaWrites

twitter.com/author_erica

instagram.com/authorericaalexander

pinterest.com/authorerica

www.goodreads.com/author/show/15143372.Erica_Alexander

amazon.com/Erica-Alexander/B01LRQQG80

bookbub.com/authors/erica-alexander